D1591153

THE EXPIRATION DATE

© 2019 Vanessa Arias

The Expiration Date

Published by: Brown Leaf Publishing LLC
Interior Design: Vanessa Arias
A CIP record for this book is available from the Library of Congress Cataloging-in-Publication Data

Trade Paperback ISBN: 978-1-7336273-0-6
eBook ISBN: 978-1-7336273-1-3
Printed in the United States of America

THE EXPIRATION DATE

V.L. Arias

To my parents,
for going along with every kooky idea I ever had.

To my husband,
who understands my mind, my emotions and my determination
to the fullest degree.

1

LITTLE AUSTIN BRYSON lies buried. His tombstone reads:

Our Baby Boy, An Angel
January 7, 2012 – March 26, 2018

Just hours after he slipped into the world, his father Jeremy sat shattered and numb, absorbing the piercing hiss of sandblasted granite until he was presented a completed headstone with both dates in place. He stored it in the garage for six years, knowing all along that this would be the day Austin's short life would come to an end.

The day before he passed away, Austin awoke to a cool spring morning. His parents had not told him it would be his last full day on earth. His last day to roll his trucks across the floor, his last day to ride his tricycle up and down the driveway, his last day to eat his beloved marshmallows roasted over a fire.

That night, the family of four gathered in the backyard; his favorite toys lined up on the grass. He played with each of them, one by one. Twisting, dismantling, assembling, swooshing, bouncing. A digital camera propped up on a pile of building blocks captured the final hours they shared with him, along with whatever raspy giggles he could muster up in between coughing fits. It was the only time his mom allowed him to unwind his bothersome scarf and throw it off to the side.

Just before midnight, they cuddled under blankets on the living room floor and watched Austin's favorite movie, *Finding Nemo*. They fell asleep side by side with the sounds of animated fish still playing in the background.

An hour later, his mother flung herself from a deep sleep. Anxiety had gripped her during a dream, crippling her lungs, cutting off oxygen; the strength of boulders crushing her chest. Fighting her way out from under the blanket, she sat up gasping for air, crawled to her son, and tugged his comforter back. He lay in his usual sleeping position, on his side with one hand tucked under his cheek.

But the wheezing in his chest had subsided.

She pounced, pulling his arm out from under him, flattening him, shuffling his head back and forth between her palms. He did not wake. She lifted his eyelids, called his name. But he was gone.

The pneumonia had taken Austin already, so early in the morning.

Tears streamed from her eyes. Her body convulsed with the pain of what felt like a million needles poking out from inside. As much as she prepared for this day, this exact moment, none of it helped. She had now lost her only son.

Her wails blared like sirens, yanking her husband and daughter back to a reality they so easily escaped while asleep, but upon opening their eyes desperate to understand, it was all too clear. The image of a hysterical mother collapsed over her son had culminated their tragedy.

For six years, they had known this was the day they would say goodbye to this sweet little boy, a gash through their hearts far worse than they could have ever imagined. They wept in each other's arms until the glow of the sunrise burst through the windows.

The following day they attended Austin's funeral, in place since the day he was born.

2

"SOMEONE PLEASE DO something about this," Priscilla said to no one, pacing the walkway unaccompanied, her high heels hammering the pavement. The lack of activity around their house had just about exhausted her patience. The reason she suggested to Jeremy they leave the cemetery early in the first place was to make sure every detail wouldn't be tossed up to land in a tangled mess . . . and now it had. In her eyes, it was the beginning of a catastrophe.

Over the past fifteen years, Jeremy and Priscilla Bryson had secured their spot as *best hosts in the neighborhood*, and to give up that title now would be ridiculous. In a matter of minutes, a heap of guests would cram into their two-story house, expecting to unwind with chunks of food dangling from toothpicks. Some had even traveled to the Connecticut home from as far as Maine, and as of this moment, she didn't have so much as a cocktail napkin to offer.

I can't let this happen. This has to be perfect, she thought, her eyes landing on the light blue finish of the house matching the cloudless sky above, ready for its dim into evening. Priscilla's face squeezed into a few different expressions before it settled on one that matched her fury; then she slapped her arms into a pretzel knot. She looked to be a cryptic part of an exquisite painting. A disconcerted woman surrounded by the deep green hue of an impeccable lawn, every blade of grass in its place. On either side of her, splashes of blooming perennials led the way to a front door so pristine it glistened on even the gloomiest of days. Less than forty-eight hours before, Austin had been hanging off its oversized handle leaning forward, waving at his neighbor and father's best friend, Ernesto, who lived across the street. She remembered it clearly, the burst of worry when Austin opened the door to a rush of chilled air.

Tires circling over cobblestone crunched in her ears, and she verged on hysteria. A long row of headlights had turned onto Gardenia Way, and time had run out. No way to barricade the street, keep them at bay until her plans had realigned themselves. She watched helplessly as they made their way down the curved road, saluted by puffs of precisely rounded bushes. A row of cast-iron streetlamps stood at attention, their radiance battling the gleam of the setting sun. At least their approach would be a pleasant one.

Then, the procession dismantled, swarming the vacant parking spaces near the Bryson's house. By this time, Priscilla had given up. There was nothing more she could do—until she spotted the accelerating vans she had been waiting for, zipping down the street, jerking their way around other cars.

Priscilla blocked the front door like an enraged mannequin; shimmering four-inch heels, a perfectly tailored dress, arms angled at her sides, fists digging into her hips. A look used to overstate her displeasure as caterers shuffled trays and oversized utensils into the house. She tapped on her empty wrists every chance she could, whenever she thought one might look her way, but the act looked unrehearsed. A situation like this was unfamiliar to her. So, she set out to ensure every guest knew the caterers had arrived an hour late, making Austin's funeral reception look disheveled, and it had not been poor planning on her part.

"Jeremy, can you please speak to the person in charge and tell them they need to stay on schedule for the rest of the night? This is a must. I don't want anyone leaving before the truck cake comes out or everything will be ruined." Priscilla sulked in her sleeveless dress, eyeballing the aproned servers, who in her view, strolled along with little urgency. "It's what Austin would have wanted—to do what he did for his birthday— take everyone by the hand and show them his giant toy truck cake, but they, in the least, need to quicken their steps," she said. Her attempts to mask grief with snarkiness no longer worked. She raised the scraps of a tissue to her nose, allowing a bulging tear to gain strength and plummet from her eye.

"Honey," Jeremy said, laying his arm around her shoulder. "Don't worry. I'll take care of it. Just relax, have a good time, and enjoy his memory. It's *also* what Austin would have wanted." Jeremy pulled his wife close. The warmth of his arms evaporated most of Priscilla's concerns, but he also struggled. The images of his son's tiny silver casket, no more than four feet long, swamped his thoughts at every turn. He could still feel Austin's knuckles in the palm of his hand as if they were permanently etched there when he reached in for one last touch before they closed the casket for good.

But there was no time for crying.

The repeated car door slams and thumping footsteps diverted their attention back to the caterers and the 115 people that would crowd their home within minutes.

Priscilla tapped under her eyes one last time and ran her hands over her dress, smoothing out the minor creases she had acquired during the car ride back to their house. She remained at the front door preparing to greet the swarms of people, all arriving at the same time.

Jeremy waited by his wife's side. His clean-shaven smile narrowed his eyes and cascaded over her every move until she composed herself. He then tugged his tie back into place and rushed off to the side of the house to ensure the caterers would stay on schedule, just as Priscilla asked.

"Hey, Pri, you guys need help? I'll have the girls change and step in if you'd like. They'd be happy to do it," Ernesto asked, whispering into Priscilla's ear as he leaned in for a hug.

"Thanks, Ernie, but I think Jeremy has it all under control now. I've used this company before and they're usually pretty good with keeping things on track. I just don't want anything to ruin my baby's last party." Her unexpected pause produced the sound of a hiccup. "I can't believe it, Ernie. This is my baby boy's *last* party." She whimpered, her words barely slipping through her tightened lips. A cool breeze rushed through, stirring strands of her hair as she waited to regain vocal strength. Ernesto grabbed the loose hair and tucked it behind her ear.

"We'll get through this, Pri. I promise. But for now, let's get you some help." Ernesto said, as his daughters Jacklyn and Sherry crossed the street.

Ernesto mumbled into Jacklyn's ear as she approached the porch. The older daughter then perked up and took a few quick steps toward Priscilla.

"Mrs. Bryson, if you need some help, Sherry and I can go home and change. We'll be back in ten minutes, okay?" she said, stroking her long sideswept ponytail, her enthusiastic nod unconvincing to Priscilla.

"Jacklyn, you girls are so precious. Thank you so much for the offer, but we're okay. The caterers will handle everything in no time, and besides, we'll need you to help us celebrate Austin's memory. He loved both of you so much."

Priscilla extended her arms around the teenage sisters, and their heads met in a huddle as the three fought to hold back tears. Sherry reached into the purse she had strapped across her chest, pulled out a tissue, and handed it to Priscilla.

"Take it. We have plenty. My purse is pretty much acting as a tissue dispenser today."

Priscilla grabbed it and patted around her eyes. The tissue shriveled with moisture. She tried her best to not further ruin the smeared mascara she had already applied four coats of throughout the day.

Across the street, the front door at Ernesto's house swung open and out came Mia, his wife. Her dark hair, pulled back in a sleek ponytail, not a single strand out of place, and she wore a navy-blue pantsuit she hadn't worn to the funeral. She dominated the walk to the Brysons, in high heels and with a hip swing you would expect to see only on catwalks, cars around her stopping short to let her pass. Priscilla exhaled, relieved to see her heading over. Mia was the only person besides Jeremy who could revive her mood.

"Sorry I'm late. I had to change out of that dress. I made a quick cup of tea and somehow it spilled all over me. I guess it's my nerves; they're getting the better of me today," Mia said, swooping into the small crowd gathered at the Bryson's front door and giving Priscilla the usual peck on each cheek. "Again, I'm so sorry about Austin. He's was such a loving boy, and *you* are such a strong woman . . . and I admire you for that," Mia said.

Priscilla's pout stiffened, her lips fighting to stay together, and after a few moments, she was able to relax and resume speaking.

"I'm sorry, I'm trying my hardest not to cry again. I've had a migraine all day from it. I'm thinking maybe if I hold it in, it'll go away," she said with little energy, massaging her temples with two fingers.

"I think suppressing it might make it worse, but it's worth a shot. I love you guys. That's it! That's all I have to say. Now, let's get inside and celebrate Austin!" Mia grabbed her by the wrist, and both went trotting into the house.

3

THIS WAS THE last of it. A crowd like this would never again gather for Austin. Tomorrow would begin the outline of a new life depriving Priscilla of her son. Just movement on a calendar, one day spilling into the next. In time, the clarity of his memory would fuzz around the edges, cloud until it raised the question about whether he ever existed.

Mia ushered Priscilla through the living room. A hard left, curving to the right, getting around the masses already sipping from wine glasses and looking to discard their empty toothpicks. The caterers had done their job, made up for lost time. At last, Priscilla could relax, decompress with her husband in the furthest corner of the dining room. Far away enough to momentarily curve their postures and loosen their smiles; steal a minute off the clock for themselves. Jen walked by and linked an arm with her mother's and the three stood there in silence, their deadened stares observing the bodies moving around them, listening to the inaudibility of their conversations, sensing the pity that cobwebbed the room for having lost a child at such a young age: the small boy with the giant smile. It was hard to believe they had already lived one full day without him, but their sights insisted his existence—that he still walked among them, that he played on the grass with the other children, that he ran by them quicker than their eyes could focus. The unfair tricks a mind will play.

On the way home from the burial, Jen imagined her brother in the clouds, bouncing up the layers, propelling himself to the highest point, sitting down and crossing his legs at the ankles as he watched them weave to and from the cemetery. Jen broke down a few times in the car, unable to keep the plaster of her mask in place, the one that channels bravery. Worn to prove she is capable of living with the weight of her brother's death strapped onto her back, with the shame that threads through her spine for being the lucky one out of the two. In the last twenty-four hours, her mind chose to recall specific memories as if she carried a satchel of only the most painful ones. Like when Austin came home for the first time lost in blankets. The thrill of being a big sister, her mind expanding to the adventures they would share: his first trip to the movies, riding a roller coaster, his first time on a plane, showing him how to twirl spaghetti onto a fork. At only ten years old and within minutes of his arrival, she had redefined her purpose and declared herself Austin's guide through life, only to dig around in her father's pockets and find her baby brother's Birth-Death Certificate folded into a perfect square. As hard as they tried, Priscilla and Jeremy could not protect her from the Reveal. She was too smart and too curious. After looking over it, she folded the certificate back into its uniform shape and returned it to the pocket. At the time, Expiration Dates had only circulated for a year, but at her age she understood their significance. So, her mental clock began a countdown to her little brother's death on the day he came home from the hospital.

"Mom, I'm not gonna cry anymore. I don't think I saw Aussie cry once. So, I'm gonna honor him by smiling the way he did." Then, Jen revealed a good portion of her teeth through an exaggerated grin, triggering a burst of laughter from her parents she had not heard in months.

"That's definitely what he looked like, teeth and everything," Jeremy said, and in one harmonizing wheeze they drew in deep breaths and exhaled back to their solemn state. Yet, less ruffled and more adjusted.

"Hi dears, the service was lovely." Their neighbor, Shirley Wilcox drifted toward them. "Especially that toy truck floral arrangement next to his casket. It's amazing what people can do nowadays," she said. Her silver hair shined bright against the contrast of her charcoal dress, the hemline hovering below her knees.

"Thanks, Shirley. It was a gift from my uncle. He went to the florist with a picture of Austin's favorite truck and told them, 'I want this—made in flowers!' It seems they've done it before, because he said it didn't frazzle them one bit," Jeremy recounted his uncle's story, but a chilling holler coming from the side door cut their conversation short.

"STOP!" . . . followed by a couple of thumps and simulated cries. Sandra's kids had shoved each other into the doorframe, fighting over a dollar. The four-year-old twins yanked on the bill until it tore in two. The boy then pulled his sister's pigtails, inciting more grisly screams, but their mother had had enough.

"Chris times two! You both better stop fighting and go sit quietly on the couch. I will not have you embarrass me like this today!" Sandra's shrieks cleared the space around her, the startled guests pushing back and crowding to the sides of the room, offering the screaming, pregnant lady all the space she required. Sandra's quieter child, eight-year old Brianna, clung to her side during the commotion, pressing her face into her mother's hip.

"NO!" the twins shouted in sync. "We wanna play, and you can't stop us!"

Priscilla twitched a half smile at Sandra and scooted into the mix, leading the twins out by their shoulders to the backyard where the other children played. As she walked passed her husband, Priscilla heaved a loaded glance in his direction, a thousand words spoken in a single glide of the eyes. Jeremy took his orders and cut off Sandra's chase by hopping in front of her.

"Hey, the kids are tired, and the funeral and burial probably didn't help. I'm sure it all seemed long and boring to them. Let them run around outside and burn some energy with the other kids for a while."

"Thank you—and I'm sorry. Sometimes these kids *drive me crazy,*" she said, flustered and uneasy, her dark brown curls bouncing around the contours of her face. The further they fell forward, the better they could hide her. Brianna stood at her side, leaning her head on her mother's six-month-old belly, holding a lifelike doll with scraggly hair, which every once in a while let out a dainty belch.

"It's nice to see you," said Jeremy. "Hard to believe you live right next door and we've gone months without seeing you. I assume Logan won't be joining us," he asked about her husband.

"He's working as always, but sends his regards. He's been so busy with the firm lately. You know how things can get." Sandra felt the sudden urge to leave. To snatch the twins by the back of their collars and zip her way out, but she chose more conversation. She could do this.

"The Hellingtons were right behind me. They parked in their driveway and started walking this way. I know that because my kids made a scene when they saw Janice, screaming her name, *Janice! Janice!* I was able to quiet them down a bit until Chris noticed a dollar in Christina's hand," Sandra said, chuckling, ". . . and, well, you know the rest," . . . and just as Sandra forced out every last bit of air in forged amusement, Janice took her first step through the doorway. Great timing for Sandra to trade places. She pulled Janice in front of Jeremy, regained the color of normalcy in her complexion, and disappeared into a cloud of guests.

"It's impossible you ladies aren't twins," Jeremy said of Janice and her younger sister, Lacey, greeting them for the third and final time for the day.

"I don't blame you for thinking that. All she does is wear my clothes," Janice said, knocking her elbow into Lacey's rib. "Once a kid sister, always a kid sister, right?"

"But nonetheless," said Norma Hellington, their mother, walking in from the side door, "you girls love each other." She then looked around for a seat with a slow spin like the ballerina of a jewelry box, her skirt lifting with the flow of the breeze. She had arrived too late to claim a chair.

"Priscilla's out back, and the kids are waiting for Janice." Jeremy gestured toward the back door where children could be seen in their tiny suits and dresses. The kind worn by formal teddy bears. Misused by the kids as they stumbled across the grass and through bushes. Some even did cartwheels.

Norma looked out back. "I see she's got her hands full," she said. "She needs my help, but before that, let me ask you—and I only know because I overheard him telling someone—does Ernesto's whole family really have the same Death Date? He, his wife, and their two daughters?"

Ernesto appeared next to them as if the receptors of his senses alerted him of such talk.

"Hey, Norma, where's the Mr.?" he asked, popping his head in between them.

"He was right behind me, probably stopped to talk to a

few neighbors who were toasting by the side of the house," she said, but Barry was already on his way, taking an extended step in through the side door.

"Hey, Ernie," Barry said, extending a palm, but Ernesto grabbed his wrist and pulled him in. Barry went missing in Ernesto's arms.

"This is becoming a habit," Barry said, grunting as he emerged from Ernesto's affectionate squeeze.

"It didn't seem right giving you a handshake after our numerous embraces throughout all the services," Ernesto joked, keeping one arm wrapped around Barry's shoulders.

Without the group noticing, Jeremy had slipped away and come back with a tray carrying four glasses of wine.

"Here you go, guys. Some wine to help us forget our troubles . . . at least for a little while." They each held up a glass for a sloppy and out-of-sync "Cheers" and took a swig.

"Lacey, there's some sparkling cider for you in the kitchen," Jeremy told the Hellingtons' youngest daughter, still a year away from legally consuming alcohol.

As she commenced her search for cider, Jeremy leaned into the group:

"Ernesto, your family's Expiration Date . . . Norma overheard you talking about it. Go!"

The announcement set off sparklers in Ernesto's eyes. "Yes, it's true. We all have the same Death Date. We thought it was an error on the Bureau's part, but it wasn't. At least we know we'll be together when it happens, *if* it happens that way." He went for another gulp of his wine, snapping his head back as if taking a shot of bourbon, and then spruced up the edges of his goatee. The Hellingtons, meanwhile, concealed their thoughts of what he had just admitted with a series of uncomfortable smiles. Although they had known each other for several years, Barry and Norma never expressed much interest in knowing Ernesto's Expiration Date or anyone else's for that matter, but the Arroyos' bizarre circumstances met them with obvious interest.

"By then, I'll be seventy-eight. So, we have plenty of time to figure it out," Ernesto continued, trying to ease their concerns, but his affirmation kicked off a flurry of under-breath remarks by the other guests, mostly assumptions of how the Arroyos would meet their fate.

One couple whispered to another, "It could be a fire. That's a scenario that kills a whole family at once." Another man told his wife, "It'll probably be a car accident. How else does an entire family get wiped out?"

4

SANDRA'S WALK HOME under the evening sapphire sky was a quick one. Her house sat next door to the right of the Brysons', making it easy to shuffle a set of wet twins back home after their unexpected romp through the sprinklers.

"I can't believe you kids turned the water on. You are *not* allowed to touch things at someone else's house. How many times have I told you," she scolded them through gritted teeth, waving an ineffective finger in their faces.

Yet, as the three kids skipped ahead of her on the sidewalk in complete disregard of her tongue-lashing, she couldn't help but giggle with every soggy step they took. She watched their shoes squirt at the heels, while mulling over the list of bedtime stories she had promised them, eager for their snuggles while she read.

Just as the four of them stumbled into the house, the tin foil atop of the paper plates Sandra carried jangled with the jolt of her arms at the unexpected sight. Logan's eyes caught hers and locked them in as if snapping down a trap.

"Seriously?" he howled. "This is what awaits me after a long day at work? No food, an empty house?"

Sandra found it hard to turn away, his biting glare buried under hunched brows. The informality of his clothing told a tale of how long he had waited: no blazer, dress shirt untucked and only half buttoned, the cuffs undone. At least two hours.

"Honey, I was at the Brysons'. Remember I called to tell you? Austin passed away, and we went to the funeral reception. It was appropriate for me to finally show up to something, don't you think?" Nearly every word ended in an upturn, a way to wiggle out the tension knotted between them.

"I brought you some food." She uncovered the plates piled with vegetables and pasta. "Do you want me to heat it up?"

Appeasing him with leftovers would not work. She could tell.

"So, my stay-at-home wife brings a cold plate of food from the neighbor's house, then shoves it in the fuckin' microwave, and I'm supposed to be happy about that? Is that what you're saying?"

Sandra leapt in front of the children, her small stature towering over them, unable to ignore their gurgles of shock, the sudden downturn of their lips. Like a brick wall, she stood between them, stamping her feet down as if to call upon the hollows of the basement to aid her.

"Kids, go get ready to shower." Sandra patted them on the back and directed them up the steps before swinging back around to confront her husband.

"At least wait until the kids are out of the room before you start cursing. Maybe you should show them an ounce of respect, if that's even possible." Her eyes slid away quick enough to disconnect from his and, on her toes, she reached for dishes from an overhead cabinet.

"Honestly, Logan, the least you could do is say hi to them before going in on me," Sandra said, stabbing into zucchini chunks with a fork.

"Forget it. I'd rather go to the pub where I can have some cold beers and eat a decent meal." He rolled down his sleeves, re-buttoned his shirt, and tamed his short hair with his long fingers, none of which wore a wedding ring.

Beads of disappointment rose from her skin. Her lips formed words before she even knew what to say.

"I—I'm sorry, honey. I'm just aggravated." Her firm exterior cracked at the surface, one long split down the middle. "I felt so awkward at the Brysons', then the kids turned on the sprinklers and screamed and yelled. Some guests got wet and it made a mess of their yard, and that's why I'm in a bad mood." She hurried her explanation in a single breath. The faster she spoke, the less time it would take for him to understand.

But Logan said nothing. He grabbed the sport coat draped over a chair and charged through the door, slamming it behind him.

Sandra dropped into a chair at the kitchen table, running through a summary of a hundred other explanations that could have fared better, following the grooves in the wood with the fork as the untouched remnants of the buffet called her from the beeping microwave.

The rev of Logan's obnoxious engine soured her stomach. Why had she not tried harder? At least he had made the effort of coming home.

She listened as the car backed out of the driveway, cruising away from her, away from the family, away from their home where her arrogance had ruined yet another night.

Why had she not left the Brysons' house sooner? All

of this could have been avoided. Now, the kids would go another day without their father.

From upstairs echoed the sounds of mischievous laughter, running water, and an excessive amount of splashing. Somehow, she managed to keep calm. Perhaps the memories of what life was like before the Reveal kept her propped up enough to stand firm, but with the good memories always came the bad.

And there it was again, the breaking news of seven years ago flashing into an empty space in her thoughts. The awful experiment government officials tried to keep secret. At the time, it seemed to have solidified an unbreakable bond between her and Logan. It was that night, Sandra remembered, that Logan had strapped his fingers around her folded hands, assuring her everything would be okay as they watched coverage of the Expiration Date release. Even the anchors reporting it appeared wide eyed and tense. The color of beets under the sheet of their skin. Every channel: a new theory, a new revelation. No escape from it for days, and an all-out war against the government the way people carried on in the streets.

Screaming.

Crying.

Looting.

Setting fires.

The following day, schools and offices closed, offering grief counseling in preparation of the inevitable. As petrifying as that night was, love coiled them together. The will to survive, stand shoulder to shoulder, hand in hand.

Sandra withdrew from her memories, ran a paper towel under cool water, and tapped it across her forehead. Counting back from five, she recalled the rumors that stress and anxiety directly affected the Death Dates of unborn fetuses. She needed to settle down.

Sandra dropped three inches after kicking off her clunky heels, tied her spirals back in a loose bun, and raced up the stairs toward the dribbles of bath water. That night, she tucked her kids in, one by one, kissing each on the forehead, making an unprecedented promise, before clicking off their bedroom light:

"See you in the morning, my babies. We're out of toast. I'm sorry, but we'll just have to have ice cream for breakfast." Their sleepy and collective gasps poked a pinhole in her ballooning guilt for continuously nudging them into the line of fire. The line meant to keep them safe.

Sandra dug her toes into the soft carpet of her walk-in closet and searched for a clean pair of pajamas. Ones that fit this far into her pregnancy. She tiptoed into the bathroom and closed a hand around the towel bar as she climbed into the tub, cradling her belly with her free arm. The misty streams from overhead doused her hair and poured down her face. Then the tears came, flowing just as fast as the spray of the showerhead. Her shoulders fluttered, her eyes blurred, and the twitch at the sides of her head felt like the whacks of a hammer. Another battle lost. She leaned back against the shower wall and slid down it, until she rested crouched at the far end of the bathtub.

That's how Sandra flushed out her frustrations every night, in a flood of tears after full days of having to mask her misery with artificial smiles.

Thirty minutes later it was all over. The full-time mom crawled into her bed in complete darkness, guided only by the short beams of light that crept in through the gaps of the curtains. She laid in the center of the bed and hummed along to the tune of her unborn baby's kicks until she fell asleep.

5

A T THE TIME Sandra headed home from the gathering at
the Brysons', Shirley wasn't far behind. She watched the
mom and her three kids walk ahead as they turned down the
path leading to the side of their house.

It had been thirty years since Shirley's two girls hopped
alongside her, dressed in ruffles and twinkling shoes, like
Sandra's kids except . . . they were never dripping wet on the
way home from a funeral reception. In fact, the girls would
whimper at the sight of scuffed shoes or tangled hair ribbons.

Shirley smiled through watery eyes, her mind reminiscent
of a time when her girls stood no taller than strollers they
had grown out of, walking on either side of her, their delicate
fingers clipped onto hers.

Even though the flashbacks weren't as clear anymore,
Shirley grasped at them every chance she could as a way
to enjoy her daughters together again, even if in her own
memory.

The night had turned muggy. Fog had closed in on
Gardenia Way. The tops of homes blended with the nighttime

sky and trees rested like silhouettes, calm and motionless, behind the thick haze. Shirley turned toward her home and jingled her keys, thrusting them in her hand with the force of punches.

Nothing.

She stomped the concrete with her wide heels.

Still nothing.

Maybe the sound didn't travel well in this climate, deadened by the density of the air. Sandra deserved a gold star for successfully dodging her at the Brysons' and perhaps, Shirley thought, getting her attention now would obligate her pregnant neighbor to stop for a chat or, at least, an exchange of pleasantries.

In one final attempt, Shirley smacked the keys into the ground and pings of metal carried through perforations in the dampness. Two of Sandra's kids granted Shirley a half rotation, but like a spring, turned back around almost immediately; their mother's grip pressed firm into their arms. By the time Shirley arose from her plunge to retrieve the keys, Sandra and the kids had vanished.

Mist coated Shirley's silver strands as she stood facing her door, sliding over key after key in her crowded palm. Like Sandra, she too balanced a heavy plate of food she had brought for her daughter. Tara hadn't been home in days, and lately, Shirley had found it difficult to keep track of her. Afternoons that turned into nights of calling Tara's unsavory friends. Numbers she acquired while secretly sifting through her daughter's cell phone.

In all of Tara's thirty-eight years, this was her longest disappearance.

Eight days.

For certain, it would be another night on the phone for Shirley, who called out for her daughter several times as she walked through the threshold before abandoning hope for a response. Welcomed home only by the hiss of the oscillating fan she had forgotten to turn off when she left for Austin's funeral that morning.

Making space in the refrigerator for the plate of pasta she knew Tara would never touch, Shirley caught a glimpse of flailing arms through her kitchen window.

Logan.

She lifted the window two inches, making the muffled words a little clearer.

"So, my stay-at-home wife brings me a cold plate of food from the neighbor's house, then shoves it in the fuckin' microwave, and I'm supposed to be happy about that? Is that what you're saying?" she heard Logan bark at Sandra. His face was a bright pink hue, from what she could tell.

Shirley grabbed the stepladder tucked away by the fridge, flipped it open, and took three wobbly steps to the top. From there, she had a perfect view into Sandra's kitchen, but it was all over by then. Logan was barreling out of the house and huffing his way down the steps. The way his clothes hung on him, she suspected he had already guzzled his way through a few beers.

She slumped her way down the step stool and dropped to the floor. Another worry she did not need: Logan catching her snooping on them. She crouched down and slammed her back into the cabinet below the sink, hiding. It was hard for her to make sense of his outburst on such a disheartening day. A six-year-old boy had just died, his neighbor, the son of his wife's friend . . . former friend.

As much as Shirley didn't want to admit it, she had become fearful of him. Maybe it was the hold he had over Sandra, the perpetual smug look on his face, or the lack of respect he exhibited toward his wife and kids in public and behind their tightly shut doors. That kind of attitude, for an old-schooler like Shirley, was unheard of.

On the floor, Shirley hugged her knees, listening, waiting for the evening silence to swallow the hollow sound of Logan's muffler. She reached for the angel pendant hanging from her necklace, kissed it with her coral lips, and held it pinched between two fingers.

"My beautiful Angel, please watch over Sandra and the kids . . . and *please* help Tara find her way home to me, safely," she whispered.

Her youngest daughter, Angel, had passed away within days of the Expiration Date release. Tara gave her mother the angel pendant in memory of her sister. Later that night Tara tried to kill herself.

Before heading to bed, Shirley dialed a few numbers she remembered off the top of her head, looking for her daughter. Three sent her to voicemail, and two had the decency to pick up, but greeted her with "Leave me alone, ol'lady," and "Tara's not here; stop callin', gramma."

Tomorrow morning, she'd go about her routine: toast a couple of English muffins and steep two bags of chamomile tea. The same as she has done for the past few years. If Tara never made it home, she'd eat at the kitchen counter alone, in silence; the morning news on mute, an ear on the front door. Upon her last buttery bite, she'd sweep up the crumbs, cover Tara's untouched dish with plastic wrap, and pile it in the fridge on top of the eight other breakfast plates Tara had missed since she'd been gone.

Mid-morning, she'd sit at the bay window in the living room, rereading Sunday's newspaper, erasing and rewriting letters of a crossword puzzle, and watching the streets for Tara.

It was no wonder Shirley and Sandra had been such great friends; they kept each other company during bouts of abandonment. But most recently, Shirley's solitude had intensified since her neighbor stopped visiting and became unrecognizable, a different person; like the seizing of a body, displacement of a gentle soul, and the installation of an enemy. It had all happened in a handful of minutes the last time they were together. Sandra was at Shirley's venting about Logan, the children, her mother . . . letting all her complications bubble to the surface, until she realized what she had done . . . what she had said. In her haste, she put the wine glass down; splashes of red slopped over the rim, dripping onto Shirley's coffee table. She tried to take it all back, the words she had let slip, but it was too late. Repulsion had already sketched creases across Shirley's face, crinkling, folding as she tried to relate, to accept without judgment. With more time, maybe just seconds, Shirley could have done it, but Sandra had already gathered her hat and coat and rushed out into the blistering cold without saying anything more.

6

ONE NOTCH LOUDER and the chimes and overlapped sirens would have sent Jeremy tumbling off the bed. Buzzes and reverberation broadened inside the bedroom, reaching its boundaries, smacking the walls and bouncing off to slam into Jeremy's head with full force. The catastrophe: a pushy alarm clock he had set the previous night for six in the morning, an hour earlier than usual. In segments, it all came back to him. A slow process as if he had opened the cover of a book and, page by page, took the time to remember his life. Where he was. Who he was. Who he needed to be. An extra hour to acquaint himself with this new Jeremy. One who had never before existed. Different from the one before his son's death. It would take some work: regulate loosened mannerisms, adjust the way his cheeks hung, and increase tolerance for voices he did not care to hear. All this before a dreadful arrival at work. The first since Austin's death.

He flipped onto his stomach and dug his face into the pillow, shifting and repositioning until it fit right, until it hindered his breathing, cut off oxygen. He emptied his lungs and held his breath. Is this the discomfort Austin felt? How could no one have been there to ease his son's last breath? They were all asleep when he died. He snapped his head back and the air enveloped him once again, refreshing his heated cheeks, alleviating the sting in his eyes, filling his lungs to capacity. Jeremy's fingers groped under the comforter beside him: empty. Priscilla had already woken up and dragged herself out of bed. The aroma of freshly brewed coffee this early implied she too anticipated a rough morning without her son.

Through a hazy view, Jeremy watched the scrambling in the sunlight; specks of dust on a chase spinning circles in a small space, precisely the activity in his mind. Disjointed thoughts in a whirl. No way to flush or eject them into a space far away from his. No way to repel the steady flashes of his deceased son, the imbalance that thorned their lives. Austin buried at only six years old. How had he even contracted pneumonia? If only a switch existed; one flip and his brain would power off. Then, he could carry on as if nothing had ever happened. Desensitized. But he knew that even with a wired switch and a short circuit, it would be impossible.

It seemed like only yesterday Jeremy had rushed his wife to the hospital with a baby boy on the way. He would complete the set they had waited for, a girl and a boy. Eight hours later, Austin Aaron Bryson was born with a full head of hair. Moments after being wrapped in a light blue blanket, he surprised them by scrunching up his forehead enough to reveal his gray eyes.

By that time, it had already been a year since the Bureau had started sending out the red envelopes most feared receiving. Inside them was a red sheet of paper printed with a name and an Expiration Date. Further down the page you were asked to *Plan Accordingly*. The highest form of insensitivity he had ever experienced: this is when you'll die, and make sure you work out the kinks before you go.

But at hospitals, the government software was already accessible and Death Dates were printed right on birth certificates.

That day, the clock seemed to spin faster than any other in his life. A day in which he wished to move the slowest, stand with his arms stretched over his head power-lifting the sun, holding it at its highest point to keep it from slipping off to the side and bringing an end to the day. He took several walks around the medical facility in procrastination, turned into every crevice that presented itself, even a breath-holding stroll through an alley stacked with garbage bags. Before every lap, he inspected the shelves at the gift shop, the tips of his fingers brushing over pastel-colored fleece, rose petals, leaves, candy wrappers. In his nine visits, he never purchased a thing. Left empty handed with eyes of the cashier on his back.

He then sat alone in the cafeteria with a cup of the day's soup, the spoon trembling in his tight grasp and a half-bitten sandwich laying in defeat on a paper plate. His wife rested three floors above. *I can't let her see me like this.*

At 3:55 that afternoon, the vibration in his pocket meant his time was up. Still, he used up every millisecond to the seconds he had available, delaying his walk to the administrative area, to the counter that would tell him how long his son would live, when he would die. He appeared at the office window two minutes before they were to close. He squirmed in front of it, his lungs stiff as if the air he drew in filled them unevenly. Trickles of perspiration burst through his scalp, skirted around follicles, and plunged off his forehead at the moment the clerk reappeared. A white envelope flashed in her hand.

Through the carpeted corridors, his legs pumped in

a hurry. The certificate weighed heavily in his hand like a stone too large for his grip. He slammed his way into the men's room, knocking into a young boy on crutches. The child pegged backward to let the man rush through. Jeremy welcomed the extra space and continued on his path to a private stall.

He peeled off the envelope and unfolded the warm sheet of paper, reading the date over and over again. Multiplying, adding, subtracting, thinking somehow it had been miscalculated.

The month.

The day.

The year.

The more he looked at them, the less sense they made. He turned the page upside down, right side up, sideways—but pain had already shoved through his limbs, nudged the pit of his stomach. His body knew the truth before his mind could accept it. He collapsed inside the confining walls and dry heaved into the toilet. His newborn, the son he had waited for his whole life, would live a mere twenty-two hundred days.

The whiff of overly toasted bread danced on his taste buds. He exited his memories and sunk his knees and hips into the mattress and flipped himself over. The date on that paper had come and gone. Nothing else to do about it.

Sitting upright, Jeremy made a mental note to confirm the delivery of roses he had scheduled for his wife. A way to express gratitude for her handling of Austin's long battle with pneumonia; a time where her courage outshined his.

That started in early January when they rushed Austin to the ER, only to be sent home a few hours later. Hospitals no longer treated patients within six months of their Expiration Date. It came as a surprise to them considering he was so young. They thought, for sure, his age would be an exception despite the law. Doctors handed them a bag filled with antibiotics, anti-inflammatory medications, and a nebulizer to keep him comfortable until the day of his death. The disheartened parents notified his kindergarten teacher before pulling him completely out of school, which he only attended for two weeks in February. That was the only time they were able to effectively mask his symptoms.

On his last day, Austin enjoyed a cupcake-filled celebration, in his honor, followed by finger painting and story time. At three that afternoon, just before their release, the teacher instructed his classmates to line up for high-fives. Their target: Austin's little hand in midair. He waited with laughter and wiggles as the line of classmates approached him single file. Their enthusiastic jumps and hand slaps were like a demolition of Priscilla's strength, imploding; the feeling of glass shards and stone fragments destroying her insides. She and Jeremy watched from the corner of the classroom, like two heartbroken busts on a pedestal. Stiff and smile-less; their bodies nonexistent, hidden behind ankle-length coats.

During Austin's final twenty-four hours of life, Jeremy recalled Priscilla's determination of never showing signs of their son's imminent death. She was upbeat and energetic, never leaving his side. They played Twister for most of the morning until he tired and took a nap to regain strength. Upon waking, he asked for ice cream with chocolate sprinkles, served on the side of deep-fried cheesecake and curly fries, something Priscilla would have never fed him had he more time to live.

Jeremy closed his eyes and waited until he saw his son again, summoning more of him. Austin giggling under a blanket pretending to be asleep, jumping on the bed, his tiny hands squeezing toothpaste onto his Spider-Man toothbrush, the daily search for his misplaced Batman sunglasses.

The memories pinched at Jeremy's chest, scratched at his throat, fluttered at his temples.

He wanted to laugh.

He wanted to cry.

He wanted to die.

Maybe, he thought, the arduous part was now. On this day. Not the months of Austin's illness, not his death, but today. The commencement of a routine that did not include Austin. A trudge through twenty-four segments. One day, then the next, then the next, getting further away from the time they spent together. The more time that passed, the harder it would be to retain proof that Austin had lived among them.

He rose out of bed, wiped the drip from his eyes, and rolled his neck in preparation for an excruciating day at work; an entire office offering their condolences and asking the same three questions: Are you okay? How are you doing? How are you holding up?

During his walk to the bathroom, he mouthed his scripted responses over and over:

"We are doing our best. We're doing the best we can. We're hanging in there."

At the bathroom mirror, he paired his affirmations with a few different smiles and head nods, his hoarse voice repeating, "We are doing our best. We are doing our best." He smiled a little deeper and peeked through squinted eyes. Almost perfect enough to encourage the meddlers to swing back around and parade off to their desks. No harsh stories to tell here. He would not recount Austin's final days or his crossover into death. Jeremy had grown bitter.

"Honey?" Priscilla appeared at the bottom of the staircase holding a coffee mug, thinking she may have heard him muttering upstairs.

"I'm up." Jeremy stepped out of the bathroom, his

electric toothbrush spinning in his mouth. He walked to the top step into Priscilla's view to show he had made it out of bed.

In the mirror, he stared at a drained version of himself after a splash of cool water over his face. Sallow skin, shaded eyes, frown lines. It was then he remembered a box he had stashed away at the top of his closet shelf.

He pulled out a pair of fuzzy slippers six sizes too small for him and dragged his feet into the kitchen.

Priscilla let out laughter of coffee and spittle that sprayed back into her mug.

"Honey, those things look so tiny on you. Are those the ones Austin picked out for you last Christmas?"

"Yes, I remembered I had them. I thought they'd at least cover half my feet, but if I could walk on my toes, they'd be perfect."

"I was there when he picked them out for you," Priscilla recalled, a faint frown threatening her smile. "He was so excited. I kept telling him they'd be too small, but he said, 'Daddy can fix them.' He thought you'd take them into the garage, put them on your workbench, and fix them enough to fit you." Priscilla's eyes puddled and Jeremy rushed in front of her, combing her bangs to one side and swiping his thumbs across her cheeks.

"It hurts, Pri. I know. He was such a happy kid. It hurts to think he had no idea what was happening. He thought he'd get better and go back to school," Jeremy said, sitting down on a stool across from her. "Things'll be rough for a while, but we have to keep it together for Jen. I know she's a teenager, but it's still hard for her."

Priscilla agreed. "These last two weeks have taken such a toll on her," she said while pouring Jeremy a cup of coffee and sprinkling cinnamon on top.

He grabbed the mug with both hands.

"What time did you get up? I was surprised you were already out of bed when my alarm went off," Jeremy said, taking his first sip.

"I couldn't sleep. So, I figured I'd get started on my day, but all I've done is stand here and drink coffee. This is my fourth cup." She raised her mug with a perky grin, proof the caffeine had already kicked in. "It's hard to believe the smell of all this coffee and burnt toast hasn't woken Jen up yet. She must be exhausted . . . at sixteen, she's already had to deal with the loss of a brother."

Jeremy spoke through a slurp of coffee.

"At least she'll be able to enjoy a long life. I wish Austin could have been around for just as long." He pressed his lips tight to fight off a nagging pout. "Now, our family's incomplete. How are we supposed to get through this?" he asked, slamming the mug down into the counter.

"Ok, honey. We have to keep his memory alive, but can't linger in depression. Here's more coffee." She shoved a fresh mug into his chest, and a small splash ended up on Jeremy's tee shirt. She ignored the mishap and bustled around the kitchen, gathering charred pieces of toast.

Priscilla's nervous ticks had a habit of manifesting themselves into chronic coffee pouring. It had happened on their wedding day, when she walked down the aisle in a coffee-stained ivory dress.

"You know, if you think about it, we're lucky we knew when he would—go. Whether or not we were aware of his Death Date, his destiny would've been the same and we wouldn't have spent as much time with him as we did. He would've been in the hospital for weeks, even months, instead of a few hours. It could have been much worse. At least this way, we were able to prepare for it. Keep him comfortable and happy," she said with a convincing nod, trying to persuade him to see it her way, but he was indifferent.

"Really, Jeremy. Think about it. Ten years ago, he would have been confined to a hospital room. Austin would've been miserable. We would've never expected to lose our only son at such a young age. This way, we were able to spend the last two weeks by his side, soaking up every one of his crooked little smiles. It was a blessing," Priscilla said, assuring him there was no better way.

But Jeremy remained skeptical. "I don't know. It's hard to talk about this only because I'm still not sure which *is* better. Knowing or not knowing. Since the day he was born, we've been conscious of the fact that we'd only have him for six years," he told Priscilla with a trace of agitation. "Waking up every single day after that was agonizing knowing it was another day closer to his death." He jumped off the stool, expecting Priscilla to defend her side, but she didn't. "Sometimes, Pri, I think it would have been easier the other way around. I don't know. Maybe that's selfish of me."

Jeremy and Priscilla met at the kitchen island and stood face to face in silence, their opposing views flickering in their eyes.

"Well, I have to get ready for work. I want to get there before everyone else so I don't have to parade through a row of sad faces." Jeremy kissed his wife on the forehead and ran up the stairs.

7

THE REST OF the morning was unusually warm for March. Birds chirped and flapped onto branches with a view into Austin's room. Jeremy and his son had spent afternoons watching them at a feeder they hung there before a fall storm knocked it off its peg.

Jeremy walked around the house, lifting the windows up halfway. The curtains expanded with every gust.

"Pri, I'm headed out. I'll see you later. Wanna go out for dinner tonight?" he shouted as he grabbed his keys.

"That'd be great, I'll make a reservation."

In his haste to get down the porch steps, Jeremy tripped over his feet, stopping short after spotting Sandra at the side of her house organizing the trash. He hurried to reclaim his balance before she looked his way . . . if she looked his way. Assuming she'd shuffle back inside without lifting her head, he pounced at the opportunity to dig.

"Good morning," he said, louder than anticipated. "Need some help?" He threw his briefcase and jacket into the passenger seat of his car and met Sandra at her driveway.

"Oh no, I'm fine. I'm a mess. Sorry you have to see me like this." Sandra crossed her robe tighter and adjusted her coiled bangs.

"On the contrary, you have that pregnancy glow most women would kill for. A few out-of-place strands of hair won't make a difference," and like a gentleman, Jeremy grabbed the garbage bin by the handle and rolled it down the driveway. He hadn't expected her to follow. After months of practice, she had become an expert dodger of friends and neighbors. So, he ransacked his brain for a conversation starter, even though he was twenty minutes late for work.

"This tree's getting so big. I remember when we first moved in it only had four large branches. Now, there are too many to count. What a difference twenty years makes," he said, looking up at the massive oak tree that shaded their encounter. A sting of embarrassment tingled across his face for choosing a tree to speak of.

"Twenty years," she sneered, "It makes a *huge* difference. It's crazy to think back at how different life was. Our kids will never experience a world like that again . . . and poor Austin won't experience it at all. He was the first to go," Sandra said, then snapped herself out of a momentary daze. "I'm so sorry, Jeremy. I don't know why I said that." She seemed sincere. "I haven't had my ounce of coffee yet. You'll have to forgive me, it's been a rough night," she said through a giggle, figuring it would be easy for him to excuse pregnancy brain having had two kids himself, but Jeremy hadn't gotten that far in his mind, stuck at trying to sort her wavering personality.

"No worries," he said, "but you're not wrong. Our kids' lives will be much different than ours were. It's only been seven years, so it's hard to know how it'll affect them as they get older." He aligned her garbage bin with his and slapped his hands clean.

Jeremy liked being the good guy. Most of the neighbors

had shut Sandra out once she became cold and distant, but he considered himself different, sympathetic. A little more understanding than the rest.

"So how's Logan?" he asked boldly. "Are you guys okay? The stress of work and a pregnancy can create tension. I remember when Pri was—"

"We're fine," she snapped. "Yes, there's stress and sometimes tension, but it's no different than anyone else's marriage. Why do you ask?" She had made their exchange uncomfortable for Jeremy. She was good at that.

"I apologize, but I'm not implying anything." He felt out of breath. "I just remember how it was with Pri and me during both her pregnancies. I was just making small talk. I'm sorry if I offended you." He glanced away, not knowing where to look, then lifted his chin to admire the large overhanging branches of the oak tree that towered over them.

Her mood shifted.

"So, what's this I heard about Ernesto's family's Death Date? Is it true?" Sandra asked.

"Yes, it is." His throat trembled. He hated to be the cause of friction. "I didn't know he had told everyone about it, although they do take it lightly."

"I guess that's a good thing. You'd think in all the years I've known Mia, she would have mentioned it." Sandra cocked her head in suspicion as if Mia had intentionally slighted her. "Are they at all concerned about how it'll happen? He didn't mention it. I mean, it can get tricky. Having to prepare for your whole family's . . . uh . . . *departure*?"

"I don't think there's much worry there, yet. At least, not at this stage. I'm sure it'll work out fine though. Besides, they have plenty of time to figure it out. About thirty-five years."

"I see. He didn't mention the year . . . or the amount of time they had left. Wow, that's a long life, huh? Lucky, they won't leave each other behind—or even grieve each other's deaths. Now that I think about it, seems like a perfect situation," Sandra said.

"Well, that's if they even get around to passing on the same day." Jeremy checked his watch. "They're on a quest to make sure it doesn't happen."

Sandra looked baffled. She released the belt on her robe and readjusted it, as if preparing to stand by the curb longer than expected.

Jeremy was ready to go. He fiddled with his watchband as a way to bring attention to the time.

"I don't get it," she said.

"You know, the *rumors*. The ones where people claim they have defied their destiny."

"What about them?"

"They spend a lot of time looking into those. Trying to figure out how they can do it too."

"But those are hoaxes."

"All of them?"

"Yes," she said, ready for a debate. "I've watched some of the videos online and all of those people are loopy, crazy. I don't think you can change your destiny. I mean, it's your destiny for goodness' sake. Most of those loons are on some serious medication. Expiration Dates have been on target one hundred percent of the time in the past seven years. There's no evidence at all that these people are being truthful," Sandra said with mounting rage.

"Maybe you should talk to the Arroyos. They know more than I do." Jeremy checked his watch with back-to-back glances, but Sandra disregarded it.

"Well, if it were that easy, everyone would do it, right? I mean, if it were that simple, everyone would be able to change their destinies whenever they wanted."

"I don't think any of us think that if it *can* happen, it's *that* simple. All I know is if there's a way to change your destiny, Ernesto's family'll figure it out. As I said, they have thirty-five years to work on it. Besides, it keeps them busy." Jeremy smiled to lessen Sandra's tensional vibe, then looked past her and waved at Shirley, who appeared at the next driveway hauling her garbage can to the curb.

"Good morning," Shirley hollered, walking back toward her front door.

Sandra did not turn to greet her.

Jeremy tapped on his watch.

"I have to get going. I don't want to be late. It was nice speaking to you. Give the kids a big hug for me," he said, opening the car door and climbing inside.

"I sure will," she said flatly and lingered at the foot of the driveway as Jeremy pulled away. She appeared lost in thought. Pensive. In another realm.

He drove with his eyes planted on the rearview mirror until Sandra's tense reflection disintegrated.

8

A s DARKNESS DESCENDED onto Gardenia Way, Ernesto pulled into the driveway, marking the end of a hectic day at the bank. He loosened the knot in his tie, undid the top button on his shirt, and turned off the ignition just as the last streetlamp flickered on.

If he remembered correctly, there was a single beer on the bottom shelf of the refrigerator door left over from two weeks ago, when the Bryson's stopped by to help christen his new top-of-the-line, stainless-steel grill. He recalled the night feeling perfect, everyone's family still intact enjoying a cool, sunny day that turned into a relaxing night under the stars. Now, they were missing Austin, and nights like those would never be the same.

"Mia? I'm home," he called out, tugging his tie off and locking the door.

"Hey, babe, how was the rest of work?" she asked, her voice cloaked by rattling silverware. "You sounded stressed at lunch. Is everything okay now?"

Ernesto's eyes scoured the living room and stopped at

Mia's tightly wound bun peeking out from behind the wall of the kitchen.

"Now, yes. Before, no. The whole branch was in complete chaos." Ernesto spoke loudly so Mia could hear him over the clatter of plates in the kitchen. "There was a woman who was missing documents to complete the turnover of assets to her sister. She started screaming, made a scene, scared away clients, and threatened to call the cops. When I came out to handle it, she finally told me she has an Expiration Date of a week from tomorrow."

"That's horrible. Was she able to take care of it?" Mia asked, walking into the living room holding an open bottle of beer out in front of her.

"Look at this—" Ernesto perked up. "You read my mind. I thought about this exact bottle all day long." He took a gulp.

"Anyway, we couldn't do it, Mia. She needed a few more signatures and said she'd try to come back with everything in a few days. There was nothing more we could do."

"That's heartbreaking. I'm sure she wanted to get everything done early so her last few days don't consist of running errands. Can't you help her somehow?"

"I have one guy working on it, trying to facilitate the whole thing for her. But we still need every piece of paper required to follow through," Ernesto said, guzzling another mouthful.

"Good. Do what you can, Ernie. That sounds like a horrendous way to spend your last days." Mia expected him to say he'd do more, but his disheartened look confirmed he had done all he could.

Ernesto's feet swelled inside his stiff shoes. He kicked them off and fell back into the recliner.

"Where are the girls?" he asked, still admiring the bottle, wiping off the condensation.

"They're upstairs. They both have big exams tomorrow. They've been studying for about two hours now, so they need a break. Are you ready for dinner?"

His head nod went lost in the three final gulps he took before pushing himself up, just as the girls trotted down the stairs.

Sherry was holding a gift-wrapped box with a flattened ribbon.

"Look what I found," she said, tears surging at the corners of her eyes. "I never gave it to him."

"Sweetheart, what is it? Gave it to who?" Ernesto asked, but felt foolish. He knew.

"Austin. I found it in my closet when I got home from school. It was supposed to be a Christmas gift, but I forgot about it 'cause I bought it in October. I can't believe I forgot to give it to him." Sherry's voice cracked as she planted her forehead on her father's chest.

"Sweetie, don't be upset. I know it's hard to believe he's gone." Ernesto felt her struggling to breathe normally, work through her desire to cry. "Those six years flew by. I remember when he crawled for the first time, across their kitchen floor to get his stuffed turtle . . . he was so determined. Feels like it was yesterday," he said, getting lost in scrambling memories.

Twenty minutes into dinner, the sadness that accompanied Sherry's newly found box still hung thick over the family of four as they quietly ate dinner, nibbling their way through their main course. The only sounds came from the clanging of utensils and the crunching of croutons.

Ernesto's internalized sorrow converted itself into anger. He viewed the death of his best friend's son as nasty, cruel. It was hard for him to talk his daughters through their grief. For him, there wasn't much to say about the loss of a boy whose first wobbling steps he recorded.

But the silence suffocated him.

Ernesto cleared his throat with a roar, ending the fifteen-minute stillness, and wiped his mouth with a napkin.

"So, you girls have exams tomorrow?"

"Yup, I have a literature test tomorrow, and Jacklyn's got biology. We've been testing each other since we got home from school. It actually helps me because next year, I'll already know what the test'll be like, so I won't have to study," Sherry joked with her family, a full school year behind her older sister.

"You know," she continued, "there was a new girl at school today and during lunch, she sat at my table and told everyone she doesn't know her Death Date. How could that be?" Sherry asked, perplexed by the new girl's confession.

"Her parents probably haven't told her yet, honey. There was a point where your dad and I thought we may not tell you until you were eighteen, but then decided against it. Even though you were ten and eleven years old at the time," Mia said, meeting eyes with each daughter, "we realized you two were mature enough to handle it. Some parents don't want to trouble their kids until they feel the time is right."

"I guess I get it, but it sets them up to be teased or bullied. When all this first started and some kids found out their dates, any time they argued, one would throw the other kid's Death Date in his face and he'd run off crying. It was terrible," Sherry said as uneasiness swept across her face, twirling the bottom of her ponytail around her fingers.

It pained Ernesto to see his daughters recalling the stress they had dealt with during the reveal. They were so young. He sat back in his chair and stared off into the dark street past the window, remembering the day the mailman arrived at his home with the red envelopes in his hand. There were only three. Jacklyn's notification was delayed, and every day that went by without receiving it felt like a dagger through

Ernesto's heart. He wished he'd never have to know when his daughters' last days on earth would be, but at the same time, the anxiety of having to wait for the last notice agonized him. He promised Mia and the girls they would open the notifications together, but instead, he secretly stayed home from work for three days until the last envelope arrived. While everyone was out of the house, Ernesto stood over a steaming pot of water, holding the envelopes over it and loosening the flaps.

With trembling hands and his pulse thumping in his ears, he read each date out loud, recording it in his memory.

Shocked that all four Expiration Dates were the same, he called the Bureau immediately to notify them of their error. While on the phone, his concerned tone turned into piercing yells, threatening to sue them for causing his family such distress with their careless mistake, enraged that his family would have to wait yet another week for the correct notices.

When the person on the other end verified they were in fact correct, he clicked the "end" button on his cell phone . . . without an apology for his rant, without a thank you, without a goodbye.

Anxiety wiped his knees out from under him.

He crouched down by the kitchen stove, tears of relief streaming down his face, grateful that his whole family would live another forty-two years, meeting their fate together on the same day, and hoped his friends across the street were just as lucky.

The girls stood from their seats and began gathering the dishes, dragging Ernesto back from his leap to seven years ago.

"Hey Dad, I want to show you a new layout we've been working on in the den. Do you want to see it?" Sherry asked, a little more upbeat.

"Sure, although you girls promised we'd all work on the new layout together."

"We think this is a better system than the one we talked about. I think you'll like this much better, and it's a lot easier to understand," she said with confidence, as she folded her tomato sauce–stained napkin.

"Plus, we wanted to surprise you. Right, Sherry?" Jacklyn shoved her elbow into her sister's ribs as a reminder that *that* was the excuse they had agreed to give their dad during their presentation.

"Yup. It's all a surprise. Just for you, Daddy, because we love you so much." Ernesto's youngest daughter opened her arms, but he didn't miss her broad smile as she went face-first into his sternum.

The girls led their father upstairs to their updated creation.

Mia rinsed off the plates as quickly as she could without putting them in the dishwasher, dried her hands, and joined them in the small hallway outside the den.

"Okay, I know we said we'd do it together, *but* Sherry had this great idea of a color-coded system. It'll help us find what we need right away without having to search for it through digital files or stacks of papers." Jacklyn stood in front of her dad with her back to the door, her fingers wrapped around the knob.

"Yes, and we can see it all clearly, side by side, and follow the patterns back and forth." Sherry clasped her hands at her chest, eager to unveil their project.

"Are you ready?" Jacklyn asked her dad.

Ernesto nodded, skeptical of what awaited him behind the closed door.

"Presenting, our new"—Sherry made a drum-roll sound—"Expiration Date defying wall!"

The den door swung open, revealing a mural of brightly

colored Post-its. Hundreds of sticky notes flapped vigorously as the rush of air flowed through the room.

"Well, it certainly is colorful," Ernesto laughed, not knowing what to make of it. "And bright!"

His eyes followed the colors from the top of the wall all the way to the bottom, near the baseboards. Then, from left to right, where the color-coded puzzle ended with a column of photos, resembling headshots.

Jacklyn grabbed him by the wrist and dragged him into the den, so the handwritten notes on each paper were more visible.

"This is how it works," Sherry said, with a pen in hand to use as a pointer.

"The pink ones are their current location with details about where they've lived, where they were born, things like that. The yellow are all the different places they've worked and/or gone to school. The orange are their birth dates, ages, and their supposed Expiration Dates, and the green sheets are basically our opinion of whether or not we think they're being truthful. You know, things that may prove or disprove their claims." Sherry slid her fingers around the wall, occasionally using the pen to point out specific notes.

Jacklyn then took over the presentation where her sister left off.

"The aqua pieces are miscellaneous things. Any quirks they may have, medical conditions. Anything that catches our attention on their video posts or social media."

Ernesto, impressed by their diligence, turned back to look at Mia, who already had a wide smile across her lips.

"Did you know about this?" he asked his wife. "How did I not know this was going on? This must've taken days. Where the hell was I during all this?"

"Yes, I knew, and if you look closer, some of my very own handwriting is on those Post-its." She walked toward the wall, pulled off an orange sticky note, and dangled it in his face.

"Okay, well, what about all these tangled up pieces of yarn?" he asked his daughters.

Ernesto's eyes followed the different shades of yarn zigzagging over the papers, neatly traveling from one side of the room to the other, ending at the pictures. They were wrapped around several thumbtacks along the way. He recognized the images as people claiming to have changed their destinies and lived past their Death Dates. The Arroyos had kept eyes on them via the internet for the last few months.

"Well, Dad. First of all, they're not tangled," Sherry said rolling her eyes, miffed that he would see their work as a mess and not a neat display of collected intelligence.

"Each person has their own yarn color which follows their path. See, we start it all the way over here"—Sherry pointed to the pieces of paper indicating their birth dates—"and it follows their journey all the way to their pictures. We do that for each person, and when the different yarn colors cross paths, then there's something they have in common and we can use that to determine if it had an effect on their Expiration dates . . . if it's even true, of course."

Ernesto began a slow, loud clap. "I have to give it to you girls. This is quite an intricate system you have here. You're right, this is a thousand times better than the manila folder idea I had that would have also involved a few of those metal filing drawers."

They laughed while still admiring the vivid masterpiece the girls had created with the help of their mother.

"Also, this is a faster way of seeing what may work. Even if the odds are against us and everyone out there, we can still gather up whatever information we have and try to help others, especially those with Expiration Dates coming up. You never know, we could save one person in our lifetime, and if we do that, this will have all been worth it," Mia said, replacing the paper she had pulled from the wall.

"I don't know what else to say except that I'm super impressed by how organized everything is." Ernesto walked toward the left side of the wall where the yarn trails began.

"Can you walk me through one of these?" he asked, strumming a purple piece of yarn that looped around two silver thumbtacks.

"Well, let's start here, at the beginning, which is the orange." Sherry used her pen to follow it back to the left side of the wall. "This is Maxine, and she was born in 1965. She *says* her Expiration Date came and went about a year ago." Her finger then followed the yarn up to a pink sticky note.

"She lived in San Francisco for ten years until she moved to San Antonio, Texas, a little over a year ago, right before her supposed Expiration Date. She worked as a barista at one of those trendy coffee shops for a while, was then rehired at a restaurant she had been fired from. She didn't say why, but apparently she loved it there and talked to the owner to smooth over any misunderstandings and—"

"Hold on, hold on," Ernesto cut her off. "How do you know so much about their personal lives? Please don't tell me you've talked to these people. Please," he said, disturbed by the idea of his daughters interacting with strangers online.

Jacklyn stepped forward, taking over for her younger sister.

"Dad, we have to talk to them. There's only so much we can find out on their social media pages. There isn't a whole lot to go on, and we need details—dates and other info—that we'd never get by only searching online. Interviewing them is the only way to get what we need." She paused, waiting for a reaction, but he stayed quiet.

She continued, "Plus, speaking to them helps us get a good read on them and whether it's something worth investigating or if it seems like a hoax. That way, we don't waste our time."

Ernesto turned to look at Mia, who had expected him to overreact. "You agree with all of this? Did you know that part, too? You let them speak to strangers? Isn't that something we taught them *not* to do when they were little?" he asked sarcastically.

"Yes, babe. The three of us have talked about this. We don't want you to feel left out, but you've had a lot on your plate with work, Austin, and being there for Jeremy. We didn't want to bother you with all this just yet, but the girls couldn't wait to show you. They worked hard on this."

Ernesto recognized Mia's stern look, scolding with her eyes, urging him to give in.

He stood silent, mulling it over in his mind, looking into his daughters' eyes as if it were the first time he realized they were no longer little girls. No bows hanging from their hair. No jumping around excitedly about the release of a new doll. At sixteen and seventeen, Sherry and Jacklyn had stepped into the shoes of intelligent, independent women and at some point, he had to let them go and make important decisions about their passion, which included the research of Death Dates. After all, he and Mia were committed to doing everything possible to help his daughters live more than just the next thirty-five years.

Ernesto pulled a chair out from under the desk, sat down, and clasped his hands behind his head. "Well, girls, I see you have it all covered. Let me know if you have anything for me to do, and I'll get it done."

"For now, I think we've done enough. Let's relax and clear our minds. It's been a tough week, and we need to get through that first in order to get back to all this, refreshed. How about we all go out and get some ice cream?" Mia suggested.

"That actually sounds like a great idea. I could use a nice fattening desert right about now." Ernesto used both armrests to heave himself off the chair and escorted his daughters and wife out of the den, gently shutting the door behind him to not rattle the papers that covered the wall.

He knew it was a job well done, and from here on out, if the possibility to live past Death Dates existed, Jacklyn and Sherry would be the ones to figure out the formula.

"Oh—and I forgot to mention," Jacklyn said as she hopped over the last two steps of the staircase, "I stopped by the Hellingtons' after school and talked to Janice about our wall, and guess what? She wants to help with the interviews. She gets to practice, and we get an *almost* professional reporter helping us. Win-win."

9

O N THE DRIVE back to her college dorm, Janice had reached the pinnacle of exhaustion, her eyes getting smaller as the street lights shined brighter. The hypnotizing highway divider streaked across the corner of the windshield as she pressed harder on the accelerator with her leg fully extended. Her father liked to tease her about her small stature. It made her look much younger than her twenty-two years, and she accentuated it with the cheerleader-style ponytail she wore high on her head. "You'll be the youngest-looking reporter on TV," her father had told her.

After bracing herself for a rough ride, it reassured Janice to see few cars on the road coming from the opposite direction. The glare of headlights speeding toward her tended to be extra troubling on this night, triggering a fierce twitch in her eye that brought on a lightheadedness mimicking one too many sips of wine. From her experience, that's the only thing she could compare it to.

The Hellingtons' eldest daughter had spent most of the day coiled inside a thick comforter, crippled by a migraine preventing her from writing an English paper due the following morning. Every attempt at flipping open her laptop was met with an unrelenting lack of focus, sparking worry in Janice of tarnishing her status as an excellent student. All this with just two months left before graduation. The last time she had had this much trouble was during the Expiration Date craze while in her freshmen year of high school.

Days after the burial, Janice experienced a decline in concentration. Her mind a dripping sponge: Austin and his short life. No room for absorption of anything else. Whenever a quiet moment presented itself, her mind would surge with curiosity of his final hours, minutes, and even last breath.

Was he scared? Did he know what was happening?
Did he feel himself fading?
Was he struggling to hang on or was it peaceful?
. . . What does that final second into death feel like?

When her thoughts crossed over into an unmanageable flurry of questions, they were loud—like screaming in her head—and they played and rewound with a shriek of a cassette player she owned as a child. Instead of becoming easier as the days passed, his death proved more difficult to process. The innocent little boy she babysat three weeks ago was now buried, alive only in her memory.

Diverting her attention back to the limited view of the road ahead, a sheet of blackness behind it, she welcomed the sight of a rest stop sign indicating it was only a mile until the next one. Forty-five miles away from school and she already needed a break, losing focus of the road she had driven on twice a week since her freshman year. The speculating, head pounding, and the hour-long ride had formed a powerful funnel cloud, violently churning around her.

To stay alert, Janice took a deep breath, but the sudden thumping and crackling against the car jarred her into full awareness. Her eight-year-old Civic had drifted into the shoulder lane, crossing the solid yellow line on the pavement and causing the tires to kick up a cloud of rocks and dust, powdering her view.

She had to stop.

Risking another near collision would only add to the four she hadn't told her parents about. As understanding as they were, she supposed it would just be another opportunity for them to hound her about dropping out of college, leaving behind the sixty days she had left to complete her bachelor's, which they claimed she didn't need.

Things'll get better once finals are over, she thought as she entered the bustling rest stop, an act that seemed to be just as distressing as driving. The door heavier as if pushing to keep her out, the air-conditioning blowing shivers down her spine, and the aroma of overcooked fried food, smothering. Even the chatter coming from the cramped dining areas exploded in her ears while walking toward the ladies' room.

With numbed fingertips, she splashed cool water over her face. From what she could see through the blurred view of her reflection in the scraped-up mirror, her eyes had filled with fatigue. An hour drive and a good night's rest until settling on a plan for the paper she was expected to hand in the next day.

"Can I have a bottle of ibuprofen? Whichever brand, it doesn't matter. I need to get rid of this headache"—she asked the clerk at a convenience counter, while holding out a ten-dollar bill—"and a bottle of water too, please."

As she whipped her head from side to side, the loosened ponytail smacked Janice's cheeks during her desperate search for an empty table in one of the dining areas. Dizzy and rocking on her heels, she stumbled toward a crowd gathering their trays. She pulled on two sections of her hair, driving her ponytail even higher onto the top of her head. Perhaps, she thought, that's what was causing the tension at her scalp—her heavy hair pulling at her follicles.

Every spoken word and glow of light caused a vibration at the back of her neck. Even the crinkling of the brown paper bag she carried the Advil in put more stress on her already throbbing temples. She sat at a sticky table and gulped down two pills.As many times as she'd been at this rest stop, everything looked foreign to her, nearly unrecognizable as she blinked her way around the structure. Unfamiliar sounds, a lot of them. Like sandpaper scraping a piece of wood. When she turned to look, it was nothing more than her tablemate cleaning pizza sauce off the side of his mouth.

Then it happened again. Unsteadiness, but this time while seated, coupled with a flicker of blindness. Her own diagnosis after searching online the last several days had led her back to the *trauma* of Austin's passing. That's how some sites had put it. Still, the more discomfort she had, the less she would tell her family. In her opinion, they were champions at formulating catastrophes from the insignificant.

A half hour later, Janice headed back to her car feeling only slightly better than when she came in. By the time she reached her assigned parking spot at her dorm, the Advil had done its work. A formulation of clearer thoughts, better decisions. She had convinced herself that quitting college would be in her best interest and likely the only way to make her family proud.

Her roommate, dressed in pajamas by the time Janice arrived, discouraged the irrationality:

"That would be crazy! Just because of *one* paper? The best thing you can do is talk to him. Send him an email requesting to meet and explain your situation. That's all, no need to quit school, I mean—you're obviously kidding, right? He's pretty easy going; he'll probably give you an extension," Sue said while dabbing pimple cream onto her face. She had already taken that class the prior semester and knew the professor better than Janice.

"Are you sure? I'm scared he's going to fail me again, then call my parents. They'll be so mad at me. I can't put them through that."

"What?—Your parents?" Her roommate chuckled, "What are you talking about? Why would he call your parents? You're an adult; he doesn't care about them. Trust me, he'll give you an extension. Besides, you've never failed a thing . . . and you told me you haven't even taken one of his classes before. Just talk to him," Sue said, fluffing her pillow.

"You don't get it, he totally hates me, he told me himself. Watch, he'll fail me no matter what and then I'll get left back a grade," Janice complained and immediately felt the heat of embarrassment rush to her face. It had gotten harder to hide the babble.

Her own words puzzled her as if someone else had spoken them. The glimpse of a passing memory from grammar school had somehow settled in her mind. Although disoriented and flustered, the dumfounded look on her roommate's face forced Janice to regain lucidity.

"Sorry," she grumbled, "I'm being stupid. I don't even know what I'm saying . . . and I'm not crying, my eyes are stinging. I'm exhausted; forget we spoke about this. I'll talk to him in the morning," she said, her head shaking away the confusion.

Her roommate brushed it off with a cautious grin, shutting off the lamp next to her bed.

Janice whispered one last thought: "Thanks for the advice. I owe you a donut, per our contract."

The ladies enjoyed a laugh as they each crawled into their beds, remembering the promise they had made to one another the first day they met four years ago. They drew up a fictitious roommate contract that stated one would buy the other a donut if she helped her through a rough patch. The original contract still hung on the narrow space of wall between their beds, barely legible, faded and dusty.

At six the next morning, Janice woke up refreshed but impatient. She watched her roommate sleep, unaware that an hour had passed when Sue began to toss and turn just before her alarm was set to reverberate throughout their tiny living quarters.

"Are you seriously up right now?" her roommate asked, her eyelids barely lifted.

"I couldn't sleep. I'm nervous about speaking to Professor Thomas."

Sue slammed the pillow overhead. "Stop stressing!" Layers of feathers muffled her demand. "Do what I said and go talk to him. You're making yourself crazy . . . and you're starting to worry me . . . for real this time." She rolled onto her back, stretched her arms, and let out a thunderous yawn.

"I think you're right. I want to get this over with. Maybe I'll take a quick nap until I have to leave."

Thirty minutes of sleep were unsatisfying. Janice opened her eyes for a second time that morning, clawing through a second wave of grogginess. Though she made it to the lecture hall on time, the recollection of it had deserted her. In the few seconds she stood in the hall waiting for her professor, anxiety had reassembled itself and stabbed at her much worse than the night before. She leaned sideways into the wall and let the cool, textured paint sooth her, but the sound of rubber soles squeaking on the glazed floor disoriented her. No way of telling where they came from. Behind her? From down the hall? From the side door?

A familiar face walked among the students that crowded the hallway, and it appeared in front of her quicker than its approach.

"Janice, are you okay?" asked her friend Rocky, whose

face seemed to zoom in and out as Janice squinted her into focus.

"I'm fine. I'm waiting to talk to Professor Thomas about my paper. I couldn't get it done."

"He should be here soon . . . you okay, though? You look a little pale, your eyes are bloodshot, you look hung over or something," Rocky examined Janice from head to toe. "Wait—or was it your neighbor? I know a few weeks ago you mentioned there was a kid with a nearing Death Date. Did that happen already?"

"Yes, it did," Janice said, the side of her face mashed against the wall. "That's probably why I'm having intense migraines. You can prepare all you want, but the deaths still affect you the same. I hope this doesn't screw up my average," Janice said through a glop that had developed in her throat.

"Girl, one paper isn't going to undo the four years of work you've put into this place," Rocky laughed. "You'll be fine. You're the only person I know that goes home sober after a party to study. Just don't make yourself sick over it. You don't look well at all, like you're coming down with the flu."

Just as Rocky turned into the doorway of the lecture hall, Janice identified the over-gelled hair of her professor. His denim jacket and tinted prescription glasses, in her opinion, made him look more like a trendy bar owner than a professor.

Janice pushed herself off the wall and met him halfway down the hall. With her chestnut ponytail wagging behind her, she then joined him at his quick pace back toward the classroom.

"Can I please speak to you for a minute?" Janice said, without the intention of waiting for a response. "I think I'm getting so stressed about graduation that I can't keep anything in my head straight. I've had these bad migraines and a funeral, and I didn't even start my paper that's due today because my six-year-old neighbor died." Janice spoke unusually fast, out of breath and nervous. "I mean, I started the paper, I just didn't finish it."

"Six years old, a baby. My condolences. I see how that can be distracting," he said kindly.

Mindful of his elevated glance, Janice presumed his eyes judged the top of her head where her ponytail hung at a slant.

"I understand; take time to recuperate and please get it to me in a week," Professor Thomas said and walked away, leaving Janice in the hallway to bask in the excitement of a second chance at the last English paper she'd ever have to write.

I'm finally doing it. She was giddy while walking into the lecture hall. *If I graduate magna cum laude, there's no way I can fail! I'm actually gonna do this! The right way!*

As she zigzagged her way through a row of seated students, preoccupied by her elation, Janice collected a series of strange glances and sneers from classmates, oblivious that she had actually spoken her thoughts out loud.

10

A T THREE IN the afternoon, on a day that could rehabilitate her marriage and Logan's relationship with their
kids, Sandra found herself face to face with chocolate
pudding smeared all over the walls.

Brianna had carried an open pudding cup into the house,
a gift from a teacher for being the day's class monitor. The
second-grader placed it on the coffee table while she shrugged
off her backpack, but by the time she went to retrieve the
container, the twins had gotten ahold of it. Excited to
demonstrate their artistic abilities, they chocolate-painted a
family portrait on the wall above the cream-colored couches,
adding a spotted dog to the drawing, which they didn't have.

Something that would have infuriated Sandra long ago
warmed her, driving a smile straight through her lips even
in her fatigued state. She had been suffering from swollen
ankles and lower back pain since the morning.

Instead of becoming angered and frustrated, she laughed
herself to tears at the chocolaty mess, dabbing the wetness
of her eyes with the cuffs of her tee shirt. It would take

hours to clean. Before filling up a bucket with soapy water, she snapped pictures of it and scrolled through the images, her finger sliding across the small screen, her shoulders shaking with silent laughter. Another powerful reminder that the twins were much more than just a handful.

Sandra's memory toppled with embarrassing trips to the supermarket, like last year when they knocked over a tower of discounted toilet paper. Sandra worked swiftly to restack the display before it brought on any undesired attention. Little did she know, Christopher and Christina had snuck off into the next aisle, pulled out individual rolls from the displaced packages and rolled them on the floor like bowling balls until the store manager put a stop to it. That same afternoon she grounded them, forbidding their use of tablets and DVDs for the following seven days. When they protested, she also eliminated cartoons and desserts. The only way she kept them busy, while running errands and cleaning up around the house, was with scribbling pads and crayons. At first, the twins had more fun peeling the labels off all sixty-four colors.

Sandra inspected the newly decorated wall with the flourishing thought that she had only herself to blame. All those doodling punishments the kids endured had likely created the chocolaty masterpiece.

The time she spent contemplating the proper method to remove the artwork and the laughs she had at its expense had left her with a little over two hours to get everything cleaned and back in its place. She would not let something as irrelevant as a pudding cup ruin a night that had taken two months to plan. It was too important.

Both nervousness and excitement had swirled in the pit of her stomach all day and blended to awaken an anxiousness she had only experienced the first time she went into labor. The basics now incited those same feelings; Logan getting home early, Logan having dinner with the family.

Sandra had the night's agenda tucked away in her mind like a secret . . . dinner, a movie, the harrowing talk with the kids, a second movie, and a sundae. The ice cream was meant to take their minds off the conversation they had sandwiched between both DVDs. To top off the rare evening, she would surprise her children with a day off from school.

Sandra filled a bucket of warm water, squeezed dish soap into it, dug her hands into rubber gloves, and dragged a sponge across the wall, creating thick streaks. The pudding art had become a display of chocolate arches. Getting the living room clean, washing her hair, and starting on dinner seemed impossible once she glanced at the time on the cable box.

During the first hour of scrubbing, her mind swooped into different scenarios of a day-to-day existence in which she could trust Logan to resume being a good husband and the type of father the kids deserved. Not that he had asked.

Through their actions, the kids convinced Sandra they had obliterated their father from their minds; they never asked for him, they hadn't uttered the word *dad* in months. How could she have let this happen?

For her, it was simple.

The kids would undeniably get to know the Logan she had married, a man enamored with the idea of a simple family life, and forget the crumbled version he had become.

Determined to make the next few months easy for him, she planned a series of expedited baby steps that would bring them right back to where they started, although it could not take more than three months. That's what led to the first jam-packed evening. Next time, she supposed, snagging him for two consecutive nights would come with less resistance.

The chocolate splotches lifted off the loveseat with ease, as she recalled an argument with Logan a few years back about paying extra to have stain repellent applied to it before leaving the store, but the wall differed, holding on to the pudding as if it had craved a dessert after all these years. Two hours of scrubbing made it look worse than the chocolate stick figures she had tried to eliminate.

Her belly felt heavy and her ankles nagged. She stood back to assess the saturated wall and concluded that putting more effort into cleaning it would not make it less chocolaty. She untied the bow of her apron and shimmied out of the neck strap. The wall would need a fresh coat of paint.

With no time left to wash her hair, Sandra tucked her thick, disobedient curls into a shower cap. For tonight, she decided on a side swept ponytail to help tame the fluff on her head.

After clearing a spot on the fogged mirror and reacquainting herself with a mascara wand, it crossed her mind that she was being selfish, a fool. Taking a path that could complicate her children's life even further seemed cruel, but she had to take that chance. Sandra quelled the badgering thoughts, vowing to move forward with no regrets.

"Kids, get down here and help me set the table. Your dad should be here in a half hour," Sandra called out to her children from the bottom of the staircase, her jitters evident in her screechy tone.

The kids' accelerated footsteps down the stairs sounded like a thousand pounds of a hammer, as each shoved the other out of the way to be the first to reach the landing.

Their mother disrupted their race with a pile of placemats, napkins, and paper plates she entrusted them to distribute. Although Sandra contemplated using her special china for such a delicate night, she opted out, expecting she'd be the one stuck at the kitchen sink.

The three kids walked steadily around the dining-room table, each with a task of putting down what they were carrying. Brianna set the placemat down, Chris followed her with the plates, and Christina was in charge of providing napkins, placing one beside each dish. Their mother had never seen them so orchestrated before.

Lost in her own thoughts in front of a simmering pot of pasta sauce, Sandra analyzed her wrecked marriage and family life. *How did things get this bad?* she wondered, stirring the sauce with an oversized wooden spoon. *What more could a husband want?* She revered herself as a great wife and an even better mother. She gave him three beautiful kids that he never had to clean or pick up after. Had she pushed him so far over an edge that justified a disconnection from his children?

As she reached for the knob to shut off the burner, her phone chirped with Logan's designated ringtone. With the only clean knuckle she had available to slide across her screen, she answered the call on speakerphone:

"Hi honey, are you almost here?"

"Nope, not even close. I'm working late so I won't make it home for dinner," Logan said. His tone crackled like ice.

She wiped off her hands, reached for the phone, and took it off speaker.

"But Logan, you promised to be home tonight." Sandra scaled back the harshness in her voice with every passing syllable. "Why are you doing this? Today was the day we were going to talk to the kids. We can't keep putting this off. We're running out of time."

"I have to go. I'm late for a meeting," he said, without acknowledging her objection.

"No!" Sandra yelled. "It's time you make us a priority, come home! You don't have to do it for me, but the kids are entitled to have their father around, especially now. Tell your client you've postponed the meeting until tomorrow," she demanded while undoing her hair and finger-brushing it up into her usual bun.

"Sorry, work is work. It pays *your* bills," Logan said, and soon after, Sandra heard the two dreadful beeps concluding the call.

She stood frozen in front of a splattering pot of sauce. Coordinating this one crucial evening had taken up valuable time and spanned across several moods. Trying again was not worth the agitation. The night she had planned would change everything, but if his conscience hadn't pestered him by now, then it never would.

With her back facing the doorway, she took a few deep breaths and exhaled away all the uncertainty. As much as he had tried, Logan wouldn't ruin this evening. She turned off the burner and grabbed a serving tray.

During dinner, Brianna told her mother and younger siblings about a girl in her grade who owned a pony; at least that's what she had told her classmates.

"I wanna a pony!" Christina demanded. "If she can get one, so can I," she said, detecting indifference from her mother.

"A pony isn't easy to take care of. You have to feed it, give it baths, walk it for exercise . . . " Sandra told her as she stood up with a napkin still draped across her belly.

"No way! The pony won't fit in the tub, and my bed is too little; we can't sleep on it *together*," Christina said, stunned by the amount of work a pony would add to her short list of chores.

The kids giggled hard enough to pulverize Sandra's idea that they needed Logan present in order to complete a family dinner. The twins even snorted a few times before winding down their laughter.

Sandra, suppressing shame and guilt, gathered the disposable plates before the next phase of their night, slightly modifying the schedule. The movies would be played back to back. No talk in between.

The kids slurped up their pasta spirals without a flicker of a thought that their father hadn't joined them. She wondered if things would be easier this way. At this point, it had to be considered.

After dinner, Sandra pushed the coffee table off to the side and placed a drop cloth over the pricey area rug. On top of that, an old bedsheet, assuming it would be a messy night of ice cream eating. She held out two different DVDs for the kids to choose from. The winner would be the one with the loudest cheers.

Lying between the twins with Brianna perched in front of them, Sandra leaned back on the chocolate pudding sofa, pondering the crucial discussion she and Logan needed to have with their three innocent children. She could no longer count on him. He was too far gone. It seemed that no amount of fighting would fix it.

With a twirling snowman on the flat screen, Sandra checked her phone for text messages and missed calls, still hoping Logan would reconsider, but ten o'clock came and went. No new notifications from him, no flash of headlights illuminating the living room as he turned into the driveway. Instead, the windows remained dim and her cell phone quiet.

A half hour later, the kids fell asleep on the living-room floor on top of their makeshift bed. Tiptoeing around, Sandra picked up their bowls and pulled out a couple of facecloths to clean their mouths, waking them with her slimy wipes. Draping a thin blue blanket over them, she waited for their slowed, heavy breathing to kick in and then crept up the stairs.

Without bothering to flip any light switches, she sat at the edge of her bed for a moment, staring out into the dark night, the sound of passing cars whooshing down the street. It wasn't supposed to be like this.

She slid off her bed in a seated position, supporting the underside of her belly, and headed into the bathroom.

The showerhead burst into a steamy drizzle as she turned the knob, leaning forward, allowing the water to gush over her head. She let out a few gasps followed by a steady stream of tears, as she did every night. Her silent sobs and shallow breathing were not a good mix in a slippery tub.

So, she sat . . . sat at the far end of the shower with her knees drawn to her chest, the spray of the showerhead barely trickling over her. She continued to weep until she felt hollow. Tomorrow, she would start over.

She slithered back down the stairs, kissed her kids on the cheek, and wiggled her way under the blanket, falling asleep almost immediately.

11

SHIRLEY LOOKED AT herself in the mirror of the luggage store, trying to decide which rolling bag would look better with her new sun hat. She stared at each of her reflections in the three-way mirror holding two different colored bags.

"I like the olive one; it suits you," the bushy-haired sales associate said, tilting her head to one side to get a better view of Shirley's reflection.

Her name tag read "Kathy."

"It's earthy, and it looks great on you, although you could never go wrong getting both," Kathy said with an assertive wink. "You seem well traveled. What kind of luggage did you use before this?"

Shirley cackled, throwing her head back as if the question had been a joke to laugh at, though it thrilled her to have given off that impression.

"Dear, I'm not well traveled at all. I've only been to two states my entire life—and that includes the one we're in right now." Shirley laughed. She had an inkling the woman's sales routine included flattery. "I haven't left Connecticut in over sixty years. This'll be my first time traveling as an adult. My first trip at the age of seventy-three. Better late than never, I suppose. With a death age of ninety-three, I have twenty years worth of vacations to plan, but I have to make sure I don't run out of cash," Shirley said, swiping her fingers together gesturing money.

"Wow—you'll see a lot in twenty years, for sure. That's exciting; I'm happy for you," Kathy gushed. "Too bad we can't all be as fortunate as you . . . to live a long, healthy life, but it makes me happy when others can. That's what life's all about, right? Doing what makes you happy? The sad part's when the people you love do the complete opposite; they curl up into a ball and wait for death, feed it, but I guess when you only have a few years left, it can get to you," Kathy said, sliding the charm back and forth on her necklace. She then placed the pendant between her teeth and gave it a chomp. "Still, you have to make a decision to keep living, or life would be pointless. I mean, before, we all knew we'd die someday, but it didn't stop any of us from *living* . . . waking up, going to work, going shopping, to a movie. Now, everything's different, but the outcome's exactly the same. We all know exactly how much time we have left, and it's like some people can't die fast enough, like they want to get it over with. It's crazy!" Kathy screeched, her eyes in a bounce between Shirley's reflections. She seemed repulsed and agitated, but immediately altered her mood.

"I apologize for my rant, I get myself all worked up for no reason." Kathy cleared her throat. "Anyways, who'll you be traveling with, your family?"

"No, I don't have much family left. It's just me and my daughter for now. Eventually, it'll just be me for fifteen years," Shirley said as she plopped an oversized sunhat on her head and stared into the mirror. "I lost my husband before the Reveal, so it'd be nice to do everything we had planned on doing together. But trust me if this were *back then* and we knew his Expiration Date, things between us would've been different. We would've taken advantage of the days we had left together." Shirley turned to look at Kathy and found her with her head hung low, peeling off her chipped nail polish.

"I miss him every day," Shirley continued. "We never made time for each other, focusing on work, making money, and paying bills. We figured there'd be plenty of time to travel and enjoy life and each other when we retired, but he never made it to retirement. One day he had a heart attack while I was in the shower. When I went into the bathroom, he was watching a baseball game, excited about a homerun someone had hit, and when I came out, he was gone. The paramedics said he probably didn't feel a thing and for that, I'm grateful." Shirley wiped under her eye, thinking she had felt the drip of a tear.

By now, Kathy's eyes had stuck to Shirley's reflection. "Wow. I'm sorry; at least it was peaceful . . . and I don't mean to pry, but how old was he? How long ago was this?" the sales associated asked. Her arms crossed her chest tight enough to make it look like she was hugging herself.

"Dear, I'm an open book. You're free to ask all the questions you'd like," Shirley said amiably. "He died seventeen years ago. He was fifty-six. I know it's hard knowing the exact day you'll leave this life, but if you don't make the most of it, it'll slip away and you'll never get another chance." Shirley had been in this position before, talking to strangers about her life experience, the lessons learned, but they had not all been as receptive.

"Even though I agreed with the Bureau notifying the country of their Expiration Dates, it was hard once we received them," Shirley continued. "They sat on the kitchen table for a whole week before anyone even touched them. We knew eventually we'd have to, but we definitely took our time. Neither of us knew how we'd react, and of course, we were afraid," Shirley remembered. "But I know how you feel. I've seen people waste their lives on something that, in the end, won't matter at all. The majority of people out there are chasing fancy cars, men chasing young girls behind their wives' backs, women chasing their husbands' best friend, it's a travesty. They don't chase the people they love and the time they have left with them. They don't take the things that are actually important into consideration at all."

The sales associate remained fixed on every word that crossed Shirley's lips.

"You know, dear, when we received the Bureau's notices, our youngest daughter's Expiration Date was exactly six days after we opened them. At first, we were confused and called to find out if there had been a mistake. The Bureau was overwhelmed with the number of calls they were receiving from people thinking there was a misprint. It was so new for everyone they couldn't fathom the dates actually being real. Well, six days later, my daughters spent the whole day at my house, trying to evade death. My oldest, who was thirty-one at the time, sat on the couch with her arm wrapped around her little sister . . . because if you were going to get to Angel, you had to get through Tara first. Later that night, right before midnight, Tara convinced her sister to go out and celebrate. According to Tara, she had helped her sister beat death. They drove to a bar one mile down from my house . . . *one mile*. On the way there, they were hit by a drunken driver and Angel was killed instantly." Shirley glanced away from her own reflection to look at Kathy. Her eyes expressed unexpected shock.

"I kept telling Tara, 'You can't dodge your destiny; you have to accept it.' But I guess no one thought Angel's destiny included being convinced by her older sister to get a drink at the bar. Life is crazy that way."

Shirley waited for a reaction from Kathy, but there wasn't one. She then exhaled into a regretful giggle. "Oh dear—I've done it again. I didn't mean for you to get upset. I tell my stories not realizing they can have an adverse effect on people. I try, as often as I can and probably not in the most appropriate places, to make others think about how their decisions can impact everyone around them, especially those closest to them. And you're right, before all of this, we all knew we'd die someday, could've been that same day or in fifty years, but that didn't stop a majority of us from giving our best before we made it to the finish line. Lately, I see nothing but hate and a lack of compassion for the very people they're supposed to love. It's disheartening. From the day the Bureau announced those dates would be released, I thought it was a great idea and that it'd give most people a real reason to live, but things have drifted severely since then."

Kathy took a deep gulp and repositioned her black cardigan, which had started to bunch up at her waist, but said nothing. Shirley assumed the topic may have been too sensitive and personal to discuss with a saleslady.

On instinct, Shirley changed the subject. Facing the mirror again, she stared at her disconcerted reflection, tilting the hat on her head a few different ways and acting as if their conversation had never happened.

"I like the color of this hat. I think I'll take the darker one too. You can never have too many sun hats while on vacation. Right, dear?" Shirley attempted an encouraging smile to snap the sales associate out of her unexplained trance.

Ready to leave, Shirley piled up her sun hats and turned to look at Kathy, who had sprung fresh tears by the time they came face to face.

"I'm sorry if I've hurt you. I sometimes find myself too liberal when it comes to this. I didn't mean for you to get upset. I thought we had similar views, and it was nice to be able to talk to someone who saw it exactly as I did." Shirley grabbed a tissue from the purse she had strapped across her chest and tapped under the sales associate's eyes. "Can I get you some water or something?"

By now, Shirley had figured it out. She recognized the look on Kathy's face.

"No, I'm fine, and I'm the one that should be apologizing. Please don't get me wrong, I'm totally *that* person. I like being inspired by stories like yours, and I'm committed to living—100 percent—to the fullest. However, as I said before, some of us aren't so lucky," Kathy said, every blink ejecting a new tear.

"I have exactly three years, four months, and twelve days to live. So, as much as I strive to maintain a positive attitude and to find my true purpose for being here, meeting a person with a long life is upsetting. I'm not sure why. I don't hate you, but I *am* envious."

"Dear, don't be, we all have our battles. Some lasting longer than others. Our Death Dates are hard to accept, but your outlook's exactly what'll get you through it. I know you look at me and think I've had a long and healthy life with another twenty to go, but my life hasn't been easy by any means. My oldest daughter, Tara, the one who feels responsible for her sister's death, is now thirty-eight, and since this happened seven years ago, she hasn't been the same . . . caring, career-driven . . . it's all gone," Shirley said, seeing a hint in Kathy of what Tara once was.

"It hasn't been easy, dear. She's been on drugs ever since. I once saw her using cocaine, and after that I found a needle in her bedroom. Her sister's death affected her, but she chose to go down a dark path when the correct path was there for the taking. So be proud of who you are, be proud of how you carry on. If you love the people in your life, it'll come around full circle. I don't wish my daughter's behavior on anyone. Because of how she's chosen to live her life, it's affected everything around us. I can't have a party or invite friends over, we don't talk, we don't go anywhere, we don't have that mother-daughter relationship. Most of the time, I don't even know where she is. It's a stressful way to live, but I'll never stop trying with her."

An apologetic smile broke through the solemn expression of the sales associate. She pulled her short, frizzy bob behind her ears and walked to a smaller mirror hanging on the wall where she cleaned up streaks of eye make-up.

"I'm sorry—sorry you have to live like that. Plus, I feel like I made you my personal therapist. You should bill me for your time," Kathy said, erupting into deep laughter.

Shirley picked up the olive rolling bag she had placed on the floor and pushed it toward the register. "I'll take your advice about the olive bag. You are a *very* convincing saleswoman."

After Kathy rang her up, the two women hugged by the glass door. Shirley grabbed her new bag and set off for the bus stop.

12

SHIRLEY HAD NOT checked the time when she left the luggage store, and as she waited at the corner for the bus back home, she noticed the crowd becoming more substantial. She sat on a weathered wooden bench at the tail end of rush hour, narrowing the space she consumed; she drew the new rolling bag closer to her side and tucked the shopping bag between her knees, crushing the big floppy brims that spilled from it. She had suddenly become more aware of those traveling alongside her, surrendering space and learning to be more compact with her belongings. Accustoming herself to the crannies of airport security lines and window seats of airplanes. From what experienced flyers had told her, there would not be much elbow room, and if she snagged an armrest, they suggested she should fight hard to keep it.

The flow of traffic had decelerated, each car moving slower than the last. A hypnotizing sight from where Shirley sat, her mind streamlining to a time when her husband hand-wrote plans for their future. A list of all they would see starting the day after his retirement. Together they added to it, scribbling ideas in bullet points on a scrap of paper. It clung to the refrigerator door for ten years until the day he died. That night, Shirley snatched it from its magnet, punched it into the garbage, and watched as paramedics lifted her husband's shape onto a gurney and rolled him out of their home.

Regret is never easy. A wish of never having thrown out her husband's only impulse. A man who contemplated and planned every detail of their lives until an urge struck him to race toward that refrigerator list with a sharpened pencil in hand. Specks of excitement fell within every one of his scrawls.Shirley spent years sorting through her memory. A longing to re-create it down to the way his letters rested across the page.

- Rent a fancy RV, the kind with sleek interior and luxurious décor
- Drive south, making stops along the way
- See Graceland

The rest of her husband's plans had disintegrated. No amount of racking her brain had summoned them. Still, what did it matter? Because what she and her husband had not anticipated back then was the burden of a drug-addicted daughter. A circumstance that gladdened Shirley he did not live to witness what Tara had become.

Commuters closed in around the distressed bench where Shirley encapsulated herself, their impatience and fatigue detectable: grunting, tapping their feet, their eyes jumping from the bus schedule to their watches. A choleric world compared to what Shirley created for herself inside her limited space. Like an aura of protection bubbling around her to keep the hissing at bay. *What you want is what your eyes will see*, Shirley had told her neighbors when they cringed about her journeys on the city bus, but the different people she met along the way made getting around town exciting. The one broad smile among a horde of sour-faced commuters.

Eleven months earlier, she had made the decision to let her license expire. Now, the old Chevy she shared with her husband sat idle in the driveway. The last time she sat behind its wheel, she had stranded herself in Hartford, some twenty-five miles from home, giving in to her night blindness. Back then, she made a promise to never again be further away than a few miles from Tara. On the worst of her recent days, she instead had prayed for ten thousand miles between them.

The bus showed itself in the distance behind a congestion of different-sized vehicles with puffs of black smoke as Shirley's mind billowed with the idea of scrolling through resort websites and choosing the one with the most pictures of beaches and palm trees. With her lack of experience, how else was she expected to choose? Her first stop: Florida, a state she heard people of her age should live, not opposed to moving somewhere she thought would be better suited for her lifestyle.

Shirley got to her feet, the tips of her sandals teetering at the edge of the curb.

A few good Samaritans saved her from a clumsy boarding while lugging her purchases up the three steps, and after a forty-five-minute ride, she arrived at her stop and disembarked under a vermillion sky.

"Mrs. Wilcox, I assume you're going my way," Jeremy said, yelling through the passenger window from the driver's seat as he turned onto Gardenia Way. "Come on in, I'll give you a ride."

"Thank you, Jeremy. It's been quite a day. How're Priscilla and Jen?" she asked as they pulled away from the curb.

"Eh—" His head wobbled from side to side. "They're coping. We try to spend as much time as we can together to make it easier on us."

"That's the only way to do it. As long as you stick together, you'll get through anything. My family was also close before my husband passed away."

In the six years they had known each other, Jeremy had heard about Angel's car accident several dozen times and little about Tara. But Jeremy prided himself in not being the meddling type.

"So, how's everything going with you? I see you went on a little shopping spree today. Going somewhere?" he asked.

"Yes, I'm making travel arrangements for myself," Shirley said shyly. She felt silly traveling for the first time so late in life. "I've been putting it off, but I think it's finally time I dip my toes into the traveling pool. You know I've never been on a plane, right?"

"Is that so? I had no idea. I personally hate flying. Plane rides can get tricky during turbulence, but I'm sure you'll do fine," Jeremy said, glad they had arrived at Shirley's house when they did before he sparked a fear of flying in her.

"This ride usually costs twenty dollars, Mrs. Wilcox, but for you it's always free."

"Sounds like today's my lucky day."

Jeremy grabbed her two bags, dropped them at the front door, and within a few strides, made it back to the passenger door to help Shirley out of the car and up the porch steps.

"Would you like me to help you inside with these?" he asked, tipping his fictitious hat impersonating a bellhop.

"No dear," Shirley said, waving him off. "Thank you, but you've already done enough. I don't want to take up anymore of your time. Now, go on and get home to your girls; they're waiting for you," she insisted, drawing his attention a couple of houses away where Priscilla and Jen waved from their front lawn.

"Well then, have a great night, Mrs. Wilcox. Let me know if you need anything," Jeremy said, crouching back into the car.

Shirley already regretted not taking him up on his offer to help her inside. The new bags felt as if they had somehow filled with sand, resistant and heavier than when she had left the luggage store, and as Jeremy slammed the car door two houses away, she stumbled up the last step and wrestled the disobedient bags through.

The first sight from inside her home fired through her like a cannonball. She dropped her bags and threw herself onto the rug.

"TARA! WAKE UP! WAKE UP! WHAT'S WRONG?" She flipped her daughter over by the boney shoulders that poked through her tee shirt and laid her flat on her back. What looked like blood smeared across her mouth, after close examination, appeared to be day-old lipstick. She tapped her daughter's cheeks several times, but her head jiggled as if on loose hinges.

Shirley's heart thumped louder than her thoughts, overpowering them into disarray. She wanted to cry, scream, and at the same time, she wanted to do nothing. Walk upstairs without dinner and sleep until tomorrow's sunrise, but her fingers had acted on their own, fluttering across her phone.

"9-1-1, what's your emergency?"

"Please, help! I think my daughter's—unconscious. I'm at—"

She stopped before giving her address.

"—nevermind!" Shirley ended the call before the dispatcher's instructions. An empty bottle of pills rested in the crevice between two couch cushions, discarded after having completed its one task. Shirley felt herself holding in vomit. The flavors from lunch sizzled at the back of her throat. Through quivers, she thumbed Tara's wrist for a pulse, but could not hold still long enough to distinguish her daughter's faint palpitation from her own through the tips of her fingers.

Tara looked gray.

Shirley tilted her daughter's head back, took a deep breath, and began filling Tara's lungs with a few hard blows into her mouth.

Nothing.

With interlocked hands, she pushed down on Tara's chest twenty or thirty times, adding a dozen for good measure after losing count. Her mouth hovered over Tara's, she blew two more quick breaths and waited.

Tara let out three gurgled hacks. Yellow foam spilled from her mouth.

Tara was alive.

"Sweetie, wake up!" she cried, pulling up on her eyelids.

Shirley sat back on her heels and looked over her daughter; a bizarre version. Hair dyed black and cut bluntly around her face, left to look like a tangled, mispositioned wig. And perhaps the scribble on her arm, blotchy and puffed, was a new infected tattoo . . . or had she tried to cut herself? Was that not a teen epidemic? If not for the faded black tee shirt and dirty jeans with the hole at the knee, Shirley would not have identified this person as Tara.

Then, the commotion outside the house stunned her stiff, the laughing and shouting crystal clear. Kids on skateboards passed like a rumbling cloud, their projected hollers making it far into the living room where Shirley had seemingly brought her daughter back to life.

The door was still wide open.

Aggravation crackled through her bones wanting nothing more than to shut out the rest of the world, forget everything and everyone in it. Her mind excited her with the idea of leaving on a plane and never looking back, but once the thunderous sound of miniature wheels on the pavement diminished, she pounced on the door and slammed it shut.

It took thirty minutes: the jerking of the car up the driveway, around the house, and into the backyard. One of the side mirrors now hung by a clump of colored wires.

Back inside, Shirley reached over her head and into the linen closet, yanking on a thick comforter and ignoring the folded towels that tumbled out with it.

"I can't believe this is my life," she mumbled, walking down the steps. The twin-sized comforter trailed behind her like the train of a wedding gown, gliding over the floor, following her through turns and swivels.

Shirley dropped to her knees, flapped the blanket into place, and rolled Tara's skeletal frame into the center. Her consistent heroine use had put her at the average weight of a twelve-year-old girl.

She had done this before when Tara was a newborn and she, an inexperienced mother; folding the corners over her body, over arms that resembled fallen twigs. Tight tucks on each side. Shirley swaddled her daughter as she had nearly four decades earlier. This time, easier than the first. Tara had been a squirmy newborn.

Shirley gripped the top end of the comforter and tugged backwards, sliding her unresponsive daughter across the kitchen floor and into the yard.

The biting breeze tossed Shirley's silver hair around in different directions, catching on her eyelashes and lips. The sun had gone and left behind a chilly evening, tranquil and soundless, the surrounding houses lit only by the glow of their windows.

From inside the car Shirley wrapped her arms around Tara's boney chest and hoisted her in. She pulled, grunting and moaning, inch by inch, until Tara's small frame lay across the back seat, her knees twisted and bent to fit.

Spotty vision on the darkened highway left Shirley unable to spot potholes before speeding over them, bucking off her seat. It reminded her of a mechanical bull she had ridden on her twenty-first birthday. Yet, this was a ride to the hospital, and her only living daughter lay in the backseat.

She would risk everything to avoid the embarrassment of another ambulance blaring its sirens in front of her house. How many more times could she tell neighbors she had accidently set off her senior alert tag? The last time it happened, their distorted smiles implied they had not believed the story.

With less than a mile to go, the hospital building became visible, towering over the condo complexes that stood before it.

Shirley braced herself for another harrowing visit to the emergency room.

The third of the year.

The first in which Tara was unconscious.

13

THE COLD AIR of the hospital discouraged Shirley's sluggishness. She had been awake for almost twenty-four hours; the moon, now receding behind a slow burn on the horizon, had kept her company throughout the night. That and the steady beep of Tara's heart monitor.

Shortly after arriving at the hospital, the drug addict had her stomach pumped while her mother watched from ten feet away; Shirley grabbed at her own neck, cringing while her daughter gagged on the long tube nurses forced down her throat. Tara had attempted to kill herself for the ninth time since her sister's death.

Over the past few years, Shirley had cautioned her daughter, *Your destiny is your destiny. If that's what's in your cards, then that's what'll happen. You can't change the path that was written for you. Embrace it and move forward or bad things can happen.* But her words never quite took ahold of Tara, who carried on untroubled by her mother's declarations.

Though she would never stop trying, Shirley had

convinced herself there were no more ways to inspire her daughter.

Movies she rented sat on the coffee table unseen.

Popcorn, unpopped.

Books went unread.

Gifts returned for cash.

Dinner reservations Shirley made for two had only seated one.

What more could she do?

Tara had five years left to resurrect a worthy existence. Yet that's what she hated about herself the most, having a Death Date nearly twelve years longer than her sister's. Guilt that ripped through her the day they tore open those red envelopes. Six days later, Tara went to the police station to formally take responsibility for Angel's death, hoping to be arrested.

Spears of daylight pierced through the desolate hallways of the hospital. At this time of the morning, the emergency unit livened with sporadic grumbles, troubling coughs, and yawns. They seemed to be coming from one person, maybe two at most. These days, there were fewer patients due to the Six Months Policy the government had imposed. Access to the bureau's software kept hospitals informed of patients who should be treated and those to be sent home. The healthcare industry's way of preserving resources so they weren't wasted on someone who couldn't be saved.

Shirley had spent seven years trying to persuade Tara to live free of guilt and regret, but that seemed to push her further into a life of self-destruction. As the years went by, she stopped caring about her boyfriend, her career, her family, and then herself.

The grumbling Shirley had detected in the hallway erupted into a familiar roar, penetrating through her exhaustion. She wiggled her way out of the chair, bracing her back and shoulder now sore from dragging her daughter across the house. Grabbing the aluminum cane the nurse had loaned her, she limped toward the hallway, her shoes squealing on the freshly polished floor.

Norma, Janice's mother, stood hunched over the front desk of the emergency room in mismatched sneakers, a fleece jacket, and yoga pants that were stretched out at the knees. She grasped at her stomach as if suffering from abdominal pain, but her shrieks didn't seem to rouse the callous-looking receptionist sitting behind a computer monitor.

The forceful snap of Shirley's cane reverberated through the hallway with every hurried footstep she took toward her neighbor.

"Norma? Is everything okay?" she shouted, approaching the waiting area.

Norma's head floated up. Discolored streaks cut through her rosy cheeks. Her eyebrows, thin and sparse.

"Are you okay? What's happening?" Shirley asked, scanning the area for Barry. "You don't look well. Are you alone?" She had never seen Norma without well-blended foundation and perfectly penciled-in eyebrows.

"It's Janice!" Norma cried, bubbles forming at her nostrils. "She collapsed this morning. They don't know what's wrong with her." She gulped her words and held a soggy tissue to her nose.

"What do you mean they don't know what's wrong with her? Is she conscious? Is she awake? We need to find out." Shirley raised her tone demanding attention, but the oblivious receptionist either didn't hear or couldn't be bothered to look up.

"She's conscious now, but we panicked when we couldn't wake her. I don't know—what—I'm going—to do," Norma's words faded in and out, but Shirley restored her focus, tugging on her shoulders to draw her back to the present.

"She nearly fell down a whole flight of stairs," Norma said. "I was getting ready for work and from one second to the next, she was on the floor. I caught her as her knees buckled. Her arm went through the banister, and it could be broken. We called the ambulance right away." Norma inhaled deeply through her nose, slurping up the slime that clogged her airflow.

"She told us she's had bad headaches at school. So, I hope it's just the stress of graduating. Hopefully, that's *all* it is," Norma said as she blew her nose into a used tissue. "I'm so sorry. I didn't ask what you're doing here. Is everything okay?"

Shirley's repeated story about tripping off her medical alarm would not work again.

"Yes, everything's okay, dear. Tara had a seizure, something from childhood. She also has the flu. She hasn't been eating much," Shirley said, boldly. "But she's better now. She's resting."

Seconds later, a man in a long white coat appeared at a set of double doors looking for *Mrs. Hellington.* The frantic mother's steps progressed into a light jog through the waiting room, skirting around scattered chairs to meet him.

"That's fine." Her scolding tone overpowered the soft-spoken man. ". . . Whatever you have to do. I'll be right here when she's done. Come out as soon as you can to get me. I want this resolved immediately," she instructed him as he turned to disappear behind the swinging doors.

Norma followed the winding path between the chairs back to Shirley.

"He said they're taking her up to the fourth floor for a CAT scan and a few other tests. Apparently, she fainted at school the other day, but this is the first I'm hearing about it. She only told me about the discomfort she had driving at night and the migraines, but nothing about fainting. Nothing whatsoever . . . how could she keep that from me?" Norma raised her voice at Shirley, attracting the eyes of the lazy receptionist, who watched until Norma reverted back to her panic-stricken demeanor.

"I'm sure she didn't want to worry you. The stress of papers and finals right before graduation can be detrimental to your body. It can lower your immune system too. Fainting spells are your body's way of telling you to slow down." Shirley's justification for Janice's condition made sense to Norma, but the attempt at calming did not work. There had to be more to it. Tension puddled in her knees, which weakened under her own weight. She fell back into a chair, her sobs heavy enough to be mistaken for hacking and asphyxiation. She cried for several minutes, wiping her slippery face with the sleeves of her jacket as Shirley watched on with her own desire to breakdown. She had yet to shed a single tear over Tara.

Upon her last sniffles, Norma pulled down the bulging zipper of her fleece jacket that had ballooned around her neck and fished around in her pockets for more tissues.

Shirley walked cane-less to the young woman at the front desk and returned with a fresh box. She had every intention of cutting Norma off to check on Tara now that it had been twelve hours since her sedation.

"It's just so hard . . . " Norma continued, pulling on a lump of tissues from the slit on the box, ". . . when your child gets sick." But she noticed Shirley had immersed herself in the actions of a few people down the hall. "I mean, you know what it's like, your daughter having a seizure and all. You try so hard to protect them from everything, but it's impossible."

"It always is, dear. Try to stay calm. Is anyone else here with you?" Shirley asked, distracted, her eyes locked on the activity by Tara's room.

"No, Barry was trying to get into the ambulance with us,

but I told him to stay home with Lacey until she wakes up. She's also under a lot of college stress, worrying about papers and exams. When she gets up, he'll drive them both here."

"I hope I'm not out of line asking this, but is it safe to assume her date isn't today or within the next few weeks?" Shirley's face flushed as the words slipped from her mouth, supposing she had overstepped boundaries her neighbors had never crossed when asking about Tara.

"No—not today," Norma replied flatly. For her, Expiration Dates were personal, not to be spoken of. Like marital problems or income.

Shirley regretted the intrusion, disappointed for not taking into consideration that doctors were running more tests on Janice. If her Death Date were close, the ambulance would not have transported her. A cup of fresh coffee, she thought, would help sharpen her lethargic and sleep-deprived brain.

"Well, that's good news. She'll be fine. She's a great student, and I'm sure the stress has overwhelmed her," Shirley said, unhooking the cane from the armrest and positioning it at her side.

"If you'll excuse me, I'm going to make sure Tara's okay and that she hasn't woken up yet. I'd like to be there when she does. Even when your kids are nearing their forties, you still try to protect them with all your might," Shirley said with a weak smile, but the pout across Norma's lips persisted. She limped away while Norma's eyes supervised the double doors that at any moment would spit out that lanky technician.

As she looked around the colorless waiting room, different shades of gray and white blending into the fluorescent light, Norma conceded to the harsh reality her family faced. In just over a year they would lose Janice at the age of 22, merely a child in her eyes.

In one uncontrolled thought it became indisputable; this

would be the day Norma would look back on and remember what it was like to still have Janice alive and in close proximity, even if at a hospital. It would be a day she would cling to once Janice had passed—and until her own memories went dim—but she did not want to think about it while her daughter was alive. Norma revived from her thoughts with the help of a TV in the corner of the waiting area that brightened with a rerun of a black and white show she had seen before, although she couldn't remember the name. Her attention then fell on the receptionist at the front desk, who never glanced up from her cell phone unless someone required her attention. Norma's senses stirred, setting out to absorb every detail of this exact moment so it would remain vivid in her memory . . . because among everything horrible that happened, Janice was still alive.

The anxious mother repositioned herself in the cramped seat to face the hallway Shirley had feebly walked through. She watched her gray-haired neighbor turn into a brightened doorway. Shirley had selflessly sat next to her, making an effort to soothe her when no one else did, even though she had her own ill daughter in a room just a few steps away.

Norma jumped to her feet and slapped on the receptionist's counter.

"Hi, I'm waiting for my daughter's test results. If someone comes looking for me, I'll be down the hall. I have a friend here who's tending to her daughter."

"Okay, no problem," said the annoyed receptionist, flipping her hair behind her shoulders to reveal small pictures of ducks on her blazer.

Norma knocked on the open door of Tara's room, surprised to see half of it concealed by a long gray curtain. "Hello?" she called out faintly, taking a fraction of a step inside.

Shirley peeked out from behind the curtain and lurched

forward to meet Norma at the doorway, contradicting the labored movements she had been making all morning.

"Hi, did you get Janice's results back?"

"Not yet, but I wanted to make sure you were okay. Do you need help with Tara?"

"No, no dear. Not at all. She's resting, and I'm being as quiet as possible. I don't want to wake her." Shirley stood square, blocking the doorway without the company of her cane. "But thank you. I'll be fine; there's a nurse on this side of the building that comes in every forty-five minutes to check on us," Shirley lied. She hadn't seen a nurse since the previous night when they finished pumping Tara's stomach, but Norma crossing the partition would expose her to Tara's fading track marks.

"Okay, then—I'll head back to the waiting area. I'll be there if you need anything," a puzzled Norma offered, still trying to peek past Shirley's disarranged hair.

"Great. I'll come out and see you in a bit," Shirley said while steering Norma out of the room with one hand on her arm.

By the time she crossed back into the waiting room, Norma had stopped questioning Shirley's odd behavior and reclaimed her seat by the TV. An hour passed before the double doors flipped open again. The same technician appeared, this time holding a thick folder.

"Mrs. Hellington, would you like to head into my office so we can talk about Janice's results?" He pulled a pair of thin-framed glasses from his chest pocket and placed them on his face. Norma followed the technician through the doors, her right foot tingling from sitting cross-legged for so long.

"Please take a seat." He pointed at two chairs pushed up against the wall of the smallest office Norma had ever seen. Not a comforting room to receive news about her daughter's health. No certificates or plaques or health posters. Just bare walls flickering under the fluorescent bulbs.

"Mrs. Hellington, we do have some bad news. We discovered a brain tumor in her frontal lobe. That's what's causing the headaches, dizziness, fainting, and of course, this morning's seizure. We believe her health'll decline over the next year, leading up to her Expiration Date." His explanation seemed half robotic, half compassionate.

Norma's head dipped. Her eye sockets landed in her palms. She rubbed them until they tingled, until flashes of neon colors appeared, hoping to wake up to an alternate ending to her daughter's life. Something less brutal.

"Why? Why is she going through this? Isn't the fact she has a year left enough?" Norma gurgled as she fought to catch her breath; her head trembling, voice cracking, her tears slow and steady.

"I'm sorry to bring this news to you. Usually, physicians'll have these talks with patients and their loved ones, but most are attending a conference this week. It's a shame to see such a young, vibrant person go through this."

Norma had no interest in his proposed words of comfort.

She sat immobile at the edge of her seat, her face still buried in her hands.

The technician walked around from behind his desk and placed limp fingers on her back. "Mrs. Hellington, would you like to see her? I can take you upstairs. Then, we'll have to come back to the office and sign a few forms."

Norma strained to raise her head, somehow feeling unbalanced though she sat firmly in a chair. The technician guided her toward the elevators that carried Norma up to where her daughter lay in an unfamiliar bed with a terminal brain tumor.

FINAL NOTICE

Janice Hellington
Expiration Date May 21, 2019

Please plan accordingly

Janice: 389 days until death

14

THE CAR RIDE from the hospital was silent. Not because of the devastating news Janice had received about her brain tumor, but because of the comments she had made to her mother in front of the technician who sat trapped behind his desk during their blowup.

"Mom, I don't want to fight with you. This should bring us closer together, not tear us apart," Janice said, breaking the ten-minute silence.

"Yes, of course," Norma said calmly, having had the chance to cool off before leaving the hospital. "This'll be hard on all of us, and I absolutely agree with you. This *should* make us closer, but what you want to do will—without a doubt—tear us apart. We'll want to be around you all the time to take care of you, to make sure you're comfortable. Your father's already taking this news badly. Wait 'til he hears about your plans. *He's* the one that didn't want you wasting time on college IN THE FIRST PLACE!" Norma shouted her last few words, slamming her hands into the steering wheel. Rehashing the argument had infuriated her even further, but that was not how she wanted to handle this. So, she kept her eyes fixed on the road ahead and exerted all her energy into scaling back her anger. For a moment, she regretted raising Janice to be exactly like her, persistent and defiant.

"I'm sorry," Norma said. "I can't pretend that I'm happy about it or happy for you. Maybe I'm selfish, but you've already been away from us for four years when we begged you to stay home and go to school online. Now, look at what's happened. Our final year with you will be harder than the last four. That doesn't make any sense." Norma's rage peeked through what she tried to pass off as a level-headed perspective. Yet, she clenched her fist so tight around the steering wheel, her knuckles had gone pale.

"Let's talk about it when we get home. You're getting upset again. Everything's gonna be fine Mom, I promise." Janice turned on the radio, filling the car with deafening guitar riffs. She smacked the preset button and found something soothing for the migraine that began to ripple at the side of her head.

When they reached the driveway, Lacey waited at the bottom of the porch steps with a face that looked like it had cried for days. In two skips, she made it to the car, collapsing on top of Janice in a lopsided embrace before she had a chance to get out.

"I love you so much! I can't believe this is happening," Lacey blubbered, digging her wet face into her sister's shoulder. Every one of her tears slid off Janice's graphic tee shirt.

"I'll be okay. We all knew this was gonna happen. Stop crying, please," Janice said, grabbing Lacey by the elbow and peeling her off. It hurt to see her little sister worried. It would be easier if they agreed on disregarding the diagnosis and carrying on as if the tumor did not exist.

"Please, stop crying. Come on, let's go inside and have breakfast." Janice felt guilty for being annoyed and frustrated.

Lacey did not want to be difficult. She wiped away the tears with the back of her hand and led the way into the house.

When Janice stepped through the threshold, she caught sight of her father standing in the middle of the living room, his eyes radiating concern, much different than his usual invulnerable presence. It caught her by surprise.

For the first time she saw him not as her dad, but as a person, a regular person susceptible to pain and sadness. He looked helpless and *human*, something that affected her much worse than the discovery of a brain tumor. Her chest caved. She howled like a wounded creature and fell into him. Barry held her tight, rearranged his mood, and returned to his impervious nature, vowing to be nothing but brave in his daughter's eyes.

"Everything'll be fine, sweetie. Good thing they found the tumor early and gave you medication. Is it working?" he asked, his fingers curled around the fabric of her tee shirt.

"Yes," she said, lifting her blotchy face off her father's chest. "It actually took the nausea away and my vision isn't as blurred, but I have a headache. Obviously, as time passes and the tumor grows, the dosage will increase and eventually stop working," she explained, repeating what the technician had said.

Relief from the symptoms that had disrupted Janice's last weeks of school thrilled her, but her family's crass looks ruptured that sliver of optimism.

"Come on . . . are you guys serious?" Janice complained. "We've prepared for this and knew I'd be the first to go. I'm actually happy to know *how* it'll happen. I don't have to curl up in the corner of my room and wait for a meteor to crush me." Janice produced a hiccup of a laugh, but her little joke did nothing to rouse even the slightest smirk in her family. Instead, they stood as an organized bunch, facing her with glowering stares, reminding her of a vintage photo.

"Can't we move on and act like this never happened? This diagnosis doesn't change anything. I'll continue my life the way I planned. I'll get a job and enjoy that job, my life, and my family until my last day. What'll happen to me is inevitable. So, if we're not enjoying the time we have left together, then we're wasting it. Stop worrying about me." She gauged their reactions one by one. Her mother still appeared angry, Lacey's eyes were nearly swollen shut, and the look of defeat had resurfaced on her dad's face.

"Okay?" Janice squealed, motioning for them to muster up a response. Her patience had weakened and caused a numbing sensation to rise in her cheeks.

Norma took a slow walk to the recliner by the front door and sat, her way of buying time before speaking.

Taking the pressure off his wife, Barry went first: "Yes, we'll do that for you, but you have to let us know when you're not feeling well so we can take care of you. That doesn't mean we'll keep you bedridden; it means we want you to feel better so you can get back at it the next day. Okay?" Barry's raised eyebrows indicated to Janice they had their own list of demands.

"That sounds simple enough." She nodded. "You know, I wanna be that family you see in soup commercials. They're always so happy sitting at the dinner table ready with their spoons, and there's no way you could imagine them any happier until that steamy soup comes out. That's how I've always viewed us. I wanna be that soup family every day." Janice reached out for her sister and father and waved her mother in. They wrapped their arms around each other, squeezing together until they bumped cheeks.

But Norma did not give in.

She took a giant step back, slid out of the huddle, and returned to the recliner, kicking off her mismatched sneakers. Janice recognized the look on her face. She had seen it often as a child right before being reprimanded.

"I don't want to ruin the moment, but this isn't done. There's more to this. Janice, I think it's only fair you tell your dad and sister about your plans . . . *all of them.*"

Janice had mistaken their group hug for a truce.

"Mom, it's not something we have to make an issue of right now, but fine; let's get it outta the way." With unwavering confidence and her chest puffed, she turned to face Barry and Lacey. "I've applied to a few out-of-state jobs. There are two news stations that'll give you a chance as an entry-level production assistant to be on air if the opportunity presents itself. You guys know I want nothing more than to be a reporter. If I get to do that once in my lifetime, then my dream will be fulfilled. It's something everyone should strive for, whether it's right down the street or in another part of the world," Janice said with her arms folded, preparing for more conflict. Her ponytail wiggled from side to side whenever she moved her head.

Over time, it became illegal for employers to ask about an applicant's Death Date, classifying it as discrimination. She would keep hers a secret if it granted her the chance to be on air before she had to quit and prepare for death.

"Janice, I don't think that's fair at all," Norma said. "We're your family, and we want to spend as much time with you until—you know."

"However," Barry chimed in, "*we* understand you following through with your aspirations. Now, how far are these states you're applying to?" A smile finally broke through his anguished disposition.

"No! Hold on—Hold on—" Norma interrupted. "I'm not agreeing to this. She's my daughter, and I need to be by her side at all times." She directed her anger at her husband this time for giving Janice what she believed to be his blessing to move to another state.

Norma was desperate.

Was she the only one thinking logically?

Was she the only one taunted by images of her daughter lying unconscious in the parking lot of her job or in the stairwell of an apartment complex?

She refused to let Barry make her feel like the irrational one and fired at Janice: "You can't deny us your time. We're your family, and from day one—the day we received those god-forsaken notices—we promised we'd stay by each other's side until the end . . . and now, you're not holding up your end of the deal!" Norma hollered. Through her fury, she thought she saw Janice hold back tears. "I cannot and *will not* let this happen. You are *not* allowed to leave the state in pursuit of a job you consider more important than your family!" Norma shouted. She bolted for the stairs in a huff, stomping her way up.

From downstairs, the three could hear her heavy footsteps above, pacing the length of the bedroom. Barry felt responsible for his wife's outburst and chased after her.

"I'll go talk to her. This'll be hard on all of us, but we'll figure it out."

Two hours later, Janice's parents turned up at the kitchen doorway looking drained and teary-eyed. They seemed to have worked out their differences. Norma had changed out of her fleece jacket and yoga pants and into a gray tee shirt and shorts she only wore around the house.

"I guess we can have a family meeting now," she said, calling her daughters back into the living room. The girls had waited in the kitchen since their parents locked themselves in the bedroom.

The four of them gathered on the couches, each taking the spots they normally sat in while watching movies.

Norma spiraled into the recliner.

"Janice, I'm sorry for losing my temper before, but you girls are everything to me. We have less than thirteen months left with you, you're sick, and now you'll have to battle this tumor until next year. It won't be easy and you'll need help. There'll be a point where you won't be able to stand on your own anymore—"

"And that's when I'll come home. I hate that I have to burden you with the final stages of my cancer, but I want nothing more than to be taken care of by my mom. You said it yourself, I have thirteen months. Let me make the most of it. I'm not as fortunate as you guys. You'll be able to spend the next twenty, twenty-five years together. I'm not that lucky and have this much left compared to you." Janice squeezed two fingers together. "Please, please, please let me do what I have to do," Janice begged her mother, looking to her father for help, but he had no more than a shriveled smile to offer.

"Sweetie, if you let me speak, maybe we can get through this quicker," her mother said with a half-smile. "After giving it some thought, I now understand what you're going through. I'm not there yet—the end of my life—so I'm not sure what I'll be feeling then. I only hope I can be as strong and determined as you are to make my mark on this world. However,"—Norma lifted a finger in the air warning Janice of some ground rules—"if you get one of these out-of-state jobs, will you promise to call home every night and let us know you're okay?"

"Oh my gosh, yes. Of course, I will. I'd want to talk to you guys every night anyway."

"Will you promise to let us know if you're not feeling well or if you faint or anything like that?"

"Yes, without a doubt."

"Will you promise to fly home to see us every so often, before you really start to get sick?"

"Well, I guess I can promise if I have the money."

"We'll pay."

"Then, yes."

Janice's dimply grin dispirited Norma for a brief moment, seeing the little girl in her that did cartwheels at the playground right after going down the slide head first. The seven years since receiving the Bureau's notices had sped by. It took effort to picture Janice as a grown woman.

Norma's memories drew her away, muddling the progress she had made during her talk with Barry, but distressed and unsettled, she continued, "Your dad and I were talking, and we have an idea that'll go over pretty well with both you of," Norma said. "How about we take a trip the day after you graduate? So, it'll be a graduation gift and a way to create memories before you head off into the news world."

"Mom, that's an excellent idea," she said, relieved. "Like old times."

The next day Janice woke up before dawn with a nauseating headache that impaired her ability to get up and take her medication. She remained in bed until she recovered her balance. An hour later, she took a few uncoordinated steps and gulped down two pills with a bottle of water. Afraid it would brew more worry in her mother, she decided to keep quiet about it when she walked into the kitchen to a stack of chocolate chip pancakes. Her favorite.

15

THE SUN HADN'T come up yet, but Priscilla couldn't manage to stay asleep any longer. She'd counted backwards, forwards, and even did some division along the way to get herself back to a drowsy state, but nothing worked. Her battle with insomnia had worsened, and at one point, she had considered medicating her anxiety away, something she avoided despite pressure from her doctor. She attempted to meditate, though she was not certain how. The books, yoga classes, holistic centers, therapy sessions . . . none of them had helped.

So, after extensive counting and a few internal ohms, she conceded.

It was time to get up.

Reaching for her cell phone, she tried willing the night to be further along than she anticipated, magically speeding past the crucial hours and ending up somewhere in the six a.m. range or perhaps morphing it into a deceptive night of struggling for sleep. It had happened before, a fatiguing eight hours of sleep that felt like two. Anything was better than the restlessness she had experienced since Austin's death.

She threw the bedsheet over her head and thumbed around for the button to check the time on her phone. It was 2:03a.m.

What felt like an entire night of pillow flipping and deliberate yawns had only been an hour and twenty minutes.

Before her thoughts went astray, she started to map out the next five hours to keep herself busy—some laundry, dusting, meal prep—but her mind wandered anyway, and the uncertainty pin-balled around in her head again.

Would she ever regain control of the life that was tumbling away from her faster than she could chase? Would the torturous memories of her only son dwindle on their own without having to forcefully repel them in order to feel sane again?

Asleep or awake, her mind replayed a grainy slide show of Austin's life . . . and then his death. Lying on her back, her eyes stranded on the dark ceiling, the irrepressible cycle began for the fifth time since going to bed. Her memory back at the day Austin was born, in labor for thirty-two hours.

If only she could stop it right there. Slam on the pause button, protect him inside her womb forever because everything after that was excruciating.

The footage fast-forwarded in segmented flashes.

Austin's delivery.

Austin crying.

Holding him tight against her chest.

Waiting.

Still, for as many bad thoughts she had about his Expiration Date, her positivity had kept her tranquil. Never doubting her whole family would be around for a long time. After all, they were good people. If it came down to karma, she was confident it would pass over them in a heartbeat.

Once nurses had carried Austin away, Priscilla fell asleep in her hospital room, but soon after Jeremy came stumbling through the door, incapable of delivering the tragic news he carried up with him on a folded piece of paper. Stuck to his sweaty palm he waved it around, grunting, and she knew almost immediately.

"What is it? What is it, Jeremy? What is it?" Her voice grew more irate with every second that Jeremy remained silent, the words scratching the surface of her throat.

"What—is—it, Je-re-my?"

He wanted to tell her, get it over with. She deserved to know right away, but his words were stuck, balled up in his mouth. Unable to find his voice, his jaw hung loose, his tongue slipping out. Before he could say anything, Priscilla reached for a small plastic pan at the side of her bed and vomited.

Her hysterical reaction snapped Jeremy out of his malaise, and at last he confirmed what they had both feared.

"He's got six years, Pri. Only six years." His voice cracking, words jagged, not bothering to clear the lump of phlegm caught in his throat since he had collapsed in the bathroom.

"No! No, no no! It's not pos-si-ble! No!" Priscilla said through unbearable shrieks.

Jeremy dove to his wife's side, plummeting beside her, smashing his knees against the clammy hospital floor. He couldn't make Priscilla's pain go away. All he could do was hold her; the vibration of her wails numbed his chest. The intensity of her cries alerted nurses, who rushed to the foot of her bed, attempting to calm her because they knew too. They always knew, even before the parents did.

An hour later, just as Priscilla's howls faded, a new mother down the hall picked up where she left off. The woman's overpowering sobs riddled the hallways as nurses and other hospital workers carried on without flinching.

These were the new sounds of the maternity ward.

The anguished cries of the newborn's parents had replaced the sweet cries of newborn babies.

"Hey,Pri, you up?" Jeremy whispered. Her rapid and heavy breathing gave her away. Lost in her memories, Jeremy's voice catapulted her back to the dark bedroom where she lay.

"Yup, I've been up for about a half hour."

"Me too," Jeremy sighed.

"Did I wake you? I tried not moving around so much." She reached down her side to find his hand.

He wiggled his way closer and gripped her hand tight.

"No, Pri. I'm up every hour or so. I can't stop thinking. Even though I've immersed myself in more work than I can handle, it just won't stop." Jeremy released Priscilla's hand to rub the anxiety off his face.

"I thought I was okay," Priscilla said. "But it's getting worse as the days pass. I keep thinking, 'I haven't seen Austin in two days. Now, I haven't seen him in four days; I get further and further away from him. I don't know how to handle it anymore." She took a big gulp to loosen her throat. "I'm not sure how to move forward and continue a normal life when our family is incomplete. Years ago, when I forced myself to not think about dates, life seemed perfect. Now, I'll never have that feeling again. Our family'll never be the same." Priscilla's throat tightened again.

"Pri, those memories are there forever. I don't know why we were dealt these cards, but we were and we made that little boy's six years of life incredible, like he made ours. No one can ever replace him, but if we think it's right for us, we can always try for another. That's something we should talk about."

"That's ridiculous. How does that make sense? What

if it happens again? Or even sooner than six years? I can't go through this again. That's definitely not an option." Disgusted by his suggestion, she disengaged and sat back to face the blank TV screen at the opposite end of the room.

"We can always adopt, Pri. I wasn't done being a father to a small child yet. Saving one who needs a family would be fulfilling for all of us." Jeremy's words were assertive enough to make Priscilla consider it for a moment.

"That's not a bad—no. We can't. We'd be setting ourselves up for a similar situation. It's illegal for adoption agencies to disclose Expiration Dates before the adoption goes through. It can happen again. Honestly, Jeremy, I won't go through this a second time." She returned to her icy disposition, folding her arms across her chest, crossing her legs at the ankles.

"Pri . . ." Jeremy sat up. Through the darkness, she saw the softest expression she had seen on him in days. "It's something to consider, Pri, but at another time. We're still mourning our son's death and we should do that for as long as we need to. No one will ever replace him, but we *can* have another child, if that's what we decide is best. We have to give it time and figure out what'll work for us as a family." He grabbed Priscilla's hand again and leaned in to kiss her forehead.

Without further discussion, Priscilla mellowed and curled up in Jeremy's arms. Her eyes still wide, but her mind a little more relaxed. Or perhaps, exhilarated . . . if she had the nerve to do it all again, would an adoption agency disclose Expiration Dates if they offered more money?

16

A S THEY DRIFTED off in each other's arms less tormented after their talk, raging voices coming from beyond the curtains plucked them out of a near-tranquil sleep, zapping through them like the shock of an electrical current.

"I can't do this anymore," the man howled.

"You have to; it's your responsibility," shouted a woman.

Through drowsiness, Jeremy sorted out the voices. Sandra and Logan were arguing at four in the morning, rowdier and later than usual. He had witnessed their battles in the past, but this sounded different. Raucous. Vicious.

Jeremy flung the comforter out of his way and sprinted five feet to the window. His fingers split two slats of the blinds and through them, he could see a set of raving shadows. Obscured, animated arms crossed paths as they argued, but never seemed to make contact. The shadows disappeared from one window on the first floor of the house and continued in another as Sandra followed her husband from room to room demanding he take responsibility. But for what, Jeremy was uncertain. His hatred for Logan always led him back to the same conclusion—he should take responsibility for his crumbling family and for once, behave like a decent father and husband.

Jeremy pulled on the cord, and the blinds slammed into each other a quarter of the way up; then he slid the window open enough to poke his head through.

"What are you doing? They're going to see you," Priscilla said, hushed and repulsed.

He slammed his index finger onto his puckered lips, sparking a ferocious look in her eyes. Ignoring Priscilla's mumbles, he put his ear to the cool breeze and listened. Nothing more than mingling leaves and the hum of a car on an adjacent street.

Then it started again by the kitchen window.

" 'The hell do you do all day? You'd think a wife that doesn't have to work would at least have something for me to eat," Logan roared.

"I would have a meal for you if I knew whether or not you were coming home." Sandra's voice sounded strained. Jeremy imagined her face red and her eyes bloodshot from building pressure. "Please, let's fix this. We still have time. The kids need you right now," she begged. "I need you; I want us to be a family again."

A pause.

"Logan—honey—we're running out of time, whether you want to accept it or not. This *will* happen and they need you in their lives before it does. We have to face it together and do what's right, if only for the kids." Sandra's silhouette approached Logan's, her arms out, preparing for what looked like an embrace of reconciliation.

"Jeremy, please. It's an invasion of privacy. It's not your business. Close the window and shut the curtain before they see you. You'll only cause more problems for her." Priscilla spoke through gritted teeth.

Agitated by her interruption, Jeremy rolled his eyes without looking in her direction. He stayed facing the shadows, but the movement had ceased. No actual embrace, no waving limbs. Just two dark figures side by side.

The night had gone still.

The shouting stopped. No passing cars. No crackle of leaves.

Sandra and Logan stood in their kitchen, their shapes a little murky from where Jeremy watched. Two full minutes passed that felt like twenty, but the argument appeared to have reached its end. He threw the curtains behind his shoulders and as he pushed the window shut, Logan's large shape collided with Sandra's. The smack of flesh against flesh rang between the houses.

Jeremy spun and rushed through the bedroom door as if fire nipped at the soles of his feet. The way he hoped any man would if Priscilla faced danger in his absence, fast enough to have his tee shirt and pajama pants lag behind him.

"He hit her! He hit her! I'm going over there!" His booming voice and heavy footsteps shook the scaled picture frames along the staircase on the way down.

"He what? Jeremy, be careful. I'm coming with you." Priscilla ran after him, grabbing a jacket and fumbling her way into his size twelve sneakers she found by the front door.

Jeremy tramped through the grass with a vision of dragging Logan out of the house by his boney ankles, but Ernesto was already at the door, slamming the sides of his fists into it. The brass knocker bounced and clanged with every thump.

"Open the door now!"

"What are you doing here?" Jeremy asked Ernesto, who was too enraged to notice him.

"Open the door! Get out here, Logan!" Ernesto's nose

skimmed the door. His breath left a moist mark on the paint. He pounded his fist until it went through the threshold, losing his footing and falling into the house.

Logan had opened the door.

He stood tall in front of Ernesto, arms arched at his sides like an action figure with no muscles. His body, long and lanky in slacks and a polo shirt.

"—The hell do you want?" His raspy growl seemed to ricochet off the lampposts.

"We saw what you did to Sandra, and we're calling the cops. Did you think we'd let you get away with putting your hands on your pregnant wife?" Ernesto tried to match his height, and on his toes, met Logan eye to eye. Jeremy stood hunched two steps below them, his hands nervously gripping the metal railing. He backed his way down and moved away from the porch.

"Get out of my way, Ernesto. You have some nerve banging on my door at this time of the night." Logan shoved his way through, but Ernesto jumped back, down all six steps, and blocked his path. He stretched his arms out, his fingertips reaching for the handrail on either side of him, but he could not feel them.

"I said, 'Get the hell out of my way,'" Logan snarled, "and stop sticking your nose where it doesn't belong." Logan sprayed his neighbor with saliva as he hollered over him.

Wiping the spit off his cheeks, Ernesto figured he could do the same.

"You smacked your pregnant wife," he yelled with enough force to produce gooey strands that swung from his mouth. "If you want to know what it feels like to get smacked, then take another step." Ernesto's snug undershirt emphasized his broad shoulders and powerful chest, but ducky pajama pants and fluffy slippers camouflaged his lower half.

An unimpressive version of Sandra appeared in the

doorway. A shred of what neighbors were used to seeing. The skin around her eyes bulged. She had either been crying or hadn't slept . . . or both. Her belly erupted through a torn seam in her long nightgown, and the sloppy ponytail at the top of her head looked fried and full of static. They could see a fading imprint on her left cheek.

"Guys, what are you doing? Why are you here? Please go home; I can handle this," she said, reaching for Logan and pulling him back into the house by his elbow. He yanked his arm, swinging it violently into the door behind him and shattering its small window.

"Get off—I've had enough of this!" Logan's feet tangled in his hurry to get back into the house. One leg swung itself around the other, and he stumbled out of view. Had he been drinking?

"You see what you've done?" Sandra said, sweeping her shoe across the floor to gather the broken glass.

"Guys, I appreciate you defending my honor, but I'm no damsel in distress. It would be easier for me if no one else got involved. Just stay out of it." She had changed her tone and spoke softly, but her anger glared.

What was she mad at?

Who was she mad at? Them?

Sandra scanned over their baffled looks. All their mouths rested with lowered jaws. She then swirled back into the house with her nightgown spinning at her ankles and closed the door.

Ernesto and Jeremy finally caught eyes as if noticing each other for the first time and contemplated their next move, but before they could get a single thought in, the door swung open again. Logan took two hops down the steps and pushed his way through the men, keys jingling in one hand, his jacket and briefcase dangling from the other. Ernesto jogged backwards a few steps and postured in front of him, but Logan's momentum forced a path. Ernesto stumbled back, but his quick legs kept him stable.

"Where are you going? You can't leave until the cops get here." He jumped onto the grassy area at the edge of the driveway, cutting Logan off for a second time.

Jeremy and Priscilla watched from a few feet away.

"You're not going anywhere! You can count on it!" Ernesto shouted in his face, but Logan swung his arm around, shoving Ernesto to the side.

Ernesto lunged toward him, locking his hands around Logan's thin waist. Like a collapsing skeleton, he tumbled onto the grass. One more push and Ernesto had him pinned down flat on the ground by his shoulders.

"Call the cops, Jeremy! He's not getting away with this!"

Logan squirmed under him, and Jeremy dug around his pockets for a phone he knew he did not carry.

"You're attacking my husband! Get off him!" Sandra shouted from deep inside the house. From what they could see, she moved back and forth in search of something, but within seconds she occupied the doorway again with a phone to her ear. "I'm calling the cops! You're attacking my husband. He's done nothing to you!"

Jeremy wanted to protect his best friend. He charged Ernesto and pushed him off Logan, who then crawled away like a spider and jumped into his car. His tires shrieked as he peeled out of the driveway and down the street.

Ernesto and Jeremy, with a few heavy breaths between them, helped one another up from the grass, dusted off their pajama pants, and readjusted their tee shirts. Ernesto's scuffle with Logan had produced a bloody lip.

"You have some nerve coming to my house and starting a fight with my husband. Who the hell do you two think you are?" Sandra said. The curls on her head bounced with fury.

Priscilla had had enough. She stomped through the driveway in Jeremy's large sneakers.

"What's wrong with you? You have two men defending you, a pregnant woman, from an abusive husband, and *they're* wrong for doing it? Consider yourself lucky he didn't do something worse. Who knows what would have happened if we hadn't shown up. That could have been you with a bloody lip." Priscilla pointed at Ernesto, who stood behind her.

Sandra did not react. Instead, she stared down the street in the direction in which Logan had driven as if there were no one else around and she had just watched her husband ship off to a war.

"What's happened with you?" Priscilla asked. Frustration elongated every word. "You're a completely different person. Why won't you let us help you?"

Sandra's demeanor changed as though sinking into herself and into all that had happened. Her eyes watered, and a little sweat glistened at her hairline. Patting her belly, she said, "I'm not feeling well. I have to get into bed." She hadn't looked at any of them. Her eyes still floated down the street. "I have to go before my kids wake up. I'm surprised they haven't done so already with all this yelling. Goodnight." Sandra disappeared behind the door. Her footsteps could be heard making their way through the living room and up the stairs.

Priscilla, Jeremy, and Ernesto looked over one another, shocked and confused.

"Should we—wait for the cops?" Jeremy looked down both sides of the street for flashing lights.

Ernesto did the same, walking to the edge of the curb.

"I hope they don't come blasting the sirens. Mia and the girls are asleep. I was up watching yesterday's soccer game and when I shut the TV off, I heard yelling. I looked out the window, and I saw their light was on. So, I walked out here and stood in front of your house to make sure she'd be okay," Ernesto recounted, shoving his hands into the pockets of his pajama pants. His bones still trembled from the jolt of his brawl with Logan. A little blood had crusted on his lip.

"What just happened?" Jeremy couldn't process all that had transpired in a matter of ten minutes. "Did I miss something? I feel like I missed something. Why is she defending him, even after he slapped her? I assume that's all he did, right?" Jeremy glanced up to the second floor of Sandra's house where a light went out. "I mean, we didn't see what happened afterwards, but I'm assuming that's all it was—or who knows what happened while we were at the front door."

"That's what I was thinking. Maybe there was more that we didn't see," Ernesto said, craning his neck to look further down the street. "When are the cops getting here? Seems like she called a while ago, no?"

"Maybe she didn't call," Priscilla said. "She may have faked it . . . to defuse the situation. I don't think she wants either one of you to go to jail."

That reassured Jeremy. No one had ever called the police on him before.

"Let's hope she didn't," Jeremy peeped. "I don't need the extra stress. A lawyer and a bank branch manager go to jail over defending a pregnant lady from her abusive husband. It would be a great trial," Jeremy said, forcing a chuckle through his lips.

"Yeah—and I have the perfect suit for it," Ernesto laughed, feeling over his split lip with the tip of his finger. He could tell Jeremy possessed a fear of police. "Don't worry about it, man. She was probably bluffing. If she did call, they would've gotten here by now. It still boggles my mind that she defends him, having three small children in the house.

And him, I mean, how bad could it be that he never comes home?"

"He's probably broken her will. Why else would she stand up for him after he slapped her? I'm beside myself," Priscilla said. She turned to walk toward her house, her giant sneakers crossing like skis. "Let's head back inside. We can talk about this tomorrow. Good night, Ernesto."

"Good night, guys."

17

NORMA SAT AT her desk in the den, laptop open, scrolling the mouse with velocity, excited about the news she would deliver at dinner. After finalizing the plans, it took a great deal of effort to keep from calling her husband and daughters.

She sat nestled in an oversized executive chair, barely filling the space between the armrests, her toes pointed and reaching, but unable to skim the plush area rug beneath her; much like she had felt lately, small and insignificant surrounded by an immense world. No way of controlling a sliver of it, even if it was the sliver she had given birth to. Her firstborn had transformed into a courageous woman with goals of her own. Goals she would diligently cram into a single calendar year.

Their surprise getaway would be a momentary distraction, a way to supply memories to last a lifetime, but a lifetime for Janice had barreled toward them quicker than Norma could manage.

Mornings imposed the most challenges. Opening her

eyes to another day closer to Janice's Death Date induced misery and renewed guilt.

Had she done enough for her daughter?

Had she taught her everything she needs to know about life and death?

Had she given her the appropriate support?

. . . And at twenty-one with such little life experience and a time limit on that life, did she really need to let her go? Even if Janice had promised to not move more than three hours away.

She despised it, the rapid spin of a world in which she lived waiting to bury a child. Sunrises into sunsets, weaving in and out of the days that would lead her to Janice's final one.

But that was yesterday and all the days before it.

Today, she woke up to an altered mindset as if the dawn had infused her with resilience, determined to try a little harder, cry a little less, tuck away the angst. Relish the year she had left with Janice, instead of wasting it on anticipation.

How had she *not* had this awakening before? It felt easy and lasted hours. So far, a fluid day without pangs of depression and she had already made it halfway into the afternoon. Something in her had changed. Something inside her brain. Perhaps, the release of a chemical that encouraged good spirits. Enough left over to make the evening playful and unveil her plans with homemade lasagna, though she rarely cooked; wanting to do it all. Chop the garlic, season the sauce. Prepare it herself, not from frozen. A way of executing her bravery, to appreciate each second that rolled by. A silly first step, she thought, in practicing gratitude.

Two and a half hours later, the tomato sauce bubbled around the noodles and it was done. The aroma of roasted garlic crisping over pieces of bread escaped the hot oven and snaked through every room of the Hellingtons' home. Somewhere along the way, she acknowledged it should have taken half the time, but cooking had always been problematic. Her reflection in the kitchen window proved it, a petrifying version of herself. A sleek ponytail that had frizzed, smudged eyeliner on her temples, and an apron covered in splatters. She had gone to battle with a fussy can of tomatoes.

Norma sat at the dining room table, oblivious to the beeping oven timer and the chime of her cell phone. Finding herself in the exact spot she had sat in when she learned her eldest daughter had eight years to live, but the two weeks leading up to it may have been worse.

Angered over the Bureau's decision to release Death Dates, Norma had set out to reject them. Her daily walk to the mailbox did not produce red envelopes. Instead, she left them behind, ignored and untouched for fourteen days. When Barry questioned her, she claimed there had not been a single red envelope in the correspondence she retrieved, her secret way of protesting the Bureau's decision. The next day, she snuck outside and with a thick black marker, wrote on each one:

RETURN TO SENDER

Eight days later, the post office delivered new red envelopes, and those, too, lived in the mailbox for days. She did, however, open a white envelope with a $5,000 penalty. The Bureau had started fining protestors for refusing to accept their Expiration Dates. She gave in. Norma walked to the mailbox for a second time that day, pinched the corners of the envelopes, and carried them inside like dirty rags. For three hours, she sat at the dining room table in a standoff with the Bureau's notices, as if waiting for the envelopes to make the first move; forgetting to order dinner, turning up the volume on the TV to drown out the cries she heard from neighbors also in the midst of accepting the bad news. Dazed in her seat, she lit cigarettes one after another without raising any to her lips, letting them burn out into a long row of ashes.

Once her matchbox had emptied, she summoned the courage, grabbed the first envelope, and tore it open. It was addressed to Janice. After taking note of the date, she folded the notice, placed it under a napkin holder, and calmly went about her day. Denial had set in. That night, the rest of the family looked over them, but her instructions to Barry and the girls were clear: The dates should be ignored and never mentioned.

For some time after she became a conspiracy theorist, debating with others about the validity of the dates and those who acquired them. Years went by before she realized four of them had pulverized behind her, four years she could have savored. Her lax attitude had permitted half of the remaining time she had with Janice slip away.

Lacey barged through the front door, slamming her books down on a side table near the entrance, rattling a bowl of dusty potpourri. She searched for her mother through her thick bangs, which she hadn't bothered tossing aside.

"Mom? Mom? Where have you been? I tried calling you."

"Honey, I'm right here." Norma waved with a spatula from the dining room.

"Can you believe I got my first C ever? I bet it's because I couldn't get to my eight o'clock class on time. I have to get a new car. I can't have it stalling every time I need to get to an early class."

"Sweetie, we'll have to get it checked. Either way, you'll get Janice's car next year," Norma reminded her, but the words were like a blow to Lacey's gut.

"Right, well, that's not how I'd like to get a new car. My sister passes away and—oh joy, I get her car." She sucked her teeth. "I hate this," she said and then disappeared up the stairs.

Twenty minutes later Barry and Janice walked into the house. They had exited the highway at the same time coming from opposite directions.

"You're right on time. The lasagna's done, and I have some lemon-infused water chilling in the fridge and—strawberry cheesecake."

"Wow, sounds like a special day," Barry said, apprehensively. "What's going on?"

"*You* cooked instead of ordering?" Janice asked with genuine interest. "Yup, sounds like something's up. Let's hear it."

"You will, but after dinner. Besides, if my lasagna gives you indigestion, my little surprise'll help. It's all part of my plan." Norma winked at Janice and grabbed an oven mitt, wincing at the heat that rose from the oven door.

"Wow, this *must* be special," Janice said. "When did you get all this stuff?" Janice looked over a pile of pastel-colored dishes on the dining-room table.

"We've had it for years. The plates were stored in the cabinets over the fridge. I guess there was never an occasion special enough to make me climb up there and get them."

"This better be worth the hype, Mom." Janice backed out of the kitchen, her eyes shifting between the plates she had never seen and the pan of lasagna. ". . . although, I've never known you to disappoint."

Norma noticed how easily Janice moved backwards.

"It looks like the medication's helping."

"Seems like it. I felt a little queasy today, but it passed quicker than I could worry about it," Janice said, while walking to the living room to head up the stairs.

Barry unbuttoned his shirt as he followed Janice.

"Hope you made enough, because I skipped lunch."

"Again? Why?"

"I had a ton of meetings. Plus, the pizza place up the block from my job's closed for renovation. From what I hear, the owner met his Expiration Date. It's been shut down for a few days, but I think his sons are taking over."

"Poor boys . . . well, there's plenty. It'll be on the table by the time you head back down," Norma said, absolving herself from any talk of Death Dates.

Despite having taken a few shortcuts, using dried basil instead of fresh, onion powder instead of chopped, her homemade lasagna impressed her family's taste buds. As they took their final bites, Lacey tapped her fork against her margarita glass, half filled with lemon water and a yellow umbrella hanging off its side.

"Okay, what gives? Why are we having dinner with all this stuff? Seems somewhat mismatched, no?" Lacey's eyes drifted over the odd place settings. "We have an Italian meal paired with margarita glasses and no margaritas, but this tiny umbrella was a lovely surprise in my lemon water." She gave it a twirl. "And then there's the cheesecake, which we never have unless it's someone's birthday."

"You guys don't get it?" Norma said, looking over their expressionless faces. "Did the theme not translate well?" She maneuvered around to grab her purse from the counter and pulled out two folded sheets of paper. "I wanted to wait until after dessert, but here it is—and I know your dad and I mentioned it, but somewhere along the way it got lost in the shuffle. Today I finally made the reservations. The day after Janice's graduation, we'll be *celebrating* in the"—Norma flipped open the papers, revealing a purchase confirmation with all their names—"in the . . . Bahamas!"

The news had not affected the girls' expressions. She wondered whether they had heard her correctly.

"Hello? *Buhh*-hamas, we're going to the Buh-ha-mas," Norma enunciated.

The gears in Janice's mind meshed, rotating slowly. Her mother had planned a vacation for them . . . for her. . . because of her. They had never traveled further than where their car could take them. Though Janice showed more confusion than excitement, the announcement had actually saddened her. Lacey, waiting for Janice to speak first, procrastinated with excessive mastication of what had already turned to mush in her mouth. Unsure of what to say, she nodded eagerly with inflated cheeks, but decided to hold off on further gestures and wait to take Janice's lead.

"I have to say, I'm a little shocked by the lack of excitement. It took four days of research to find the perfect resort . . . *four* days," Norma said, demanding appreciation for the hours she had put into the arrangements.

"So, we're going on vacation?" Lacey asked. Her eyes lingered on Janice. Barry and Norma noticed the odd undertone between the sisters.

"Mom," Janice said, dispirited, "I don't know what to say. Why are you spending money on a vacation like this? I already feel guilty about all the money I've wasted on school. You've both sacrificed a lot to put me through four years of college I didn't need."

Several weeks before, Janice had felt herself a burden when her parents handed her the last portion of her tuition, something she had confessed to Lacey.

"Honey," Barry said, "you can't worry about money. We're glad to have put you through school, and whatever guilt you feel should've never existed in the first place. This is a vacation for all of us, to spend time as a family before you go off to work. We *all* need this."

Janice released her contracted shoulders, rose from her seat, and in silence, walked around the table to give her father a hug. It would take some time to extinguish her feelings of guilt bunched in her throat, but the excitement soared in the pit of her stomach. She then took steps toward her mother, tripping along the way.

"Oh, honey. Don't fall," Norma said, but Janice did fall, collapsing onto her mother's chest. Norma propped her up by her underarms, but the twitching made it impossible to keep her upright. She rolled her onto the floor, gripping the back of Janice's head.

"Call the ambulance!" Norma hollered at Lacey. "Hurry!"

She grappled Janice onto her side, their arms and legs fluttering, crisscrossing one another, shins banging against shins, until Janice's spasms died down.

18

"I WANT TO ENJOY the next five years we have together. We'll throw spit balls on a map, and wherever they land, we'll go. Remember how you'd do that to your sister's posters when you were teenagers?" Shirley said, feeling foreign and out of place in Tara's bedroom. The rough carpeting scratched her bare feet on the way in, like sandpaper, but a closer look revealed dozens of burn marks where Tara had put her cigarettes out. The butts still sat inside some of the scorched holes.

Shirley gulped the stagnant air, thick when it hit her lungs, as she glanced over the empty boxes of cigarettes scattered throughout, some toppling out of open drawers. Tara hoarded them, the only hobby she had left.

"Please check yourself into rehab and when you get out, we'll take our first trip," Shirley pleaded with Tara while sitting at the edge of her bed. Desperate to connect with her daughter, Shirley reached for her hand. It flopped around several times before landing on her lap. Although skittish,

Shirley stroked the star tattoos on her daughter's knuckles but sensed the disinterest radiating from Tara's fingertips.

"Just think back to when you felt the happiest and we'll pick up from there. We can get back to that. Your sister'd be so proud of you. She would've never blamed you for what happened, and she's probably looking down at you right now trying to convince you of that. She knows you tried to protect her, but you couldn't . . . no one could."

A grimy-looking Tara sat up in bed, her twisted tank top covered in coffee stains. A purple duvet lay lifeless across her lap, flattened and limp, no actual comforter inside it. Shirley inhaled its musty odor, different from the other smells she had encountered in the room. Her daughter's hair appeared crimped on one side, showing an inch of light brown roots that abruptly stopped at the black dye that covered the rest.

Shirley had tried everything, but stirring up old feelings of Angel pushed Tara into a deeper funk, and getting her out of it at this point seemed impossible. After seven years of fighting with Tara, Shirley was days away from surrendering and leaving Tara to be swallowed up by the drugs she desired more than her own life.

"Mom, I don't want to be rude, but you're invading my space. I have a migraine, and I'd like to get back to sleep if you don't mind. I'm sure you have better things to do than to weigh down my mattress." Tara turned her back to her mother and curled up in a fetal position, tucking a pillow between her knees.

"How long are you going to sleep? It's three in the afternoon. You've been in bed for a week. All you do is eat and sleep." Whenever Shirley spoke to Tara, the creases by her eyes multiplied.

"Fine!" Tara shifted in her bed with ferocity, bouncing the mattress, nearly bucking Shirley's feeble body off. "Okay, I'm awake, now what?" She threw her hands up, startling her mother, who dodged the presumed slap she ultimately thought she'd bear, but Tara had not tried to hit her.

"I'm sorry. I want my daughter back. You're all I have and all I need. If we could get back to being mother and daughter, we could make these last five years count. That's all I ask Tara, to live for us, for you . . . for me." By that time, Shirley had reached the bedroom door and lingered by it, not expecting a response but a reaction. Tara refused to give her either.

As she walked down the hall to her own bedroom, music blared behind her. As much as Shirley tried, she could not ignore validation that her presence, in Tara's eyes, agitated her more than the physical pain of detox. She had not wanted to go back to sleep or ease a migraine; she wanted her mother gone, out of sight, and made it blatantly obvious, in case her words didn't sting enough. Tara was malicious that way, a punisher, but Shirley mentally got back at her by making a bogus decision that she would never try again. That had been Tara's last chance.

Taking refuge in her bedroom, Shirley locked the door, jiggling the knob a dozen times before she determined herself undeniably safe from Tara's rage. Her daughter's last drug binge had initiated a rapid disintegration of Shirley's travel plans. The thought of abandoning Tara to visit a handful of states tarnished what she believed to be her purpose for being the longest living member of her family. She had to stay put and fight to rehabilitate Tara of her grief because that, Shirley suspected, would eliminate the drugs.

She met eyes with her reflection in the smudged mirror that hung behind the door. Her silver hair, almost shoulder length, looked thinned out and ragged. In amazement that five days of stress could be this deteriorating, she sized herself up, taking notice of every new ripple and crack that had developed on the skin around her mouth, some by her eyes. She hoped it would be a few days before neighbors stopped by, because her bloodshot eyes made it appear as if she had shared drugs with her daughter.

She sunk into the bed, cradled by satin pillows that slithered out from under her as she lay back, already having scrapped the promise that she would never again try with Tara. In the midst of sorting out all the worries that muddled her mind, Shirley contemplated returning the new olive rolling bag that had stood untouched in the corner of her bedroom since the day she brought it home. It had already begun to bother her with its constant demand for attention; the tags dangling from its handle flickered hastily every time she opened the closet door. The bag that had given her such joy to purchase, she now viewed as obstructive, a distraction, and in a matter of seconds she decided it was too bulky and she would return it the first chance she could.

Thirty minutes later, Shirley found herself fixated on a talk show, staring at the screen absentmindedly until she roused with a new plan to lure Tara out of her room. A routine like any other, she went through a checklist of things her daughter may warm to. After making a few calls and scribbling notes on a pad, she made the final call and within an hour, a Napoli's Restaurant delivery van appeared in the driveway.

On the slow walk down to collect her order, Shirley slammed the bedroom door, banged the banister on the way down with a hairbrush, and stood behind the closed front door until the delivery man rang the bell two more times. All things she thought would prompt Tara to peek out the window.

Shirley's idea worked, as if the garlicky aroma had wound itself up the staircase, snaked under Tara's bedroom door, and hooked at the nostrils, enticing her down the steps. Tara appeared in the kitchen pacing behind Shirley as she opened the steaming tins of eggplant rollatini. Although Tara had come out of her room, the white paper bags imprinted with the logo of the Italian restaurant she had enjoyed some time ago did nothing to diminish the puckered look on her face. Shirley moved fast to serve the takeout, eager to get the dishes on the table before Tara had a chance to clomp back up the steps.

"How did you even find this place?" Tara asked in a hoarse voice, pouting over her plate. "I can't even remember where it was. Somewhere in Hartford, I think." An elongated yawn swallowed up half her words.

"Yes, you're right. But they opened one not too far from here. One of Mia's friends manages it. I remembered you liked this place when you worked at that accounting firm. Do you remember how often you'd have it?" Shirley asked, feeling accomplished. Warmth had settled in. Her next step would be to conjure up memories of Tara's happier times, some three years ago when she was sixty days clean, reestablishing her career and enjoying Napoli's on a near daily basis.

"Is it as good as you remember?" Shirley asked through a pressured smile. "You loved eating there. You had it all the time."

Tara shrugged. "I mean, it's fried, cheesy food, Mom. It's hard to get that wrong."

"I'm just asking, Tara. I've never had rollatini before," Shirley snapped, the heat surging through her pores, but the annoyance in her tone stimulated Tara's malice.

"Fine, then, what's the catch? Obviously, there's more to this than you wanting me to enjoy a nice meal." Tara slammed her fork down on the plate. "Okay, so what it is? Come on—"

"Why are you so hostile? Why does everything with you have to be a battle? Is it wrong of me to want my daughter to live a good life? A life free of drugs?" Shirley felt the beginnings of a crevice distancing her from what she had wanted to accomplish. "I'll never stop trying. You're all I have left."

Tara disengaged and resumed chewing a small piece of garlic bread she had pinched between her fingers, but Shirley took advantage of her silence.

"I know you carry immense guilt over your sister's death, but you don't seem to understand. That's how destiny works. It was going to happen whether you were there or not. If you can get past that, you can begin to let go of the guilt and start healing.

"I'll help you if you go to rehab. Tara, things have to change; you know hospitals won't continue to treat you if you're on a destructive path. You *know* that. You carry all this guilt for your sister, but where's the guilt you should be feeling for me? The person who's here now, standing in front of you . . . trying to help you cope with all that's happened." Never having had the chance to speak this long to Tara, Shirley did not know what to do next. By this time, under normal circumstances, Tara would have punched through a wall, slammed her plates into the sink, or stuffed an overnight bag, but she said nothing, and for a second, Shirley thought she saw her express regret with a twitch at the corner of her mouth.

But in thirty seconds, it was all over. Tara jumped out of her seat and charged down the hallway, rummaging through a box on the floor of the coat closet marked "garage sale," stored there for years.

Extremely terrified to react to Tara's strange outburst, Shirley fought the urge to chase after her. She waited at the dining-room table, her eyes on the wall that separated her from the racket in the next room.

"You're not getting it, Mom," Tara said, the thud of footsteps making their way back to the dining room. "Why do you think I'm like this? Huh? Why do you think I try my best to numb myself? Why do you think I don't care to be here or to talk to anyone? I'm not interested in living my life. If I could change one thing about my destiny, it would be to take my own life whenever the hell I damned well pleased." With Tara shouting at close range, the spray of garlicky saliva landed on Shirley's face. "I don't want to live. I want to be dead—in the ground—or wherever you want to put me. Having to stay alive after killing my baby sister is of no interest to me. It was bad enough living after Dad died. There's—no—point. But you know what the worst part is— you—*you've* lived all the same tragedies alongside me and all you want to do is have fun. You have a million friends, just on this one block. You laugh all day, go to parties. Why aren't *you* sad too? Why aren't *you* having a hard time living too?" Tara paused for a few seconds, then responded to her presumed rhetorical question.

"Yeah—exactly! So if you wanna go on your little traveling journey, then be my guest. I want nothing to do with you."

"That's not fair, Tara!" Shirley said, tasting the already soured, semi-digested tomato sauce that rose to the back of her throat. "How dare you act like I don't care about my family. How *dare* you!"

Tara sneered, "I *dare*," and pulled out an open bottle of pills from her sweatshirt pocket. Pellet by pellet, they landed in her mouth. She chugged the pile with a heavily poured glass of wine that sat next to her mother's empty dish.

"No! Tara—" Shirley's screams overpowered her own head, clouding her perception and for a moment, leaving her to sort out whether it had actually happened or if she'd imagined it.

Tara's legs buckled. Landing on all fours, she locked her elbows to support herself. Two feet away, Shirley gripped her chest, a paralyzing pain emanating from her back, like a spear impaled between her shoulder blades. She could still see the outlines and perfect edges of the table, silverware, the gleam off the water glasses. Nothing had gone fuzzy. Her awareness had not been affected, no time lapses. She knew exactly what happened, but now her throat narrowed as she labored to keep filling her lungs with oxygen. She did not want to have a heart attack.

Meanwhile, Tara's grumbles turned into gagging, then the disgorging of her dinner. Her head snapped back and forth as her mother looked on without a way to help her. Shirley managed to make it to the kitchen counter, clenching her throat and feeling the airflow decrease with each step. Fumbling with her cell phone, she dialed number two, every ring muffled amid the dizziness.

"Hey, Shirley," Jeremy answered.

"Please," she wheezed into the phone. "*Help*—"

"Shirley? Are you okay? I'll be right over!" The call disconnected before Shirley lost her grip and dropped the phone onto the kitchen tile, shattering the screen. While clinging to the counter, she could hear violent heaving, followed by splashing in the next room.

A minute later, Jeremy burst through the door, using his emergency key for Shirley's house.

His eyes took a quick survey around. Violent images had crossed his mind in the thirty seconds it took to get there, one that included Shirley at gunpoint, arms tied, masked men standing behind her. He grabbed her by the arm and walked to the love seat in the living room, supporting most of her weight with his clenched fist.

"Shirley, you have to calm down. I need to know what's happening," he asked while brushing silver strands from her face, the moaning coming from the next room distracting him. After three deep breaths, Shirley's color returned.

"Tara—she took pills." With every word she wasted breath on, she worried about losing consciousness. "Lots . . . of . . . them."

"Okay, I'll go check on her. Are *you* okay, though? Is something hurting you?" he asked, taking the initiative to feel around her ribcage, down her back and under her breasts.

Shirley managed to find her words.

"I think I'm having a heart attack. She took pills in front of me—been on drugs for seven years—my heart's too weak to handle this by myself." She hoped he'd turn away instead of watching her fight to stay alert. Unwillingly, her mind recalled the savagery of Tara's actions, provoking a flow of tears that she hid in the bend of her elbow.

"Don't worry. We'll get her help. Stay here, try to calm down and continue breathing. I'll go check on Tara." Jeremy followed the moans, still wearing the button-down shirt and black slacks he wore to work. In the dining room he found Tara curled up on her side, her face lying in a pool of vomit, her skeletal arms wrapped around her stomach.

Jeremy grabbed her rigid humerus, pulling her to a sitting position with ease, his fingers maneuvering carefully around pieces of undigested pasta.

"Tara, are you okay?"

Her head rolled around, as she tried to keep herself from falling to the side. "Huh?" she moaned. "I'm okay." She sounded drunk.

"Just—my"—her words dragged—"stomach. I threw up—pills."

This was Jeremy's first time meeting Tara.

"Okay, well, let me move you to the wall. I'll bring you a pillow so I can check on your mom." Jeremy shoved his hands into her armpits and dragged her backwards to prop her up against the wall.

"Please don't call the ambulance," Shirley hollered from the living room, her words more defined than before.

"Well, I want to make sure you're okay. Tara'll be fine. She threw everything up, so don't worry about that. She needs to sleep it off," he said as he walked back into Shirley's view. He grabbed an oversized pillow from the opposite couch, walked it into the dining room, and tucked it under Tara's arm.

"I'm taking your mom to the hospital. If you need to throw up, fall forward so you don't choke. But judging from what I see on the floor, I think you're done."

He tucked his shirt in and adjusted his pants while texting Priscilla to meet him at the hospital.

"Alright, Shirley. We're going for a ride." He swooped her up in his arms like a forklift and carried her out to the car.

Ten minutes into the drive to the hospital, Shirley's muddiness lifted, her chest pains receded, and her breathing normalized. "Thank you so much, Jeremy. I'm so sorry. I don't know what I'd do without you. You really *are* like the son I never had—the son I need."

He did feel like her son in a lot of ways. The enormity of her words stirred through his soul. "Shirl, I'm here for you. Glad you're both okay."

"I think I had a panic attack. This whole thing with Tara is starting to break me. I don't know what to do with her." Shirley sat crouched in the passenger seat with her eyes closed.

"Sometimes there's nothing you can do. She has to be willing. If I remember correctly, she's got five or six years until her Expiration, right?" Jeremy asked, unsure whether the pair lived together, only having seen Tara come and go a handful of times in all their years on Gardenia Way. Shirley had kept her well hidden.

"Five years. Only five years," Shirley muttered, her eyes shut tighter than before.

"Right. We'll have to get her help. I'll talk to Pri about it and we'll get it done." Jeremy knew little about Shirley and Tara's relationship, but he determined this to be too big a task for a seventy-three-year-old woman.

The burden of a junkie daughter tethered to Shirley for almost a decade had broken free, her secret life unraveling in front of Jeremy. Although it was disconcerting to accept that her daughter's struggles would pass as whispers through the ears of her neighbors, it felt good at the same time to finally have someone on her side, someone she could call on for help.

19

A MASSIVE GRAY CLOUD rippled over Gardenia Way, the intimate neighborhood spread beneath its threat of a fierce electrical storm. The crackling sparks across the sky illuminated the darkened afternoon, rushing Ernesto's daughters out of the house to avoid getting caught in a downpour.

"Did you bring the power cord to my laptop?" Jacklyn asked her little sister as she opened the front door to a damp breeze, blurring her vision. "I don't think it's charged; we're gonna need it." She held the laptop tight at her chest while her fingers strained to wrap around her cell phone and a small tripod, her nerves transmitting a false sense of unpreparedness.

"Are we forgetting anything? I should've made a check list. Did you pack the notebook?"

"It's called a legal pad, and yes, it's in my bag with the charger. So, can you calm down now?" Sherry whizzed by her through the open doorway, jumping down the last porch step onto the sidewalk. "Let's hurry before we get zapped out here. It's starting to drizzle."

For weeks the girls had practiced interviewing each other, then alone in the bathroom mirror while drying their hair. At first, their inexperience reflected lip-glossed smiles and a plethora of hand gestures, but endless research on the skill of reporting sculpted their vision. At sixteen and seventeen, they exuded the confidence of trained professionals, cloaked in school uniforms. Their first face-to-face interview in their quest to live past Expiration Dates would begin with Shirley.

"I'll record while you interview, right? The next time we switch? Is that how we'll do it?" Sherry asked Jacklyn, combating a strong gust that smothered her words.

"Yup. Should I read from my notes or ask whatever comes to mind?"

"Do what Janice said, pretend you're having a conversation. It should be easy enough if we're starting with someone we know."

The girls walked, shoulders bumping down the block toward Shirley's house. Their backs hunched like umbrellas hovering over their electronics, shielding them from the possible drench of a spring cloud.

"Don't be scared to screw up. It's the only way we'll learn." Sherry tucked her face away from intrusive winds, her hair flapping and twisting above her head.

They stepped off the curb onto the cobbled street just past Jeremy's house.

"Remember, this is no different than doing a school project, except we could be saving lives . . . so, no pressure."

Sherry waved off her sister's comment. Jacklyn's edginess over this first interview had poked at her too many times over the last weeks. Something about it being recorded and in-person had doubled their jitters.

Shirley opened the door. They had made it on time for their first interview. Four o'clock.

Bumping into one another and sliding through narrow spaces, the girls took more time than anticipated to set up. Neither of them had ever used a tripod before. The phone kept snapping its way out every time they let go; all sorts of dials and knobs were needed to secure its steadiness.

"Would you ladies like some green tea? You kids are into that, right? It promotes weight loss and—" Shirley smiled, trying to recall the rest of its benefits.

"Sure, that would be great, thank you. You don't have to sell us on green tea, Mrs. Wilcox. If it promotes a healthy weight, then I'm in," Jacklyn said, patting her flat stomach but mostly welcoming the extra minutes to get settled.

Shirley put one hand on her hip, the other behind her head, and shook her waist. "Oh, honey, with that figure you have nothing to worry about."

It was the cutest thing Jacklyn had ever seen.

"Okay, we're all set, Mrs. Wilcox. We can start the interview whenever you're ready."

"Great!" Shirley yelled out. In the stroke of one breath, she smacked her hands together and tucked her hair behind her ears. "I'm ready for my YouTube debut. You'll have to show me how to use it again; I've already forgotten." Shirley's one-sided smile revealed a large crease over the site of a dimple she once had. Scooting to the edge of the couch with perfect posture, she folded her hands on her lap, her elbows spread wide in perfect angles. The thick layer of foundation indicated she had taken some time to get ready. It made her fair skin the color of honey. Her hair flashed silver every time it caught the light, and a touch of peach lipstick made its way unevenly around her mouth. No trace of her night at the hospital a few days earlier. That had ended with a prescription for anxiety medication and a check of her blood pressure.

Nothing more. As the nurse at the emergency room had put it, she's "healthier than most people half her age," and that made Shirley flip the pages all the way back to the center of her book. The chapter where her younger self collaborated with joy, laughter, and optimism to wash away the negative. It granted her a change in perspective and how she planned to carry out the rest of her living years without the sludge of what Tara spewed. A path that would no longer drag her unwillingly as she scraped her nails, desperate to catch a hold of something that would keep her still, her knees skidding on the surface of what she was leaving behind. Since that night at the hospital, a voice she had never heard before had fiddled with her mind. A reminder that selfishness is not as bad as everyone says.

Two weeks and Tara's sobriety had reached its most recent peak, but nothing else had changed. She spent most of her time in bed, poking her head out of the bedroom to demand coffee and food comprising the extent of their interaction since the night Shirley returned from the hospital. She had stopped begging for her daughter's attention. The worry she carried since Angel died lifted from her speck by speck, floating higher and higher, further and further.

"Three, two, one, and go." Sherry stood behind her phone, tilting and turning the tripod into place, nudging it until Tara and Shirley slid into the center of the screen.

"We'd like to welcome Shirley Wilcox, a seventy-three-year-old advocate of Expiration Dates. Thank you for taking the time out to talk to us." Jacklyn's rehearsed opening cruised off her tongue.

"It's my pleasure." Shirley smiled and nodded at the camera.

"My sister and I have known you a long time. We were kids when you moved into this house, and I always remember you telling us to live like there's no tomorrow, and that's always stuck with me. Yet, you're a big supporter of the Death Dates. In our pre-interview, you said it's good for people to have knowledge of their destiny?" Jacklyn glanced down at her notes.

Shirley's shimmering flyaway hairs, in full view of the camera, swayed back and forth with the air blowing from the ceiling fan.

"I lived most of my life in the previous world where no one knew what would happen or when it would happen. People went about their lives knowing they would die someday, but only a handful concerned themselves with setting goals, doing good in this world. The others were arrogant—arrogant would be a great way to describe it." Shirley's fierce eye squint scolded her audience.

"When this all started, I was naïve. I thought it was our chance to live full lives now that we knew exactly how much time we had left." Her rounded shoulders spoke disappointment. "Never did I imagine people letting themselves crumble because they only had four years or fifteen years left. Why waste that time?"

"So, you were for the release of dates because you thought people would make better choices?" Jacklyn wanted the audience to understand Shirley's motives.

"That's correct, but I failed miserably, and I don't know which way is right. I do still think we were put on this earth to complete a task. More of us should dig deep to find that task and get it done by the time our Death Dates come up. Put your best life into action."

"Put your best life into action . . . I like that. So, what do you believe your task was to perform here in this life?" Jacklyn ignored Shirley's talk of failure. She hadn't expected it.

"I'm still looking for a clear sign. Although I'm not sure of my purpose, I do know that it gives me time to accomplish what my husband and I set out to do before he died." Shirley's smile dissolved into a reflection. "But my whole family will have been dead for fifteen years by the time my Death Date rolls around. That could mean something. I often wonder if there's a reason I'm destined to be alone without my family for that long. But I've learned that a family need not exist if your life isn't accepting of it. If your family doesn't fit with you, then you should let it go."

If there was a way to gasp with your eyes, Jacklyn had accomplished it. Shirley had swapped personalities in the time it took to answer two questions, going from the sweet old lady she used to call "Grams" to the cynic who sat before her.

Jacklyn affixed a fresh smile on her face and carried on with her scripted dialogue, even if it didn't make sense.

"Mrs. Wilcox, I admire your outlook on life. You're an inspiration to us all. Now—" Shirley's interviewer placed a hand on her own chest, initiating a pre-apology for the part her older neighbor did not agree with.

"You do know we're trying to figure out if it's possible to change your destiny and live past Expiration Dates." Jacklyn's body stiffened. She did not like to be at odds with Shirley.

"Oh, honey, you can't change what the universe has decided for you. Put your energy into the time you have. Take the opportunity that's been given to you, don't waste it."

Shirley stopped speaking and the soft blow of the ceiling fan took her place, rattling its tiny chain, composing a song with its upbeat tempo.

"I don't think there's a way." Her voice kicked up again. "But if there were, maybe there's a way to die before Expiration Dates too."

Jacklyn's heart rate surpassed the rhythm of the clanking overhead. Why had she and Sherry not practiced for contradicting responses? . . . And why did Shirley want to die earlier?

If Jacklyn could get up and walk out of the house without an excuse, she would, leaving Sherry and her laptop behind. It had never crossed her mind that if a way existed to live past your Death Date, then there was a way to die before it.

Jacklyn thumbed the papers in her hand, shuffling through them. She needed a different topic. Moisture began building above her lip and under her arms.

"Let's move on to your husband and youngest daughter. Your husband died before the release of dates, right?"

"Yes, he had a massive heart attack. He was gone within a half hour." Shirley's words flowed without a hiccup, a story she had narrated a thousand times.

"Looking back on it, were there any indications you got leading up to his unexpected death? Days before? Months, even years—" Jacklyn asked. Her confidence had dipped, constrained by the bizarre climate Shirley had cast over them.

"Back then, things were different. You'd think, 'If I only did this and that, he would still be here.' I don't believe that anymore. When it's your time, it's your time. But there were indications before it happened. For instance, he started setting up his will three months earlier, something he had put off. It just so happened he bumped into someone he grew up with who did it over beers." She smirked, her mind locked on images of her husband signing a paper with a soggy corner, a wet ring from a beer bottle bleeding onto the pages beneath it.

"I believe it was his destiny to set up his will so we would be taken care of. He always wanted to make sure his girls were okay," Shirley said. "Also, two nights before he died, we were all home early, something that didn't happen often. He had taken the afternoon off from work. The girls lived with us since they were in college. Neither one of them had a paper due or an exam to study for, a perfect night. We all watched *Jeopardy* and then played two board games. We had the time of our lives, and I won both times! Can you believe that?" Shirley clapped, flinging her head back, ejecting a thunderous laugh. This last story had captivated Ernesto's girls.

But something was wrong.

Shirley wiped tears from one side of her face.

The girls looked at each other, communicating with their eyes as an awkward moment fell between them and their subject, contemplating whether they should ask more questions or stop recording. But Sherry made the decision to continue and swirled her finger, motioning for her older sister to keep going.

"You know, there's something I just remembered," Shirley said. "It happened the afternoon before he died. He had come home from lunch and he said something that was odd to me at the time, but I brushed it off as work stress. How crazy because it just popped into my head—"

A thousand thoughts of what Shirley's new recollection could be knotted their minds. The seconds of silence dragged on like hours. At any moment, she would speak again.

This could change everything.

At Shirley's first syllable, a loud thump above them— over the ceiling fan—dismantled their preoccupied minds. The three ladies snapped their heads toward the staircase in synch, like choreography.

Shirley let out a pinging chuckle. "Excuse me, dears. I have to check upstairs. Something may have fallen."

Shirley's movements were steady and strong and much quicker than the girls had ever noticed. She had not told them she rigged the lock to Tara's bedroom. That she had slipped her half of her own prescribed anxiety pill. Crushed it with a stone larger than her hand. Over-sweetened Tara's afternoon coffee to make up for the bitterness of the crumbled medication. That she asked the Universe for forgiveness when she did it, allowing herself a single afternoon in which two young girls wanted to hear her story. After all, they had taken an hour of their day to spend it with an old lady.

"Do you think her daughter's here?" Sherry whispered to her sister when Shirley's feet were out of view, covering the microphone portion of her cell phone as it continued to record.

"I don't think so. Does she even live here?"

"Daddy says she does, but I haven't seen her in a long time."

A door creaked open, and after a short pause, they heard a subdued yelp.

Jacklyn ran to the bottom of the staircase, mouthing words to her sister, "Should I ask?"

Sherry's expression morphed into distress, shrugging her shoulders and crossing her arms. Her older sister did not need to seek her permission.

"Mrs. Wilcox? Are you okay?" Jacklyn shouted up the staircase.

"No, I'll be right down."

They could not decipher Shirley's tone—worried, *not* worried?

Jacklyn leapt back to her seat as if she had not moved.

Shirley's footsteps staggered above them.

"Girls, I have a problem. My daughter seems to have overdosed again. I don't know where she keeps getting drugs from," Shirley yelled from Tara's bedroom, sentences flowing like a casual conversation.

"Overdose? Like, from drugs?" The words had petrified Sherry's young mind. Her first thought was *I want to call my mom*.

But Jacklyn had already determined the tasks and delegated. "Okay, I'll call 9-1-1. You go help Shirley upstairs. Keep Tara warm. Check her pulse."

"No. Please, don't call," Shirley's voice echoed from

above. "I don't want an ambulance in front of my house. If she wants to die, maybe we should let her. We can continue the interview if you'd like."

Shirley slipped her hair behind her ears as she walked down the stairs, preparing for the camera again.

"Mrs. Wilcox, we have to get your daughter some help. If she overdosed, she has to go to the hospital." Sherry looked at her older sister for support. "We *need* to call for help." She searched for agreement, waiting for a voice to say yes. But the clanging of the small metal chain still sang its tune above her. Not a single breath from Jacklyn or Shirley.

"I'm calling; this is ridiculous." Sherry wanted to cry. She reached for her phone. The tripod came with it.

"Well, if her Death Date isn't for another five years—" Jacklyn said, hinting that the issue may not be as urgent as they thought. "Then, maybe we can help her here. I don't want Mrs. Wilcox to get any unnecessary attention . . . and we definitely don't want her daughter to die. We can help her here." Uncertain, she looked at both of them for reassurance "Right? That doesn't mean she'll die; she still has five years."

"No—no, things will go wrong. We have to call; we can't help her. We don't know what to do." Sherry resisted, appalled at being the only person thinking logically. She looked down at her phone and dialed 9-1-1.

Jacklyn turned to Shirley with a drawn-out sigh. "I'm sorry. She has a point. We need to get her to the hospital."

Sherry pressed the phone to her cheek, reciting her own address three times before giving dispatchers the correct one.

Defeated, Shirley wiped off the lipstick with the back of her hand. "Fine, Tara can go to the hospital. Maybe she'll die there."

"Mrs. Wilcox, sit down. You're not thinking straight." Jacklyn led her back to her spot on the couch. "No one wants

Tara to die, especially not you. She needs help, and we have to get it for her."

Shirley's over-blushed face now exhibited a thousand frown lines. If this had happened in the girls' absence, she would not have called the ambulance. She would have made dinner and sat in bed with her crossword puzzle until her eyes closed for the night.

Five minutes later, EMS workers arrived with sirens blaring and pounded on each step up in search of the overdosed woman. Flashes of blue lights and rumblings of medical talk made Shirley dizzy until the slam of the two ambulance doors confirmed Tara had become someone else's problem.

20

O N MONDAY JEREMY called in sick to the office, the first time in over a year. He did not have a fever or a stomach ache or a list of chores to complete that spilled outside the weekend. He woke up different. Balanced.

For the first time since Austin's passing, he had jogged. Two and a half miles in thirty-five minutes. An achievement he did not expect so soon.

On the walk home, he caught himself smiling. Today, the sun appeared more energized. The grooves on the sidewalk, straighter. The air he breathed in less putrid, more floral; less sooty, more distilled.

A renewed appreciation for the living in all forms: his wife and daughter, the grass coated in a layer of morning mist, the yellow tulips that peeked out from inside their leaves, the birds that dipped in and out of his way as he trotted. He had wanted happiness again and learned how to secure it.

After a two-hour stare-down with the moon the previous night while on the back porch, Priscilla deep in a dream, he had decided to change his approach. He had grown tired and discouraged. Mourning Austin's death did little to keep his memory alive. Instead, it created more memories of his death. Nothing about it satisfied Jeremy. So, upon waking the following morning, he would allow Austin to live through his own participation in life. Having lunch with the guys at the office would no longer be off limits. He would go to a movie with Priscilla and Jen, grab a beer with Ernesto. If he laughed out loud and ordered a second beer, it did not mean he missed his son any less. All the things he believed impaired his grief, he would enjoy again.

After his shower, Jeremy flipped the handle up on his plastic tool box and accompanied it to Shirley's house. Rattling around inside were the inexperienced screwdrivers he had received seventeen years ago as a housewarming gift. He knew he'd need them some day.

In the thirty seconds it took to walk to Shirley's house, Jeremy managed to greet surrounding neighbors, those rushing off—the time on the clock granting them permission to speed out of their driveways, one hand on the steering wheel, one hand on their phone, no eyes on the road. The monotony of a weekday morning Jeremy gladly traded in for handiwork at Shirley's. Today, he would keep things simple.

"Good morning, dear." Shirley waited for him at the back door.

"Good morning. You look refreshed for sleeping on the couch three nights in a row." Jeremy could pick out the different shades of peach that brightened her face. Some in crescent shapes on her eyelids, others as blotches on her cheeks. Her eyebrows, a little sharper. But it was not just the make-up creating the illusion. Shirley *had* slept a lot better on the couch. The first night she did it without wrapping herself in a comforter. Just her, the loveseat, a decorative pillow, and a light breeze from the ceiling fan. That was the night of her daughter's latest overdose. Shirley's worries, struggles, and sleepless nights sped away with Tara, trapped inside that flashing ambulance. The same night the light bulb in the hallway leading to her bedroom burned out. Getting up the stairs and into bed once the sun had set seemed dangerous. Staying on the first floor until Jeremy could change the bulb posed less of a risk.

"I'm going on vacation," Shirley said, sipping from an oversized mug cupped in both hands. By now, she would have offered Jeremy some.

"You're vacation's back on?"

She stayed quiet. Perhaps, she had not heard his question.

He placed his tool box on the counter next to a pile of unopened mail and a bag filled with groceries. Clutter at Shirley's house had never caught his attention before. The date on the receipt that curled up from behind a carton of almond milk, which Jeremy managed to squint into focus, put her at the local supermarket two days earlier.

"How's Tara?"

"She's doing well, I suppose."

"She gettin' out soon?"

"Who knows."

Jeremy gathered a new box of bulbs and the ladder he kept hidden in the pantry for times like these. They walked like two connected train cars, Shirley's hand hooked on the last rung, guiding the back end of the ladder around the banister and up the steps.

"We haven't had a chance to talk about what happened that night with Sandra and Logan," Shirley remembered. "I saw everything from my bedroom window."

"Hmm—Logan made enough of a racket. Hopefully, most of the neighbors slept through it, for Sandra's sake. I don't know why she sticks with that guy. He's dangerous—smackin' a pregnant woman," Jeremy huffed, halfway up the ladder, his elbow swinging with the twist of the screwdriver.

"He smacked her?" she asked. Another worry had steered its way to Shirley, and just like that, life rearranged itself. A single detail slipping her into a reality she wished not to face. She had done just fine the last three days.

"I'm sorry, I don't think I offered you coffee. Would you like a cup?" She grabbed the light cover and handed him a new bulb.

"No thank you, I'm good. But yes, Ernesto and I saw the whole thing. Bottom line, Sandra's pregnant and he should be in jail." Jeremy's fingertips twisted until the bulb lit up. "She needs to kick him out. He's hardly home anyway. It may be rough for her at first, but she doesn't need a man like that around."

"I didn't know he hit her," Shirley repeated, as though convincing the unwilling part of herself to accept Jeremy's version of the story. The data she collected in the ten-minute conversation slung her back into a world she had happily exterminated. But now, she felt a responsibility, her cooperation crucial. She had to say something.

"What?" Jeremy asked.

Or did she?

"What is it? It sounded like you were going to say something."

She replied with a lengthy sigh.

"What?" Jeremy demanded. "If there's something more, I need to know. He could be a danger to any of us."

"I can't say. I don't want her situation to get worse. I promised." Shirley had not promised at all. The last time Sandra visited, she stormed out before Shirley could say anything.

"Is he dying? His date's coming up, right?"Contentment curled up inside him. Not because Logan was dying, but because the stray puzzle pieces had come together. Now, it made sense. Logan had chosen to face his end with violence and disruption, and Sandra tolerated it because the abuse came with an Expiration Date . . . his Expiration Date.

"I knew it was something like that," he blurted. "She's so secretive about Death Dates, it's hard to tell what's going on with her." He guided himself back down the ladder, each step a thud of pride for being right all along.

He folded the ladder and secured the latch on the tool box. The bulb burned bright behind his head, casting a shadow over Shirley.

"Hey," he patted her shoulders. "You didn't say *anything*— you still haven't said anything. I figured it out. So, don't feel bad. Ernesto and I knew all along. Why else would she be so accepting of his behavior?"

He picked up the ladder like a briefcase, inching passed the banister. Shirley followed, guiding the ladder around every bend back downstairs.

"Thanks for your help, Jeremy. I appreciate it." She stood at the door as he saw himself out.

"Anytime, Mrs. Wilcox. If you need anything else, give me a holler," he said. "And again, you didn't say anything. I figured it out. Don't feel guilty."

"Okay." Shirley complied and closed the door. She would stay out of it.

As she pinched the lock on the doorknob, her cell phone rang . . . the way it had for the past three days. The hospital had commenced its daily search for Tara's next of kin. Another day, another eight voicemails Shirley would not listen to.

No guilt to quench for refusing to go to the hospital or declining its calls. Maybe she'd have to face it at some point, but not today or tomorrow or the next. The first and only voicemail she had heard requested her presence now that Tara was in a coma, but for what? If doctors couldn't fix her daughter, then what did they need her for?

21

"I'LL BE HOME early today, around six."
A call from Logan Sandra had not expected.

His voice was like a breeze flowing through the clamor of an overcrowded restaurant. Calm. Decisive. Smooth. And with that, Sandra's fury and resentment slipped off her, descending with the gentle sway of a falling feather. It was that easy.

He was smiling. She could hear it in his tone, the merriment of a person who had found his way back. Soul-searched until the correct path revealed itself. Sometimes people lose their way, and she was positive her husband had been one of them.

But between his breaths, she detected mingling silverware, pinging of glasses, and laughter. Lots of laughter. The *pop* on his end as they hung up could only mean the firm was celebrating a victory. Typical Logan. Enjoying a lavish lunch with colleagues when she and the kids were a ten-minute car ride away.

Still, the butterflies spun themselves dizzy in her gut. His speech lacked the rancor she had become accustomed to, so her decision to not question his call came easy. In her eyes, the father of her kids was entitled to an infinite number of chances, regardless of his behavior.

Five days had passed since Logan and his callousness strode out through their doorway. Over the last month, he and Sandra had clawed at the bits of marriage they had left, leaving behind ungatherable shreds. Too small and insignificant to scoop up. Their disunion worsening as the calendar shoved her closer to the birth of their fourth child. But for Sandra, his call had initiated a reset. A do-over. Once again, granting Logan the opportunity to reinstate himself as father and husband.

As she wobbled her way up to the bedroom, which only she had occupied the last four nights, Sandra's mind replayed her husband's fifteen-second call. Looking back, she sensed a remorseful slope in his words. A tinge of regret. He missed his family, she was sure of it.

Standing before the mirror pegged inside the closet door, Sandra's eyes roved the clouded image. Through it, she bobbed and angled her head away from the streaks that hindered her view, exploring ways to boost her allure. Logan's voice had already rouged her cheeks; her eyes glistened like syrup, but she needed more. She loosened her constricted smile, released the tension shriveled on her forehead. Stress and age had found ways to lodge themselves into her most attractive features. The ones Logan had once admired: her smile, the intensity of her eyes, the crinkling on her nose when she laughed. But that was some time ago. Years. Before she became pregnant with the twins.

Turning to the side with spread-out fingers, she measured the growth of her belly. The oversized tee shirt that rippled over her would not work for this occasion.

Pressed inside the closet, Sandra's fingers dragged the hangers down the rod, one by one. Conveying fury. Every petite blouse and form-fitting dress flapped angrily on its way to the far end of the closet. Swearing under her breath, she claimed nothing would fit until she stopped at a maternity dress she had used while pregnant with the twins. Dangling it in front of her, she forced her head through the small space between the neckline and hanger, stretching the fabric around her eight-month-old belly. She had swelled past her largest maternity dress.

While occupied with a search for suitable outfits, it took heaps of effort to avoid all thoughts of why Logan had decided to announce his imminent presence at their home. Whatever the reason, she accepted it. In the weeks leading up to his absence, he had arrived after midnight and left before her alarm chirped. He slept on the couch, no more than a shadow to Sandra and the kids. Logan's obscurity slipped around corners, shrunk behind closing doors. She had stayed out of his way, making the children tiptoe through the house the one time he slept in. They had breakfast in their bedroom and crowded the small play area on the floor, boring them on a Saturday, their favorite day of the week, until late afternoon. Part of their weekend wasted. A necessary investment, she thought, to help thrust Logan further into isolation. Only then would he realize he needed his family, and for her, his call could only mean her plan had worked.

Just before six, after settling on a pink extra-large t-shirt and smearing an old eyeliner across her lids, she called up to the kids. The rumbling as they trotted down the steps roared like the sound of an inbound train. Sandra's usual "walk, don't run" insistence had plunged down the list of priorities. Since Logan's call, everyday annoyances did not seem as bothersome anymore. How could they? The children had on their best outfits and managed to keep them clean for over an hour. Christopher had even parted his hair and overused his father's gel. It looked stiff and wet.

Seven minutes after the kids had assembled at the dining-room table and waited patiently with their hands folded (and a few giggles between them), the obnoxious rumble of Logan's engine pulsated though the walls.

"Kids, hurry! Your dad's here."

Brianna, Christopher, and Christina popped off their seats, knocking the chairs against each other as they spun around them in a rush to get into their spots. Side by side, they stood in a straight line facing the doorway.

"Just like we practiced earlier, okay?" Sandra encouraged them.

Fidgeting and giggling, they clasped their hands behind their backs.

The doorknob jiggled.

Sandra directed the kids: "Ready? One . . . two"—she watched the corner of the door for movement—"three!"

Logan took a hesitant step into the house.

"Welcome home, Daddy!" the kids shouted, racing toward him, slamming into his waist, and clawing at him like playful kittens.

"Alright kids—easy," he grunted.

The children attached themselves to different parts of his legs. Wrapping their arms around his thigh. Squeezing. Laughing. Brianna dug her cheek into her father's hip, hoping to be recognized for the world's tightest hug.

Logan gave each child a faint tap on the back, as if it would burn his palm to keep it there longer, dug his hands into their armpits, and nudged them away.

Sandra watched her kids' enthusiastic faces dissolve into perplexity. The greeting they practiced did not draw out excitement in their father as their mother said it would. They could tell because his eyebrows had suddenly shaped themselves into a sharp V. Although young, they had decoded their father's crude reaction rather quickly: each withdrawing to a safe distance, Christina gnawing at her index finger the way she does when she's scolded.

Sandra's mind unscrambled, fragments shifting and sliding out of the way until it became clear what she had done. The evening's purpose had not centered on the kids, their happiness, her marriage, or their family unity. Instead, without realizing it, her intent had been to reward Logan just for coming home. Plain and simple. If he wanted to be a part of their lives again, then she would wait with the door wide open. Undo the laces on his dress shoes, tug at the cuffs of his blazer, loosen the knot in his tie. Make it easy for him. But just as quickly as her objective revealed itself it disappeared; her logic suddenly suggested she run through a mental list of things that might make Logan happy. Get dinner on the table, draw him a bath, send the kids upstairs—get them out of the way.

Before any of that, the overwhelmed mother committed herself to staying on track, keeping with the night she had so efficiently planned. Whatever it took, she would do it. Afterall, she had only herself to blame for the miscalculation, and it was her job to fix it. Trying to captivate Logan as soon as he crossed the threshold had been a mistake. That could be intimidating for anyone.

"Kids, get back in your seats so we can have dinner . . . and don't forget, if you eat every little bit on your plate, you'll get ice cream for dessert," she said.

Brianna, Christopher, and Christina hurried into the dining room, crashing into one another as they squeezed through the archway with clumps of Neapolitan ice cream sweetening their thoughts. Their minds already having wiped away the memory of their unimpressed father.

Sandra stayed on course. She tilted the stretched-out neckline of her tee shirt until one side slid off her shoulder, revealing a bra strap, and summoned the courage to add on a flirtatious smile.

"What's all this?" He looked around: a pot of boiling water, a dusty bottle of Merlot, a single wine glass, cloth napkins.

"We're having your favorite, pasta salad. It's been so long since I've made it for you, but it'll be magnificent. These tri-colored spirals are divine!" she said with immediate regret. Insuppressible nerves had forced her to use words to describe food that were out of character for her.

Logan stared at the steam escaping the lid of the boiling pot with intensity, as if it were signaling secret messages. The skin on his cheekbones was snug. His eyes, bare and desensitized.

"Yeah—I'm not staying long."

"What do you mean? You said you'd be home at six." Sandra kept a calm voice. The kids sat right in the next room.

"I did get here at six." Logan looked tired, haggard. "But, I didn't come to fight. I came to get some of my stuff."

The words he spoke did not make sense to Sandra, as if each blew from his mouth out of its turn. In her head, she had to rearrange them, organize them to understand their meaning. No matter what order she put them in, they did not add up to what she wanted to hear, but her mind forced her to see the truth. His message was clear. He had made it home early only to confirm he would be leaving for good.

She had the desire to stop breathing. Her elbows and knees locked up. Her lips curled, desperate to form a response, but no sound emerged. Gulping the saliva that flooded her mouth, she managed to push down the lunch that tried to make its way out during a wave of nausea. Then came the burning sensation in her throat, the disorientation. Nothing about the moment felt real. How long had she stayed silent? Felt like hours. A quick glance through the kitchen window determined it was still six-ish. The day before, the sun had disappeared by 6:30. The exact time she peeked out the window when she thought his car had pulled in.

Logan appeared to brace himself for some sort of backlash. Head hanging. His mouth twitched and twisted as he chewed the inside of his lips.

By now, Sandra's stiffened limbs had loosened, releasing at the hinges. She rubbed her eyes, leaving traces of eyeliner smudged across her lids and cheekbones.

Should she have a civilized conversation with him? Or counter his argument? She had to choose quickly.

"Why are you doing this?" Her voice was a mousy squeal. "Where are you going? You have children to think about. Why don't you at least care about them?" Sandra had a slew of other questions she did not have the energy to ask.

"I'm not doing this, Sandy," Logan said while turning toward the living room, but Sandra latched onto his arm before he could take a step, spinning him back around.

"You know damn well where this is all coming from," he said. "Don't play stupid with me. I've had enough of the *innocent mom* act." Resisting the urge to dislodge his arm from her grip, he gave into it and rested his back against the wall.

"Innocent mom act? You think I'm acting? I'm a neglected mother of three . . . soon to be four." Sandra wrapped her arms around her belly as if shielding her unborn baby from its villainous father. "So then what role are *you* playing? Worst father of the century? Hateful husband?" Her whispered questions came with a sarcastic chuckle.

"Why, Sandy? Why are you a mother of three, soon to be four? Deduce those figures for me," he snarled, crossing his arms, rage settling in his eyes. "You knew how all this would end, but you did it anyway, even after we agreed. You lied to me about everything. What'll happen if the timing isn't right? Huh?" he said, spinning around in place, not knowing which way to turn, ending up right back where he started. "But that never mattered to you—you were too selfish to care about that part. Then you went around like a joyous mother-to-be telling everyone we know, acting like it was an accident.

"It was repulsive. I lost all respect for you. I couldn't believe this was the person I married." His voice blared, getting heavier, spilling out of his mouth like rocks, but Sandra lunged toward him and clamped her hands over his lip. The kids were too distracted to notice anyway, playing the instrumental version of *Mary Had a LittleLamb* by clanging their forks on ceramic plates.

Sandra released his moist mouth from her grip. His teeth had marked the inside of her hands.

"You lied to me over and over again," he continued. "Getting pregnant twice while on birth control? You stopped taking them. I know what you did."

Sandra stood back. She felt herself stagger, yet she had not moved her feet at all. Everything went out of focus. The features on Logan's face darkened, as if someone had used black chalk to outline his head on the wall, then filled it in with scribbles. All of Logan's words continued to bang against each other before reaching her ears, more jumbles she had to sort. She imagined herself disappearing, finishing this lifetime, a clean break from her worries because everything he had said was true.

"Things would have been different if you kept things simple, Sandy. Brianna and I could have managed once you were gone, but purposely getting pregnant and having more children after we talked about it and agreed. You lied to me. *A mother creating more kids knowing they would bury her in a matter of years?* That's despicable."

"How dare you!" Sandra's eyes quivered behind a glossy wall of tears, yelling through quiet whispers, her finger pointed straight at Logan's face, jabbing it close to his nose.

He did not flinch.

"I did my best to suppress all the feelings about what you were doing, Sandy. I swallowed it all up, but it broke me . . . *you* broke me. You, your lies, your selfishness. I can't take it anymore. I want out for my own sanity." He pushed himself off the wall. "I guess it's my turn to be selfish." He started pacing back and forth in the small area between the kitchen and the side door. "I didn't want to do it like this, Sandy, but you gave me no choice. *You* wanted more children after Brianna. *You* chose to bring them into this god-forsaken world that would leave them without a mother." Logan's face turned a light shade of crimson, beads of sweat forming on his forehead. "*You* became pregnant with twins . . . *twins!* With only four years left. Why would you do that to your own children? And what's worse is you did it again, this time, with less than a year. *You* risked getting pregnant with a due date so close to your Expiration Date, and for what?" He paused in disgust. "What'll happen if your Death Date and due date overlap? You better hope that baby is born before your time's up, or you'll die a murderer."

He said what she had never wanted to hear.

"Logan, please! We can fix this. We still don't know what'll happen," she pleaded.

"You're fighting a losing battle, Sand. A baby can't save you. A set of twins won't either. You knew having more kids wouldn't make you live longer. Trying to manipulate your destiny, change your Expiration Date somehow by being pregnant. It doesn't work like that. You know the Expiration Dates are true. It's happening all around us, but you risked having more kids knowing it wouldn't change a thing. You didn't think about what it would do to them. Instead, you used them to try to bypass a Death Date." Logan's eyes finally landed heavily on Sandra. They seemed to push through her. "I won't be held accountable for your bad decisions. This was traumatizing for me. I can't live this life anymore, not here, not with you. And the kids, I won't become attached to them if I'm not of sound mind after what you've done. I can't take care of them by myself; it wouldn't be fair to them. They'll be better off with a loving, honest couple who can give them what they deserve."

The secret she thought she had hidden so well had been in plain sight all along. Her mind ran through a million different ways to clear her name. Defend herself. Justify it. Did everyone know, or was it just Logan? What if they found out? Would they hate her for it?

Still, with everything she had done, his insensitivity baffled her. The kids still needed someone to care for them, raise them after she's gone, and he had already decided against it.

Minutes passed silently.

The room had cooled. The chill, a choppy flow through her veins. Shuddering, her head followed Logan as he paced back and forth in the small corridor.

Darkness blanketed their town; it showed through the window. The pot of boiling water had evaporated, and the kids had lost their patience.

"Mom! Mom! Where's the spaghetti?" Christopher yelled, pounding his little fists on the table in perfect rhythm. Thump. Thump. Thump. The plates and centerpiece vase clashed against the table with every strike.

"CAN—I—HAVE—SO—DA?" Christina screamed, keeping with the melody of Christopher's thumps.

Leaning their chairs forward, the edge of the table at their chests, the kids tried to get a glimpse of the kitchen, their mother, their dinner. Sandra let out a jolting sigh and dipped out of their view.

She closed her eyes and tried to disappear, like a child playing hide and seek for the first time. Hoping to vanish, no longer exist. But upon opening them, everything and everyone was still there: Logan, his pending abandonment, the kids, her Death Date.

Her mind flashed the limited possibilities of what would happen during her last month on earth. She had planned on spending every minute she had left with her children, but now that wish had evaporated. Sandra would spend the next thirty days trying to find them a suitable home, a new mother, and fighting to keep the three kids and newborn together, nearly impossible in such a short time. The thought of the children growing up separately was excruciating, more so than being abandoned by her husband just before her final days.

Six years prior, her mother had promised to help Logan raise Brianna. That was before her accident. Now, in her condition with three added children it was impossible.

Logan cleared his throat and spoke softly, "I'm going upstairs to get my things. The rest of it can be thrown away with whatever happens to the house after."

"After? After I'm *dead* and *they're* left without parents?" Sandra pointed to the dining room where the pasta dinner and soda were long forgotten. The kids had taken up singing nursery rhymes while having a "who can sing the loudest" contest.

Logan was done talking.

He turned around and headed up the stairs. Twenty minutes later, he came back down carrying a gym bag ballooned up with his things.

The clang of his house key as he dropped it on the counter penetrated Sandra's sternum, like the ring of a final warning bell. Logan simultaneously unlocked the door and turned the knob and scurried through as if the night had sucked him out.

That was it.

They no longer had a father who would take care of them

when she passed or tell them stories to keep her memory alive. She would fizzle.

What she did was out of love for her kids. They always say a mother's love for her children is like no other. Stronger than a herd of charging elephants. If that were true, then she would live a million years. Defy all the laws of destiny to stay by their side.

Sandra collapsed to her knees.

In the next room, Brianna and Christina giggled so hard they fought for breath as they watched Christopher dance with a soup bowl over his head.

Janice: 365 days until death

22

SHE MAY HAVE slept with a smile on her face, perhaps laughed out loud half a dozen times during the night. From what Janice remembered, silly dreams had entertained her and took up most of the seven hours of slumber she had allotted specifically for this day. Plenty of rest equaled good equilibrium, a function she would never again take for granted.

Before going to bed, she rolled her neck for five minutes straight, then her shoulders for two. Her head felt light and in line with her spine. The churning at her temples had faded, and the instability that rocked her, even while lying in bed, had suspended itself. The confusion mornings normally casted over her was minimal. As if she and her terminal illness had called a truce just for today.

Sleeping through the night without the rattling inside her skull made opening her eyes tolerable and the weakness she often experienced—where the deadweight of her exhausted limbs felt heavier than the bed could hold—nonexistent. All indications of a perfect Saturday.

But aside from her subdued ailments, the morning had already set itself apart from others: the sun perforated its way through the clouds that had grayed the sky since Monday, chirpy birds flapped their wings outside her window, and the sluggish breeze tapped at the wind chime that hung on the back patio.

Slithering her way up the quilted headrest, Janice caught sight of her graduation gown draped over a chair, as if the glistening fabric had waited to greet her on a day when together they would cross the stage in accomplishment of what they had set out to do four years ago. That long, winding road had ejected one bump after another, but the thought of one day having a swinging tassel sweep her cheek kept her persistent.

At the bathroom sink her mind refined the message she hoped to instill in every young person with an Expiration Date like hers: perseverance.

Never. Stop. Trying.

Since the day she had received paper cuts on her thumb from opening that red envelope too fast, she had stayed true to her message, never seeking pity. Never the victim. Instead she wanted to exhibit strength and tackle the inevitable in which she had a severe disadvantage. Prove one could live a full life, even when that life wanted you expelled.

Leaning into the mirror, she swiped a mud mask across her face like war paint. A true hero, but it quickly hardened and formed cracks at the surface with every smirk and pucker.

After a shower in which she closed her eyes under running water without incident, Janice's wet hair dripped a trail on the floor behind steamy toe prints all the way back to her bedroom. She did things normally without having to hug the walls or use the handle her father had installed on her bedroom wall.

She applied moisturizer; a breeze.

Her wide-toothed comb yanked on her follicles; no pain at her scalp.

Her fluffy robe, heavy on her shoulders. But soft and comforting.

She put her nose to the air and followed the aroma of frosted cinnamon and coffee grinds. What she spotted as she spun off the staircase prompted an internal laugh.

Overflowing counters, open bags of flour, filled muffin tins, a smoking electric griddle. It looked as if the pantry and kitchen cabinets had simultaneously exploded.

"Good morning?" Janice called out curiously, still chuckling under her breath.

Norma and Lacey swiveled to greet her, their aprons covered in powdered handprints.

"Oh, no—we were supposed to surprise you with breakfast in bed. I thought you wanted to sleep in?" her mother asked with a dripping whisk in her hand.

"I guess I slept enough. I've been up for half an hour. Need help?"

"You're graduating today. Go relax and we'll make you breakfast," Lacey said.

"But it looks like you need help . . . and where's dad?"

Lacey pointed to the front door with a crusted spatula. "Buying orange juice. He should be back soon."

"Okay, because I have an announce—"

"What?" Norma cut Janice off mid-sentence. Mid-word. Every time she heard her daughter breathe, she prepared for the worst. However, in her mind, she had efficiently repelled all ideas of Janice getting a job that would move her out of their town. The less Norma thought about it, the less likely it would be to happen. The announcement, she speculated, could not be about that. Yet, her mind dispatched different scenarios upon the inflection of Janice's single word . . . half-a-word. In one, she would yelp in excitement, cry with pride. In the other, she would cry for real and weather a heartbreak. Both came with a pinch of anger.

Norma had made it her duty to point out challenges Janice faced in her quest for employment. Shine a spotlight on them in case they went unnoticed. The handful of Skype and traditional interviews Janice prepared for had smacked back and forth in Norma's bowels. Indigestion with every listed reference and resume adjustment.

The one job that caught Janice's attention offered a six-month paid internship with the possibility of on-air assignments on Sundays, but Norma casually tossed excuses as to why it would not be a good fit; the woman interviewing her seemed bossy; the newsroom looked dingy and unexciting judging by the photos on the website; and working on Sundays was for the inexperienced, the common worker, unlike Janice. Not in a million breaths would she ever have made reference to the job being three hours and four counties away. Two hours and three counties more than she cared for. That would have come off as overbearing, overprotective, motherly. Instead, she thought herself *strategic* and refrained from all talk of desired proximity.

Every day ended with a hard-earned high-five for herself. Not nagging Janice about long drives for a visit was backbreaking work. Stitching up her lips to a prospect that would put a good chunk of distance between them had started to deplete her reserved stamina.

But, despite her sighs, eye rolling, and complaints of yellowed walls at Janice's potential employers, Norma took moments throughout the day to put herself in her daughter's shoes. Tie the laces tight and take them for a stroll. Imagine what it would feel like to enter the last year of life as a twenty-two-year-old. A college graduate just starting to live while preparing for death. Try to understand it from Janice's perspective.

"So, what's this announcement?"

"Mom, I have to wait for Dad to get back. It wouldn't be fair."

"Fine. Then, let me find out what's taking so long." Norma hopped off the stool to reach her phone.

"Mom! He'll be home any second," Lacey snapped with wide eyes.

Norma slid back onto the stool without saying a word.

So, the three women waited impatiently:

Fingers tapping coffee mugs.

Throats clearing.

Pancakes sizzling.

Riding out the lull required more energy than Norma was able to accumulate at that moment.

"Are you girls all packed?"

"What more do we need than bikinis and sarongs?" Lacey asked.

"Sundresses. Your dad and I scheduled a couple of sunset dinners on the beach."

"What a relaxing way to spend the days before I head off to work," Janice teased.

Turbulence erupted in Norma's gut.

"What work? What are you talking about? You said no jobs had called back."

But thumps at the front door interrupted her discomfort. Whoever fumbled on the other side lacked an available hand to turn the knob, and as Norma reached the door, Barry burst through it balancing three bunches of roses in the bend of his elbow.

"Good morning, sweetie. These are for you."

He presented to Janice half a dozen roses in wrapping speckled with tiny graduation caps. "I am so proud of you. All your hard work has paid off and today—" He pressed his lips together as he had promised himself he would not cry.

"You're finally doing it. You're graduating. That's ninety-five percent of your goal."

"Thanks, Daddy." Janice rammed her head into her father's chest. "And please don't make me cry. I don't want puffy-eyed graduation pics." She pulled back and distracted her eager tears by sniffing the bouquet.

"And these are for you." He handed one bunch to his wife and the other to Lacey. "I know they have graduation caps on them, but none of this would have been possible without the two of you . . . always supportive and sticking by Janice's side. Always encouraging her. She's lucky to have you both."

"Oh, Dad, you know we'd do anything for her. It's so sweet of you to notice." Lacey winked, stood on her toes, and pressed her cheek against her father's puckered lips.

Norma stood in line behind Lacey, snatched one of the kisses her husband was giving away, and headed back to the griddle.

As Barry's three ladies shuffled around the kitchen, mixing, blending, popping muffins, he sat back and immersed himself in their movements. Lacey speaking, Janice and his wife laughing. One daughter pouring juice, the other holding the glass under it.

So natural.

Sliding around one another as each handled a different task. Never colliding, never stopping short. Like pieces of a puzzle, they fit together perfectly.

Next year, life would change forever.

He and Norma would bury a daughter. Lacey, a sister.

A being so full of life.

Courage.

Determination.

How had seven years rocketed by? How was knowing when your child would die the new norm? All the zombie and alien invasion movies he watched as a kid were discredited by his dad: *That'll never happen. It's only make-believe, son.*

But this, red envelopes and Expiration Dates, had gutted him far worse than any apocalyptic or science fiction film ever did. Seven years ago he had begun to live out his worst nightmare.

"I have a special announcement. Actually, this is more like *breaking news*," Janice said cleverly, stampeding all over her father's unexpressed memories.

After a pause, she prepared her throat, drew a procrastinating breath, and blurted out the words, "I got a job!"

A mix of gasps, hand claps, and high-pitched cheers roared in the kitchen. The noise of six instead of three. Janice reveled in the three sets of hands that tugged her at the same time.

But, she had not completed her announcement yet.

She had expected to get it out all in one breath, continue the vibration of her vocal cords, somehow divulge good news with the bad, but her throat forbade it as if it were no longer able to produce sound.

Smothered by her family, Janice caved and allowed herself to partake in the celebration. At any moment, they would ask *where*?

"Wait, there's more," she spit out in a rasp, as if speaking while exhaling cigarette smoke.

Her mother withdrew with a distrustful scoff. "What's the *more* part? You'll be a couple of hours away, won't you?"

The moment had finally arrived. The outcome of the interview Janice had snuck in without her mother noticing. All the shame and guilt that had pestered her while tiptoeing around getting ready for her move had clumped in her throat.

"It's in Miami." She closed her eyes and awaited the hisses and teeth sucking, but nothing happened. Not a single sound to decipher, just a sizzle. Something was burning. She peeked through squinted eyes. Her family stood in a murky cluster under a haze of smoke. A forgotten pancake on the griddle had not caught their attention.

The lack of outrage toward her announcement disconcerted Janice. She had not imagined quiet, failure to react. Their expressions were blank. As if she had not just told them she's moving far away enough to require a twenty-one-hour car ride.

For twelve days straight she had practiced telling them out loud when no one was home and while at school. Like an actress, she ran through her lines with her roommate who improvised with mixed responses to her news. Mostly backlash.

She grabbed the spatula, dislodged the scorched pancake from the griddle, and whipped it into the trash.

"Well, I'll actually have an on-air job. I start two days after we get back from vacation. I'm going to miss you and I love you." She raced through the rest of her announcement, her words blending together as she ran out of breath.

Smiles shrunk.

Lips drooped.

Cheeks sagged.

The reactions she had expected.

Twelve hundred miles would separate them. Her family had done the calculation. Their faces showed it.

"Guys, please. Don't make this harder than it has to be. I'll be a plane ride away, and you can visit me whenever. I have *one* year and you know how important this is to me."

"But Janice—"

"Mom, please don't."

Norma's initial reaction: *I'm the mother, you will do as I say.* She gave her husband a nudge with her eyes. Barry ignored it.

"Tell us about it. How are you on air already? Is that

what you said . . . on air?" her father asked through a twitch and a pant.

"Yes! Can you believe it? So, I had a secret Skype interview a couple of weeks ago." Janice chattered away. She told them about a Miami station and how they requested a second interview and how honesty had worked in her favor.

"I told them I wanted to make my last year as fulfilling as possible." Janice's own words had thrust her into another world, a place where illness and death did not exist. Although voiced, she had abolished the notion of this being her *last* anything. Instead, Janice envisioned the next twelve months as one exciting news story after the next. A schedule brimming with interviews and late-night coffee runs. Maybe even falling in love along the way.

"Then, I told them about my brain tumor and how I wasn't going to let that stop me, and they ate it up! They loved my drive, my passion, then called me two days later asking if I'd accept an offer for a new, minor segment on inspirational stories like *mine*. A new segment because of *my* story," she explained, half exhilarated, half poised. "Can you believe that?"

No response. Just three chirps riding in with the breeze through the open window.

What she viewed as tranquility, peacefulness over her family, was actually a role switch. Their minds were sluggish and impaired, while Janice's appeared to be sound and in optimal health.

Two full minutes passed on the microwave clock before her family could label their feelings coherently. Wavering between rage, disappointment, confusion, anger. Each emotion categorized as it ripped through the layers of reassurance Janice had dumped on them over the last several weeks, undoubtedly agreeing it would be wise to stay within a hundred and fifty miles. And now this.

"Wow," Norma uttered. "I don't know what to say. You did it. This is what you've wanted all along, and you went out and got it," she said dispassionately.

A minor sigh of relief from Janice.

Her feet pivoted toward Lacey. She was the hardest to read. Her head hung low as if dangling off her shoulders; she picked pancake batter out from under her nails.

"Lace, I know this's gonna be hard on you, but once you get to where I am, I think things'll click and you'll have a better understanding of why I need to do this," Janice told her sister.

"I know." Lacey looked up with inflamed eyes. "I'm sad, but not mad."

"Mom?" Janice mumbled.

Norma inhaled with the force of a vacuum hose. "Only because I can't believe what you've done—impressing a station enough for them to create a job for you—I'll accept it. I'm not happy about it, but I'll accept it."

Able to release another half-breath, Janice turned to face her father. She could see his willingness to tolerate her move glimmering through his squinted eyes. No exchange of dialogue, further debates, or justifications necessary. It was over.

The room had brightened, the smoke had cleared, the bird feeder outside the kitchen window bustled.

"But you have to promise. The second you start feeling pain or severe effects of your cancer, you'll let us know . . . and we'll be there to help."

"Deal."

For the next hour, they sat around the kitchen counter slicing through stacks of pancakes, Lacey straining pulp out of her juice. Janice heating up maple syrup. The climate had shifted. For the first time in a pair of years, they put aside all thoughts of Janice's impending departure and enjoyed her presence: expressive eyes, impassioned smile, earnest tone. They saw her exactly as they had seven years ago, when life's end could only be estimated and disregarded as something far off into the future.

INSIDE THE DARKENED college cafeteria, Janice stood in line adjusting the cap toward the back of her head so as not to flatten the waves she had spent an hour twirling around a curling rod. Snapping selfies with two girls fidgeting behind her, the three graduates adjusted their heights and smiles, pressing their faces together to fit into the small screen. The corners of their tasseled caps poked cheeks and lifted strands of hair before finding order and sliding neatly over one another.

"Here we go!" someone called out, prompting a scatter of former students as they strung together, shuffling and rearranging their places in line. Intentional in their postures, shoulders back, and chests out before taking steps that would put them under a midday sun.

Single file across the football field they marched, a mix of giggles and stiffened smiles. The perfect row of black gowns fragmented as it lengthened. Some strayed from their spots; others lingered as graduates accumulated behind them. Most of the distracted bumped into those ahead of them during an unexpected halt. A disarray of adults who had just earned their degrees.

Before reaching the center aisle, Janice tripped twice. Hard to tell what caused it—her clumsiness, the new shoes she did not have time to break in, her dizzy spells, or her obvious excitement. Still, she continued a proud stride of shortened steps in cadence with the swing of her arms.

The procession disbanded into ninety-degree angles as graduates streamed into aisles of vacant seats. Following the sudden bend, Janice spun on the balls of her feet, scrunching blades of grass beneath her soles as a peripheral cluster of three stood out among a crowd of composed families.

Waving.

Cheering.

Bouncing as they threw their palms out motioning for her to stand still, their arms extended, their phones aimed. She stopped and smiled for a count of three through a flutter of shyness. Then, she bowed her head and continued to her seat.

Three taps on the microphone and Janice froze, not expecting the ceremony to proceed quicker than her mind could manage. As if a flight had announced it would take off without her.

In sixty minutes they would change the direction of their tassels. She and her classmates no longer students, presumed juveniles. An automatic transformation into adulthood, set loose in a world full of responsibility, hard work, and countless endeavors.

The sun shone bright in her eyes and anxiety clobbered her enthusiasm.

Palpitations.

Beads of sweat.

Incapable of regulating the chatter of her teeth, the shivering of her thumbs.

Pessimism descended before Janice like the drop of a stage curtain, severing her from the rest of the world. Her thoughts ran miles in a few short seconds, settling on the one with the most friction; scuffing away expectations, fright basting in her bones. At some point, on her fingers, she would count the days she had left to live. After the flick of her pinky, she would no longer breathe into her lungs, see life through her pupils, or feel the earth on her fingertips. She would only live as a memory in the minds of those who loved her.

The shroud of bravery Janice had worn since the day she learned her life would end in a handful of years blew off with a gust of wind that penetrated the assemblage of graduates. Janice's eyes bounced about, consumed by the euphoria rising across the football field like a steaming pot. Soon-to-be alumni giggling, whispering in each other's ears. Sharp swinging tassels sharing in the fun. The speed at which the ceremony rolled on, a clear indication she was a mere passenger of a world unwilling to pause, for even a second, on her behalf.

These graduates had moved on without her. Their elation part of a different reality; one in which she could not participate. Instead, her timer had started. Racing breathless to a finish line she did not want to reach, as if being pushed from behind, her legs incapable of keeping up.

How had she become so unlucky?

Janice was now crying on the inside all while trying to control the development of fresh tears on the outside. She surveyed the convergence of the accomplished sitting before her. Through a blink and a trickle, a young Asian man wearing thin-rimmed glasses came into view. A sort of beer belly bulged from beneath his shiny gown, his slump forcing it forward. Infrequent blinking. Sullen and disinterested. Evidence Janice had designated for those who shared her outcome.

Next to him sat a blond girl who kept knocking into him unintentionally. Her long hair swept across his face with every spin in her chair as she waved at friends from a distance. He sat unaffected.

If he wasn't actually there, Janice had put him there: an

ally. A companion as she inured herself to the X-ing of days on her calendar.

Shame leaked into her veins for wishing him as unfortunate as she.

Janice pushed back into her seat and recaptured her courage as names were called out over the loudspeaker. One by one graduates stood from their seats, some approaching a near sprint to accept their diplomas. Others made a mockery of the moment, while a good portion walked across barely looking up from the floor of the temporary stage.

"Janice Hellington."

Every syllable, every letter pronounced in depth, reverberating through the speakers. Howls erupted behind her. It was time to walk.

The sun flashed in her eyes as she rose. The tips of her shoes pointed in the path she expected to follow, counting her steps to the staircase at the side of the stage. She took a deep breath and placed her right foot on the laminate floor, pressing firmly on her heels, her toes anchored in her shoes.

Don't slip. Don't slip.

Left, right . . . left, right.

She clutched the rolled paper with her left hand, shook with her right. Legs, sturdy. No fog eclipsing her mind. Her vision, crisp. She spun ninety degrees and waved it toward the bleachers. Barry, Norma, and Lacey leaped into the air, pointing and roaring as she turned to walk off stage.

Twenty-four hours later, they lay on a Bahamian beach.

Waves crashing.

Sea mist beading over their skin as the tide reached for them.

Each had an oversized glass at their side. Brightly colored drinks embellished with chunks of fresh fruit and tiny umbrellas.

"Should we head up and get ready for dinner?" Norma asked, her eyes peeking atop auburn sunglasses.

They had sunbathed for three hours under a cloudless sky since arriving at the resort. No grim words were spoken after stretching out on their lounge chairs. No thoughts of death or Expiration Dates, cancer or illness, as if their memories had been zapped by airport scanners as they walked through. Just laughter, deep breaths, and heat glazing over their skin.

"Call me ten minutes before you're done blow drying your hair. That should give me another hour or so," Barry said with no intention of budging.

The three ladies staggered across the lumpy sand toward the back entrance of the hotel. Their eyes puffed with rest and relaxation.

As the sun dipped into the horizon, they found their seats at their first beachside dinner against a backdrop of darkened waters.

"What a perfect night," Janice said as she lifted her champagne flute. "I want to make a toast, to a great vacation and many more, even after I'm gone." The four fizzing glasses clinked together, drowned out by the live band that exploded with the quick pulses of reggae. The female singer, her hair slicked back to form a tight bun, clutched the microphone to her lips and through hops and jiggles, drifted alongside the Hellingtons' table. She grabbed Janice by the hand, motioning for her to follow behind. Janice reached for her sister, who reached for their mother, who then pulled their dad into the mix, picking up others along the way. Without hesitation, they all joined the rhythmic train. Inhibitions drained along with their empty margarita pitchers.

Janice's caramel skin glowed under the dim lighting, the moon watching her every move. She twirled her sister around on the dance floor, bumping into her parents, who were still trying to get in synch with each other's movements. A perfect start to a week-long vacation. So perfect, Janice hadn't even crossed off the day on her calendar, marking the last 365 days of her life.

23

A FEW WEEKS PASSED before Ernesto and Jeremy coordinated a free moment to do what they claim men do best, roll up their sleeves and down a frosty mug of beer. Both arrived at the local pub promptly at 6:30, their polished cars turning into the parking lot entrance only seconds apart. Exchanging a firm handshake and a pat on the back, the two men loosened their ties and unbuttoned their collars.

"Long time no see, buddy. You look great as always. Priscilla's one lucky gal," Ernesto said. His trimmed goatee wrapped around his chin in neat, rounded edges.

"You're not so bad yourself. Every single hair on that head of yours is in its place." Jeremy planted a finger on Ernesto's hair and followed the dark, slick tracks the gel had created.

The crunch of their soles on the graveled parking lot nearly drowned out their continued banter as they walked toward the main entrance of the pub.

"So, what's been going on?" Ernesto asked as he tugged the brass handle of the door. A cool rush of air escaped.

"Work's been busy; nothing ever changes there. However, I do have some Sandra and Logan news for you."

"Great, my all-time favorite topic," Ernesto hissed. "I'm gonna need a double for this one, Joe," he told their regular bartender, who greeted them with a head nod.

Jeremy and Ernesto dragged two empty stools to the back of the establishment, away from the cackles of a middle-aged woman who appeared to have two men courting her.

"I went to Mrs. Wilcox's to change a few light bulbs a couple of days ago, and she gave me an important detail Sandra's left out."

"Go on."

"She says Logan has a nearing Death Date. That explains his behavior and why Sandra puts up with it." Jeremy turned his head to Joe, who stood across the counter between them.

"I'll have a draft of whatever you're promoting today, and I'll treat Ernesto to that double scotch."

Ernesto reclaimed Jeremy's attention by clearing his throat with the force of a revved motorcycle engine.

"So what you're telling me is—Logan has decided to be an A-hole as he rounds the corner to his Expiration Date," Ernesto smirked. "Well then, that explains everything. We should be celebrating his efforts."

Jeremy released a short breath of annoyance, craving a more serious conversation. But Joe the bartender stifled the tension, setting down their orders on cardboard coasters and sliding them toward them.

"I know what you're thinking, but we should give it one last shot. Maybe we can get through to her this time under normal circumstances, not at three in the morning when she's fired up."

"You think the early hour had her fired up? Or her abusive husband?"

Jeremy hadn't planned on being met with resistance. Or having to swallow his best friend's condescending tone.

"Think of Mia and how hard it would be if you were approaching your E.D., but now think of a woman with three kids and pregnant with a fourth. Ernesto, everyone handles things differently. Aggressively trying to help her may be what she needs."

"And when she calls the cops again?"

"She didn't call, you know that."

Jeremy waited for Ernesto's compassion to flare up. He passed the time with more sips from his mug. But Ernesto's emotions remained bland. He shook his head with the short swing of a pendulum and slapped one hand on Jeremy's shoulder. "I don't know how to break it to you bud, but I'm out. You cannot fix evil . . . or the person who protects it," Ernesto said, and that rammed into Jeremy like the horns of a bull.

In all the years of their friendship, they had maintained the same wavelength, seeing eye to eye on almost everything, including politics. Discord between them was foreign to Jeremy. Startling—like the snap of a rubber band.

Ernesto, on the other hand, could not rationalize Jeremy's insistence on obligating someone to accept his help. Though he had always known his best friend as generous with his time and good nature, this particular circumstance required Sandra's cooperation. Perhaps even Logan's. A waste of energy, in Ernesto's eyes. With the impression that Jeremy viewed him as unreasonable, he filled the gap in their dialogue with a gulp from his glass and sloshed it around like mouthwash.

"So, no?" Jeremy asked.

"I commend you for the great things you do. You have the biggest heart of us all. That's why you're the best guy I know, but it's a lost cause and I don't want you to get hurt.

You don't know what that guy's capable of, especially now that we know he smacks around pregnant women."

"Eh, I still have to give it a shot." Jeremy's grunts and groans made it seem as if he disagreed with all of Ernesto's valid points. "I would never forgive myself if something happened to her as I stood by and did nothing . . . or *because* I stood by and did nothing." Jeremy tossed back the last of his beer and paid the tab, and both men walked out of the establishment a little hardened.

Ernesto jiggled the keys in his pocket as they came to a stop behind their cars.

"Let me know how everything goes," he said. "I hope you *do* get through to either of them."

"I will. I'll give you a call later this week and we can do this again. Vodka this time."

"Now you're talkin'," Ernesto said as he leaned in for a partial hug, their arms stiffer than before.

Later that night, Jeremy shuffled back and forth in his socks near the side window, as though trying to build up static on his feet.

Waiting.

Twiddling his thumbs to wear out his anticipation.

I'd like to serve as a mediator. There's no reason your family life should be disrupted by a date circled on your calendar. It should only serve as the number of days you have to heal relationships. Logan, there's still time to fix this . . . A twice-edited monologue he would recite to his neighbor. Going over it again and again as he trampled the same four feet of carpeting. His plan did not include how he would convince Logan to have a discussion. Or even answer the doorbell when he rang it.

"He's erratic and cocky; you're wasting your time," Priscilla had said, opposing his idea after he told her at dinner. Yet, Jeremy's perceived defiance was his unique ability to accumulate enough compassion to empathize when others couldn't. Living with the knowledge of your Expiration Date was brutal, but living with an approaching one had to be downright barbaric.

At midnight, he fell mangled into the couch, plunging like a massive tree wounded at its trunk. One level above him Priscilla fought sleep, regretting her ill-tempered response to Jeremy's kindness. She dozed off fifteen minutes later while waiting to deliver her apology. Jeremy never made it to bed that night.

Six hours into Thursday, his phone alarm imposed the start of another fatiguing day. Though his body lay exhausted, his mind remained active as though he had dreamt one long dream about Sandra and Logan, a sense of not having slept at all.

His first steps that day led him to back to the window, but the only picture it painted was a placid house and an undisturbed driveway, as though the home had tried to alter Jeremy's view of it.

Every sip of the two cups of coffee Jeremy ingested that morning spilled like a stream of acid, cramping his stomach, corroding his insides, and coercing him to forgo the bagel Priscilla had laid out for him on the kitchen counter. Cut open in two even pieces. A fan of avocado slices circled over them. A way of purging her guilt, but Jeremy's distraction settled like a brick in his mind. He had not remembered about their squabble at dinner.

The habitual goodbye kiss Jeremy adhered to Priscilla's forehead read like an automated practice. Her impression: he did not care to make up or continue their dispute. Today, something else had appointed itself more important than Priscilla. And so, after he walked out of the kitchen, she slid the untouched bagel off the plate and into the trash. The gesture designed to end the friction had left her feeling insulted and bitter.

Meanwhile, Jeremy's poor night of sleep had shifted his logic. His impulse led him heavy-footed across the lawns and up Sandra's porch steps.

Blasts of wind flapped the branches of the oak tree behind him, clearing away the shade he used to take cover at Sandra's front door; the sun pounced on him like a strobe. With a light tap, he rang the doorbell as though the sound would diminish if not pressed all the way. Jeremy cringed at the two chimes that seeped out from every crack in the house with the strength of a warning signal. Quick-moving feet followed the noise, trotting down the staircase and across the main floor of the house. Sounded like more than a pair to him.

"Who is it?" asked a little girl from behind the door.

"It's Jeremy, your next-door neighbor. Jen's dad. Is your mother home?"

"MOM!" Christopher's voice rumbled across the wooden floors of Sandra's house. "JEN'S DAD WANTS YOU. CAN WE GO OUTSIDE NOW?"

"Don't you open that door yet, Christopher!" Sandra yelled from further inside.

"HOLD ON, JEN'S DAD!"

Jeremy held his hands to the door—frantic—as if trying to absorb Christopher's over-modulated shrieks. Fifteen seconds later, Sandra cracked the door with the security chain still attached.

"Hi, Jeremy. Sorry to make you wait. It takes me a little longer to move around these days," she said, out of breath.

"Do you have a sec? I know we left things weird last time, and I want to make it right. We've been friends for so long, and Jen misses the kids and Priscilla's upset—" On the spot, Jeremy fabricated reasons he thought might convince her to invite him in, but she cut him off by slamming the door. Jeremy's face reddened with humiliation. But in two of his accelerated heartbeats, she emerged. Square in the doorway after having closed it to unlock the chain. Her pink pajama pants and a large crease across her face suggested he had caught her just getting out of bed.

Jeremy overcame a hurdle he had imagined stood too tall and unsteady to leap over. His eagerness to regenerate their friendship quivered straight through the handle on his briefcase.

"Come in and have a seat."

Sandra's mood circulated through her like velvet, calm, plush, and gentle, as if the doorbell had plucked her from a mattress filled with cotton balls.

"Kids, go into the backyard and play for a bit before I start making breakfast," she called out, but they had already gathered on the floor near the back door, pushing their heels into their muddy sneakers.

She leaned back with one arm extended behind her, guiding the way until she plopped into a chair next to Jeremy, her belly settling on her lap.

"What's up, Jeremy? Everything okay? Are things getting better after Austin's death?"

"Uh—I—well—" The syllables dribbled out of Jeremy's mouth in disorder.

He took a deep breath.

"It'll take some time, but we're managing." His flesh prickled with shock. With the obstacles that besieged her, how had Austin's death maintained a spot in the forefront of her mind?

"Sandra," he continued, "I want us to smooth things over. That whole thing with Logan, when you called the cops on us—

"I didn't call, Jeremy. I wanted everyone to stop fighting and didn't know how else to do it. I was out of sorts, and it was late. I've been sleep deprived, and as you can see, I'm carrying what feels like a giant human in me, so I have a tendency to get irritated quickly." She placed her hands on either side of her belly and pressed around, as if trying to determine her baby's position.

Jeremy watched. The silence spun between them like a funnel cloud until a plane flew overhead and the kids laughed in the backyard.

"I know about your *situation*," Jeremy's thoughts had ejected on their own. Articulated sooner than he planned.

"Situation?" Sandra asked, extending her arms down and back to hoist herself from the chair.

"I'm sorry, Jeremy, I haven't asked, would you like some coffee?"

The cords in his throat vibrated through his ears as he cleared it.

"That would be great."

Jeremy stood with an outstretched arm to facilitate Sandra's final push off the chair. His limbs looser, his joints as if freshly oiled. The pressure that had solidified inside him like a block of ice had thawed, running rivers down his spine.

Relieved to have finally told her.

Relieved she ignored it.

Relieved he was not asked to leave.

As Sandra stamped her way into the kitchen, Jeremy lingered by the desk against the wall in the living room. Picture frames of all sizes staggered across its shelf.

"Wow, Sandra, great shots of the kids. Were these done professionally?"

"Not all. Some I took on my phone," she said in a raised voice from the next room. "I took the black-and-white ones. I like the way kids look in them."

Jeremy leaned in, admiring the images of the kids caught in full laughter. Two of the pictures showed the twins as newborns with Logan kissing one of them on the head.

"I had taken a few photography classes when—" she continued.

But a small pile of papers tucked a quarter of the way under the laptop distracted Jeremy, skimming over the top page:

I have an impending death date that causes concern for the placement of my children. On July 2nd, I'm due to have my 4th child. My death date is 7 days after that. Of course, you can see why I'm concerned over the care of my children and why I find it necessary to speed up this process. Furthermore, my husband has abandoned us, and my mother---

"Right, Jeremy?" Sandra called out to him.

Jeremy could not back away from the pages or lift his legs. His shoes weighed his feet down like cinder blocks, keeping him captive by the desk. He read it again:

My death date is 7 days after that

The phrase had seized his vision, examining the curve of every letter, their arrangement, their meaning.

A sour sting reignited in the pit of his stomach.

"Jeremy?" Sandra asked again.

His body unlocked. He snatched one of the frames from the shelf, almost knocking over a few that crowded around his fingers, and stepped into the kitchen.

"Hey—sorry." Jeremy pointed at the picture. "I was looking at this one and daydreaming about Austin playing with his trucks." When he looked at the image, it depicted the three kids next to toy sailboats on a lake. A lucky match to his excuse for not hearing her calling from the kitchen.

"I'm sorry. It must be hard on you. He was such a sweet boy. My kids ask about him every few days, but they still don't understand," she said while scooping coffee from a large tin.

"In time they'll understand. For now, let kids be kids," he said and turned out of the kitchen to slide the frame back in its place, relieved to have turned his back to her before his face dropped.

Holding out a yellow smiley-face mug, Sandra dragged her slippers across the living-room floor.

"I'm sorry. This is the only mug I have left. The kids can't get up from breakfast without breaking something."

Jeremy slapped his palms around it without noticing the design and sat on the loveseat.

"So, Sandra, when is your exact due date? You must be excited to be over with this pregnancy. I remember Priscilla tried all types of essential oils and tinctures to hurry it along."

"I *am* excited. Did I mention it's a boy?"

"A boy. No, you hadn't."

"I'll have two of each. Two boys, two girls."

For a moment, Jeremy wondered whether Sandra was on medication. Some sort of muscle relaxer. Her movements flowed easily, her voice rang like classical music; her harmonious presence had begun to obstruct his mood.

"Look, Sandra. I know things are rough, but you don't have to go through it alone. Losing Austin was the hardest thing I've ever had to claw myself around . . . " He gulped. "Pri, Jen, I would've never come out of it unscathed without everyone's support. We're here to help you. Please let us help."

She reclined in her chair and expanded her smile.

"Jeremy, I'm fine. There's nothing to handle. We've got it covered," she said. "I know things with Logan and me are weird. Every marriage has its rough patch. We'll be fine. In some cases, it's even a recipe to make a relationship stronger."

Sandra's chestnut eyes appeared near golden to Jeremy.

How had she mellowed?

"I know about your Death Date," Jeremy blurted. His admission soared, exploding like fireworks, but fizzled just as rapidly without the rage he predicted. He had envisioned Sandra fighting to get to her feet, accusing him of shuffling through her private papers, grabbing him by his tie, and pulling him through the doorway. But his words had not affected her. No pursing of her lips, no twitching at her eyes. Her composure remained steady as if what Jeremy said meant nothing to her. It was Sandra's turn to talk and she hadn't yet, but the sounds from outside filled the silence: the trembling of branches during every blast of wind, the kids' sneakers sweeping over the grass as they raced alongside the house.

Fighting the urge to blink away, Jeremy's eyes stung. He would not let her get up and change the subject. Not this time.

"I'll be fine, Jeremy. My life took an awful turn, not at all the way I planned. But I have to carry on and take steps forward for my children. I can't let myself be ruled by the fear of death. My husband's abandoned us. So, we'll have to adapt."

"Leaving four kids behind isn't something to adapt to."

"Then plan. We have to come up with a new plan."

"The kids know?"

Sandra huffed.

"Me, Jeremy. *I* have to come up with a new plan."

Hard to believe, thought Jeremy, that the questions he asked vexed her more than the neglect by her husband and father of her kids. Then, it all made sense; like stars twinkling between them, the answer revealed itself.

Adoption.

Those papers must be for an adoption agency.

"I apologize. I completely understand," Jeremy's voice cracked. "But we are willing to help. Priscilla and I can adopt the newborn; we can try to do it as quickly as we can so when it's time, you'll know he's cared for."

"So the only kid that matters to you is the newborn? You think I'd be at ease with only one child taken care of?"

"I'm trying to help." Jeremy backed away, sitting upright. "And you've taken what I said out of context. Of course you'd want to know all your kids are safe." The quivering through his forearms had returned. "Sandra, I'm working off the top of my head. I'm not *only* thinking about the newborn. I said it because maybe it would be easier to place the bigger kids in a situation like this where their Expiration Dates are already known. I was brainstorming." He over-embellished his hand gestures as though physically trying to erase the discord he had accidently created.

"I think it's best you go now. I have to make breakfast for my kids." Sandra rounded up every bit of energy she had to elevate herself from the couch, landing balanced on her feet.

"Sandra, please. That's not what I meant. Priscilla and I have talked about adopting a boy. It popped into my head." He felt himself begging and lengthened his posture, standing tall to rescue himself from having fallen short in their conversation. He placed the half-empty mug on the coffee table and started for the door where Sandra waited to show him out.

Jeremy scraped around for a way to correct his miscommunication.

"I'm sorry, but my son won't be a replacement to the one you've lost. I need my kids to stay together. Once they don't have me, they won't have anyone. That's only *if* Logan doesn't come back," Sandra said and watched Jeremy's shoes take slow steps to the door. "I'm offended that you'd think it's easy for me to hand my child over to my next-door neighbor who needs to a fill a void."

"That's not at all what I said or meant. You're putting words in my mouth." As he took his first step outside he turned to face her, but the door was already halfway closed. With one strong push, it was completely shut. From where he stood, he could hear the securing of the lock and chain on the other side.

Lingering between the main door and the storm door, he rummaged for ideas to salvage the discussion. Despite how it may have sounded, his intention had been to alleviate her stress, and he was sure she knew that too.

Eventually, he shrugged himself free from the storm door, allowing it to bounce in place before its gradual close.

THE DOOR ON Sandra's side had more of her handprints than the three kids had managed. It had become a habit of hers to shut out a world that had handed her misfortune; a reality she had never imagined for herself. There had also been that one time she took it out on Shirley's front door, the night she had four glasses of wine and strung together enough slurred words to tell Shirley of her plan to keep having babies as a way to ward off death.

24

Mr. and Mrs. Hellington woke up at dawn despite having sunk into the fluff of the mattress and rolled inside the plushest blanket that ever lay across their skin. The comfort had almost entrapped them to sleep longer, to miss the sunrise. Though dazed and wobbly, they ambled to the window in time for the day's first spark on the horizon.

Within a quarter of an hour, they were in open air walking along the curve of the pool, its liquid glimmering with the reflection of the morning sun. Hand in hand, the two stepped out of their flip-flops at the edge of the concrete and onto the powdered sand toward the ocean, their intertwined footprints trailing behind them.

"I feel completely relaxed." Norma sucked in a heap of oxygen through her nose with her eyes closed, the warmth of the sun dripping over her.

"This is beautiful. Look how clear the water is. Everyone always talks about it, but I can see my feet. They weren't exaggerating," Barry said, gliding his foot from side to side in the shallow water, the sides of his khaki shorts scrunched up in his hands.

"Now, I understand," Norma said, "why some people chase this lifestyle, leaving behind six-figure salaries for a life at the beach. Looking around at how beautiful this is, I completely get it now." She sprinkled water across her shoulders and down her arms. "Do you think the girls are up yet? I don't want them to miss out," she told Barry, who splashed his feet around like a toddler on his first beach trip.

"I sent'em a text before we came down and told'em to meet us on the beach so we can get breakfast." He let go of his shorts and pulled his cell phone out of his back pocket.

"Lacey texted back eight minutes ago saying she was getting out of the shower and meeting us down here. But by the time those girls do their hair and make-up, it'll be lunchtime." He slipped the phone back into his pocket, re-gathered the hem of his shorts, and puffed his chest to the sea.

They were lost.

Lost in a different life. A different time. They had the desire to laugh, to breathe, to allow their minds a break from planning, worrying, anticipating.

They danced in the water until the sun erupted over them from behind a cloud puff. Drips glistened down their shins as they emerged from the foam. At a cluster of beach chairs on the sand, they pushed two side by side with the air of being on their honeymoon. The one they had put off long enough to take two grown daughters with them. They reclined in their seats and let their minds sway with the sound of shifting waters. Just as they felt themselves doze off, Lacey cast a shadow over them.

"Hello, lovebirds," she whispered as she stood before them.

Barry and Norma's eyelids opened to a squint, but all they could see was a neon outline of their daughter.

"From behind, you guys look like a postcard," Lacey said. Her outfit resembled her mother's: black sunglasses holding back light brown hair, visible bathing-suit straps from under the halter of a sundress.

"Good morning, Lace. Where's your sister?" her mother asked, shielding her eyes from the sun.

"She was getting into the shower when I left the room. She said she wouldn't be long and told me to tell *you*, Dad, that she isn't wearing make-up today, so please refrain from the 'she'll take long getting ready because of her make-up' comments." Lacey mimicked her father's deep voice.

"Only time will tell," he said, checking his watch.

Lacey dragged a chair through the sand, positioned it next to her mother, and flung her dress off over her head. "So what did you guys do last night after dinner? Did you head to bed? Or did you go out?"

"Went right into bed," Norma said. "I was so tired after all that dancing. It felt like I went jogging. Every muscle in my body is sore."

"We were tired too, but then Janice and I decided to check out one of the resort clubs. We made friends with a bunch of girls here for a bachelorette party. They were all nice, but by the end of the night, two of them were so drunk we had to walk them to their rooms. One of the girls even broke a heel, so every other step she took was five inches higher. We had such a great time, and Janice . . . " She shook her head in amazement. "That girl has some energy! She didn't stop dancing the whole night. Never took a break and out-danced all those girls. I'm so glad she's back to her old self with this medication. It's helped a ton."

"She didn't drink any more after dinner, right?" Barry

asked, his face crumpled. "Because that can interfere with her medication or make her sick."

"No Dad, she didn't." Lacey rolled her eyes. "We ordered bottled water and that was it."

As the sun drifted off the horizon and into the sky, the beach speckled with slick, sun-worshipping bodies. Some dragged lounge chairs right into the water. Others stabbed the sand with their umbrellas or slathered their kids in white lotion.

"Okay, I'm hungry." Norma flipped her sunglasses up and looked back toward the resort.

"It's been an hour. Let me call her; she should be ready by now," Lacey said and with a few swipes on her phone, she was calling Janice.

The call went straight to voice mail.

"I bet she forgot to charge her phone." Lacey swung her legs around to sit at the side of the chair for a better view of the pool area Janice would walk through to meet them.

They waited.

Stomachs rumbled.

Another quarter of a turn on Norma's watch.

"Alright, it's getting hot. Let's call the room from the lobby phone," Barry suggested. "I'm famished. In desperate need of a bagel now, although I had *hoped* for something a little fancier and vacationy."

They gathered their things and trailed one another over lumps of sand.

Norma and Barry slid back into their flip-flops at the pool deck and walked into the back end of the lobby. Lacey lagged, dipping her toes in the chilled pool water.

Agitated and impatient, Norma's eyes crisscrossed the hotel lobby, sweeping over a gathering of bikinied women in sun hats; a cluttered line at the check-in counter. Like ants, vacationers moved quickly through the lobby, twisting and pivoting out of each other's way. The newly-arrived disappeared through corridors, bulging suitcases rolling closely behind.

Norma lunged at the first site of a phone affixed to a wall and slammed the receiver into the side of her face. It rang six times, then prompted her to leave a message.

"She didn't pick up; she must be on her way down. Let's go sit over there and wait for her." She pointed to a set of empty couches. "Breakfast is almost over, and I don't want to miss it."

Norma, trying to see past the glow still stamped in her vision, noticed a girl pushing her way around a revolving door at the other end of the lobby. "Is that her coming?"

"Mom, that's a middle-aged woman . . . and she's wearing glasses."

"Oh—my eyes are still adjusting from the sun," Norma simpered. "I'm really only seeing shapes. No faces yet."

Again they waited, admiring bathing suits and flowing dresses as they went by, waving fingers at toddlers stumbling along with plastic shovels and buckets. A way to appear composed when they weren't; relaxed when they weren't. Their heads swiveled with every elevator ding, expecting to see Janice at the parted doors, the noise taunting them and getting louder as time passed.

Over the next forty-five minutes, the same elevator dropped twelve times without Janice.

"Should we be worried? It's time to check the room. She wouldn't keep us waiting this long." For the past hour, Norma's mind involuntarily flashed images of Janice lying on the floor of the hotel room. *But with the medication, that wouldn't happen,* she told herself, *and besides, we're on vacation.*

"You guys go up and I'll wait here in case she's on her way down, so we don't miss her." Barry leaned back and crossed his legs. As far as he knew, Janice was still fumbling with a curling iron. "Seriously," he said. "Breakfast is important to me. Go see what's taking her so long."

Norma and Lacey shouldered their way into the gaps of the crowded elevator. The other occupants twisted and angled their way back to allow space for the new passengers.

Up they went to the fifth floor.

It was quiet. The slaps of heel against sandal joined the low buzz of the light fixtures. Down the hall, four doors up from Janice and Lacey's room, a service cart stood alone.

With each step the women moved quicker through the narrow passage. The hum of a vacuum cleaner faded in and out. The voices on a TV faded in and out. Finally, Lacey reached their door and hurled three knuckle raps into it.

No response.

She used the keycard to unlock it.

"Janice?" Lacey called out. Her eyes scoured the floor around the beds, the floor of the bathroom, the tub.

Nothing.

Zigzag glances from the bathroom counter to the night table to the dresser. "I don't see her phone. She must be looking for us somewhere. I told her exactly where to go, but she must be on the opposite side or something." She walked into the bathroom and tapped on the curling iron.

Cool.

No moisture build-up on the bathroom mirrors either.

"Her charger's here. She must've forgotten to plug her phone in last night or it would ring before going to voicemail."

"Where could she have gone?" her mother asked. "It's been almost two hours since you met us."

Lacey nodded. Norma's neck tightened.

"That means she's been ready for over an hour. How could we have missed her? Maybe she's had a dizzy spell and is lost or confused somewhere. Call your dad and see if he's found her. I'll ask the cleaning lady." Norma pulled out her cell phone and scanned the previous night's photos on her walk toward the cart.

"Hello? Excuse me."

A pudgy woman with platinum blonde hair peeked her head out from behind the half-opened door. "Yas, hello? Can'help you?" She said meekly in an indistinct accent.

"Hi, I'm sorry to bother you, but I can't find my daughter and she's staying in that room over there." Norma pointed down the hallway and showed her a picture of Janice on her phone. "Have you seen her? We think she left the room over an hour ago. Do you remember seeing her at all?"

"Dis lady? She'naw here?" asked the cleaning lady.

"I'm-looking-for-her. Did-you-see-her?" Norma pointed at her eyes and at Janice's picture.

"No. She'naw here. I don't see her. I come ten o'clock." The woman tapped on her empty wrist.

Norma looked at the time on her phone. It put the cleaning lady on the fifth floor only fifty minutes earlier. Janice would have left the room before then.

"Okay, thank you. Sorry to bother you."

She turned and met Lacey at the doorway.

"Dad said she's still not downstairs. I told him to start walking around because it seems like she left a little while ago. Her medication bottles are on the nightstand and there's a glass with a tiny bit of water in it, so she took her pills before she left. She has to take them every twelve hours."

"I spoke to the cleaning lady. She showed up after Janice would have left the room. She doesn't remember seeing her, but Janice could have passed by while she was inside a room anyway," Norma said, shrugging her shoulders.

They stepped into the descending elevator.

Barry stood outside the main entrance of the hotel by the revolving doors as if policing the crowd waiting to board taxis. A sixth attempt at calling Janice's phone had also gone to voicemail. His strained fingers fiddled with a ten-dollar bill in his pocket; his mind awakening to the end of breakfast hours and still no Janice.

"Hey, Dad. Anything?" Lacey asked as she pushed herself out of the revolving door. Norma followed.

"Nothing yet. Let's walk around a little bit. She'll turn up."

"What if her medication isn't working right and she's sick somewhere or hurt?" Norma's rushed words turned a few heads.

Was she scolding him?

Were they fighting?

"Honey." Barry kissed his wife on top of her head and the spectators' looks dissolved. "I think if she's hurt, we'd have heard about it. This place isn't that big. I'll go back inside and speak to someone so they can keep a lookout."

Barry sauntered into the lobby with both hands in his pockets.

"Mom, you stay here. I'll go to the pool and beach to see if she's waiting for us out there."

They deserted Norma at the front entrance, stuck where she felt the least productive. A drop of sweat trickled down the back of her neck. The sun hung directly overhead. Another twelve hours and this day would be over. Janice would surely be found by then. Norma no longer felt hunger or had a taste for breakfast pastries. Watching families cram themselves into cabs and drive away was nauseating enough. Her kneecaps weakened, all their energy swiped from them. They would not hold her up for long. She took backward steps and fell into a wooden bench.

Where was Janice?

A good portion of the guests gathered at the front entrance had left before Lacey swirled out of the revolving door again, the midday sun adding another layer of bronze across her cheeks.

"She's not back there. I saw two girls from the bachelorette party, and they're gonna tell the others. They'll be at the beach all day, so at least we have a few pairs of eyes helping us." She tried on a drab smile, but it immediately loosened.

"What the hell?" Lacey whined. "Where could she have gone?"

Norma felt unable to communicate. Not vocally, not with her hands, not even through blinks.

Just as Lacey leaned in to take a seat next to her mother, her cell phone startled her, vibrating and ringing at the same time.

"Oh—IT'S JANICE!" Relieved excitement rose from her chest. She swiped and squeezed the phone tight against her ear as if force would allow her to hear her sister's voice faster, clearer.

"Hey, where are you?" Lacey asked.

She looked down at her phone.

Had she lost connection?

She returned it to her ear. "Hello?"

She looked at her phone again.

"It looks like the call dropped."

Her tone gave the impression of confusion.

"Or she hung up."

She called Janice back. It went to voicemail.

Three more times after that. Voicemail.

"Okay, at least we know she's alright. She's gotta be lost. I'm gonna walk around, Mom. Dad's in the lobby at the front desk. Go meet up with him and I'll go back upstairs to see if she's there."

For the first time, Norma took direction. Did as she was

told. One step in front of the other, she wandered into the lobby to find Barry.

~~~

THE HANDS ON Norma's watch had taken another three full spins and still no sign of Janice.

Three hours earlier, a hotel manager stood square with Barry, flipping his tie over his shoulder as he leaned into a clipboard with a fresh pen. Barry dictated his daughter's information:

Janice Hellington.

Brown hair.

Five feet tall.

Twenty-two years old.

Dizzy spells.

Medication.

Cancer.

One year left to live.

The information would circulate among hotel staff and local police.

"Now, we wait," he said. "Let's get something to eat. We're all famished and need a break."

"I don't know if I'll be able to eat anything. Everything'll make me sick. My stomach's in knots," Norma said, an intertwining of stress and testiness.

"You need energy. Eat *something*. What good'll it do if we need to keep pushing ahead and you're lacking clarity because you haven't eaten all day?" Barry put his arm around her shoulder and led her in a spin toward the resort café. "Come on, at least some chamomile tea and toast."

Barry's sentences dribbled over Norma as if she were incapable of absorbing the information—*if we need to keep pushing ahead.* Ahead how? Was there a possibility that Janice would not turn up soon? Or by the end of the day? Would they have to sleep through the night without knowing where she was? Lacey would have to return to a room with no one else in it?

None of it made sense.

Barry had not intended on crushing a spear of hope in his wife, but they could no longer tiptoe around it.

Janice was missing.

"Hey, everything's going to be fine. The police are looking for her, and she'll turn up. Her Expiration Date is a year from now. She's fine," he said.

A subtle spark had returned in Norma's eyes. A pop in her ears clearing the way for better news. A flip in mindset.

"You're right," she said, chuckling at the ghastly progression of her thoughts. "She has to turn up. Before, we would have thought *dead* right away, but with a year to go " Norma paused to smile, a hue of confidence lifting her cheeks. "She'll turn up."

"Exactly. We'll let the police handle it from here. We know she's somewhere, and they know this place better than we do. Let's get something to eat and wait for them to contact us." Barry grabbed his wife's hand and waved Lacey over with the other. While her parents talked, she had paced the area between the front entrance and the back exit of the hotel fifty-seven times.

They set off for nourishment. Short steps through the lobby led them to a long corridor with a dining hall at the end of it. Norma turned her head a dozen times to make sure Lacey had caught up to them before they went out of sight. She would never again let her daughters wander, her mind reverting them back to little girls. An accumulation of her nerves fashioned themselves into nagging guilt for letting

Lacey and Janice out of her sight on an island they had never been to.

After an hour of shifting back and forth in her chair, gnawing on water crackers and slurping chamomile tea, Norma looked at Barry through misty eyes.

"What if she needs our help and she's calling and calling for us and doesn't understand why we're not there for her? What if she's disoriented somewhere and can't remember who she is? It's a brain tumor, Barry. Things could go very wrong."

"Honey, we know she's out there. If she needs help, we'll get it as soon as police locate her. They have a few different units on it. We need to refuel, and then we'll join them. Plus, there are ten girls who are also keeping their eyes open." Barry threw every bit of encouragement he could scrounge up.

"What ten girls?" Norma asked, looking up from a tissue she had folded over.

"The girls Janice and Lacey met last night after we went to bed."

"Dad, those girls were so trashed, I'm not even sure they recognized me when I went up to them this morning. Some looked half asleep. I wouldn't rely on them in the least." Lacey was irritated at both her father for having faith in girls he had never met and the bachelorette party for existing. "I don't understand why girls are stupid enough to get that drunk in an unfamiliar place. So drunk they had two strangers walk them up to their rooms. Meanwhile, *Janice* is the one we can't find." Lacey had crossed from irritated to angry.

"I wanna find Janice already so we can continue our vacation and forget this ever happened," Lacey said, taking a feeble bite of a panini she had specially made at the sandwich counter. It had already cooled and the bread was soggy.

As they folded their paper plates and assembled a pile of

dirty napkins, Barry's cell phone buzzed. Eager to hear they had found his daughter, his French-fry-oiled fingers lost their grip and sent the phone flying out of his hand. His determination allowed him to catch it mid-air.

"Hello? Hello? This is Mr. Hellington." He listened; every cell in his body stiff, his mouth wide open.

"What is it? What's happening?" Norma whispered to him, pulling on the sleeve of his tee shirt.

"Sounds good, thank you so much. We'll be over in a minute," he said, his breezy tone a contrast to the unsettled look on his face.

"Uh—" He didn't know how to deliver the lack of news. "They can't find her at any medical facilities. I guess that means hospitals or clinics. But they checked surveillance camera footage and she's on one of them, from early this morning. So, we have to meet them at the manager's office near the lobby."

"Oh my God. Let's go!" Norma shouted. The tips of her fingers buzzed with impatience as she gathered her sunglasses and wallet, leaving behind a pile of crumbs and an open tea bag wrapper on the table.

With a slow, steady jog they made it back into the lobby.

"Excuse me. EXCUSE ME!" she yelled at personnel behind the counter. The desperation in her voice claimed the attention of those scattered throughout the lobby.

"I'm Janice Hellington's mother. The police told us to meet them here. We need to speak to them," she continued. In her opinion, hotel staff did not move fast enough.

"Yes, ma'am." A man in a pencil-thin tie rounded the corner of the check-in counter. "I'll send someone to show you to the manager's office right away."

Moments later, a burly man with tousled hair emerged from a door marked "Employees Only" and directed them through a hallway lined with cramped, undecorated offices.

They dragged their feet through the doorway of a bare room with four patio chairs that matched those of the outdoor dining area.

"Sit. Manager come now," the large man said gruffly.

Norma's heart raced.

Her daughter was missing. Why were they handed over from person to person as if on some sort of hotel tour?

But before Norma could complete her thoughts, two men walked in. Their attire was opposite of one another—a three-piece gray suit and a light blue police uniform consisting of shorts and a short-sleeve shirt.

"Good afternoon, thank you for waiting. I'm Gerard, the hotel manager. This is Sergeant Robert Ingraham." Both reached out to shake hands with the three. "Thank you for—."

"Have you found my daughter?" Norma purposely interrupted the manager mid-sentence. The exchange of pleasantries had already taken up too much of her time.

"Thank you for meeting with us," he continued, clicking a pen in his hand. "We currently have officers checking all the rooms on the fifth floor. Then, they'll move to the other floors. They are knocking on doors asking occupants if they've seen Janice," he said. The information came with an accumulation of saliva at the corners of his mouth, an image of inexperience with a situation like this. "We've pulled surveillance tapes and see her walking toward the elevator, but once she passes the camera, we don't see her on any of the other recordings. You see—" He gulped. "There's a glitch we were not aware of, but don't worry, we have the whole department on alert."

That was sly, thought Barry of the inadequate explanation of the hotel's malfunctioning cameras.

"Hold on—hold on. Wha'd'ya mean? What *glitch*? Don't the recordings continue as she passes? She would have walked into other camera frames—like in the elevator—the lobby—the pool area. What do those show?" Barry's inquiry squawked with confrontation, the veins on the surface of his skin fluttering.

Neither man answered.

The vent overhead hummed with a breeze; died out within seconds.

"Well, sir." The hotel manager stepped forward. "Upon pulling surveillance tapes, we discovered faulty wires that interrupt the recordings. She's seen walking down the hallway from her room and then turns the corner toward the elevator. After that, she walks into the viewpoints of the other cameras with the interrupted recordings. It picks up again ten minutes later, but she's not seen anywhere after that. We've reviewed all the tapes."

The small room crowded with tension.

"I mean—I don't—" Barry floundered.

"What about the cameras on other floors?" Norma asked. "Or the lobby? She didn't just disappear. She has to be seen somewhere else; you're not looking thoroughly enough. Besides, aren't the cameras installed for security purposes? They should *all* be working properly at all times, am I right?" Norma's aggravation grew with every question. The way she saw it and as irrational as it sounded, the hotel was now responsible for her daughter's disappearance. She had paid this resort hard-earned money. What a betrayal. If the cameras had been working, they would have seen where Janice ended up after leaving the room.

"Those were reviewed as well, by our team here. She's not seen anywhere else." The hotel manager gasped trying to fill his lungs.

"So, she's still in the building? Or you would have seen her walking through the lobby. Right?" The significance of a surveillance camera glitch rippled passed Norma's comprehension. Glitch or no glitch, Janice's whereabouts should be on those tapes.

"Madam, the problem with the recordings extended to the lobby. Still, we reviewed them, and she's not on those either. The police are actively searching the whole resort. So, when the search is over, we will call you. It will take a few hours." The hotel manager hunched and crossed his arms. His posture gave the impression of cowering.

Norma had nowhere left to turn, jammed inside the four walls of a tiny room with two men who knew nothing. Her eyes ping-ponged from the hotel manager to the sergeant, unsure of which one she hated the most.

"THEN WHY ARE WE IN HERE?" The crash of her own voice against the empty walls seemed to turn the room sideways. "WHY HAVE THIS MEETING TO TELL US NOTHING?"

Barry took a hold of Norma and wrapped her in his chest.

"Please do everything possible to find my daughter. She's got brain cancer and has to take medication every twelve hours," he explained. "We're worried she's passed out or sick somewhere, so we need to get her medical attention quickly. She suffers from dizzy spells and seizures . . . and she's definitely alive," he said as Norma puffed and shuddered in his shoulder.

Both men straightened their backs and elongated their limbs, waiting to hear more.

"In the U.S. we have our Expiration Dates. You know, the date we'll die."

"Right, we are aware," the officer said.

"Hers isn't for another year. So, we know she's somewhere. We just have to find her."

"Yes, absolutely. We are doing everything possible to locate your daughter. Because of her condition, this is officially a missing person's case now and the station is working on printing up flyers to hand out in the area. If there is a better photo you can provide us with, you can email it to the station."

"Can we see the surveillance footage?" Lacey asked, her voice feathered into a croak. "The one she's seen on."

"Yes, of course."

They tightened the circle they stood in and bowed their heads over a tablet held by the hotel manager, heartbeats clacking in unison.

The silent footage began. Seconds and milliseconds raced at the bottom left corner. A diamond-patterned rug divided two rows of closed doors.

At 9:06 a.m., movement.

A door swings open on the upper left-hand corner of the screen.

Arms, legs come twirling out of the room.

It's Janice.

With steady steps, she becomes clearer, larger as she makes her way down the deserted hallway closer to the camera. A black beach dress flows behind her. Her hair is pulled back in a ponytail, and she sports sunglasses on her head. Her head is angled down to her phone as she walks the length of the hall.

When she reaches the bottom of the screen, she lifts her head to turn the corner, and in two paces she's gone, out of the frame.

Stillness reclaims the corridor.

No swinging doors. No cart. No housekeeping.

They played the footage seven times.

Had she walked straight?

Did she look dizzy? Shaky?

As much as they tried to redefine her stroll down the hallway, they couldn't.

Janice appeared fine, physically and mentally.

"So, the elevator footage is also part of the interrupted recordings?" Lacey still held out hope that she either did not understand the glitch correctly or their response would change.

Both men nodded their heads as if with creaky neck hinges.

Shortly after, the two men shook hands with the family, promising to be in touch soon. The Hellingtons formulated a strategy, changed out of their beach clothes, and marched off in different directions under dim skies. A storm cloud raged by the horizon.

Sandra: Five days until death

25

TIGHTENING. SQUEEZING.

Heat-filled spasms jabbed at her abdomen and crackled through her back.

Sandra had waited for the arrival of these pains. Two days overdue.

The car borrowed from her mother's caretaker had sat askew in the driveway for the last three days, expecting passengers at any second. Its position emanating a burst of urgency. The front wheels turned as if its driver were too busy and in too much of a rush to straighten them.

Inside were fastened car seats, a box overflowing with DVDs, a doll, and two action figures. Overnight bags rested in the trunk.

The next actions were familiar; having been practiced in between playtimes, just before bed, in the middle of the night, and while getting ready for school. Briana pinched the corner of a full-size brown paper bag and slid it off the kitchen counter. Her arms formed a hoop and it landed within them. Pudding cups, cereal boxes, and snack bags shifted inside. Christopher threw Mommy's purse across him like a messenger bag, and Christina dried and collected three toothbrushes.

Sandra and the kids hustled into the car and snapped into seatbelts. Perfect timing. Only seven minutes, one minute faster than last time. Among them, a quick cheer for a job well done, but the kids' attempt to unlock the doors and get back to their soggy ice creams was thwarted. This was not a drill.

The loaned car glided on the pavement, some ten miles above the speed limit. Smooth lane changes. Skimming and cutting around potholes. Gentle pushes on the brakes. The only jolts that swept through their torsos happened during the interrupted momentum at every contraction. She laid off the accelerator to avoid propelling them forward.

The soon-to-be mother of four exuded confidence that she had this delivery down to a science—a perk of having had the experience of delivering one child and a set of twins four years apart. Practice that kept her relaxed and focused this time around.

Her plan had materialized only three days earlier. A perfect solution to avoid imposition on neighbors she ought not to confide in. She would drop the kids off to be watched after by the nurse who cared for her wheelchair-bound mother. The nurse was happy to do it, coaxed with a five hundred dollar check Sandra wrote from Logan's account.

With her foot firm on the brake at a red light halfway thru her journey, Sandra called an Uber, which sat idle in front of her mother's house when she pulled up.

Sandra waved at her children, who watched from the large window of their grandmother's home, as she found her way into the backseat. Like a tunnel, she crawled on her hands and knees until she safely flipped her legs out from under her and landed upright. When she looked up, the kids had smooshed their cheeks and noses against the glass, tapping their little palms against it. Ample smiles hung from their cheeks, excited to meet their new baby brother. They chattered about playing with him at the nearby park when he's big enough and watching their mother cradle him from behind as he goes down the slide for the first time—something their innocent minds did not know would never happen.

Able to maintain her courageous disposition until they entered the highway, Sandra let out a gurgled hack. The driver thought she had held in a sneeze.

Then, the release. Spilling from her face.

The fear. Pain. Uncertainty. Every bit Sandra had caged inside fluttered out of her like the air and slobber of a balloon. Unlike her nightly cries in the shower. Different from the new morning cries before breakfast. A regurgitation of the life that had handed her setback after setback, obstacles paired with misfortunes. It poured from her like the emptying of an overflowing bucket as she sat behind a stranger. It came with the overwhelming need to feel hollow, empty.

With four miles to go, they sped toward the hospital. The driver flexed her toes against the pedal as a moment of discomfort overcame her. What if she knew her passenger had only days to live? That every revolution of the tires took her further away from kids who, in a matter of days, would wonder where she was when they went back to school on Monday? That with any luck, this woman would give birth in the next few hours so as not to waste a single minute she had left to find a suitable home for them?

"Are you okay? Should I pull over?" asked the petite driver, the seatbelt high on her neck. The roar of the engine muffled her words.

"I'm fine. I'm sorry. I didn't mean to make you

uncomfortable." Sandra took out a napkin she had stuffed in her pocket during breakfast and used it to wipe the wetness from her cheeks. She felt compelled to share her troubles. She would never see this woman again. The woman whose eyes she found staring at her through the rearview mirror.

"I'm having my last baby today, and this coming Sunday is my Expiration Date," Sandra confessed, sniffling as she wiped her eyes with the damp napkin that had already tended to her nose. With the admission, she felt the last bit of pressure against her chest escape. She was now empty, able to breathe deeper.

The driver offered premature condolences as her eyes puffed with sorrow and she accelerated her small vehicle toward the hospital.

Alleviated, Sandra thanked her for the kind words, leaned her head sideways on the headrest, and watched the blurred trees that lined the highway as they slid past. Her mind unfolded memories of the times she had sat in the backseat of her parents' car as a child.

How had so much time passed? *And* so quickly?

As a little girl, her lifetime seemed endless, adulthood too far to grasp.

But now here she was nearing the end of her existence. A ride down the same stretch of highway, transported by the same asphalt, escorted by the same trees she watched pass the window of her parents' station wagon more than thirty years ago.

Life-infused leaves.

Firm branches.

Tough trunks.

If only they could share a flicker of a leaf, a breath of their lives with Sandra. A single one to inhale, giving her more years, more time.

Life had become defective.

STEPPING OUT OF the elevator at the maternity ward, Sandra felt herself at the center of a flow of energy. A whole hospital floor spun around her, its detail obscured by its speed. Every one of her shortened strides came inches away from smacking into an oncoming wheelchair, bumping into a fleeting nurse, or knocking into motorized beds and medical machinery that stood unattended in the halls. She lumbered toward a wraparound counter, one hand on her belly, the other gripped around an overnight bag, and gave her name.

" . . . and I'd like a single room, please. No sharing. No roommates." Sandra's demands turned heads throughout the nurse's station as the notion of her request became more apparent. Her tone was more appropriate for checking into a ritzy hotel in the heart of Manhattan. She didn't smile or soften her scowl. Instead, she prepared to unleash impolite responses to hospital personnel—A way to avoid giving anyone the impression she desired conversation; a way to dodge questions about who would be joining her and whether the baby's father was on the way.

They put her in a wheelchair and a small woman in pink scrubs gripped the handles, her smile stiff and unenthusiastic. The nurse's unnerved look, stacked above the viciousness locked on Sandra's face, grabbed the attention of those roaming the halls. The heat of their stares seared through the pair.

For Sandra, the sounds of the maternity ward seemed louder than she remembered. Certain areas a little more active. Almost back to its regular shuffle from when Brianna was born, a year before the Death Date reveal. Four years before when she had delivered the twins, the sounds were more of a disturbance. Shouting, wailing. And when that stopped, a somber vibration pinged off the walls.

Had the shock of the Expiration Dates sorted itself out? Were more parents bracing for the worst, already having grieved before laying eyes on their newborns' Death Dates?

They turned into a wide entryway of an occupied room. A pregnant woman stood at the side of a bed, holding the guard rail; breathing and stretching as if preparing to run a fifty-yard dash.

"I *said* I didn't want—"

"I know ma'am, but we don't have single rooms available right now. We'll have to make do . . . for now. If one opens up, we'll let you know." The nurse's response matched that of a hotel manager's.

As soon as the rubber on Sandra's wheelchair rolled into her half of the room, she asked the nurse to draw the blue curtain that hung between the beds.

Ninety minutes later, she opened her eyes to a distorted woman standing at the foot of her bed. It took a number of blinks to blend the two wavy images into one. Through exhaustion, her memory had only captured bits and pieces of what occurred before she fell asleep.

Pains.

A hospital gown.

Her doctor.

An epidural.

"Good evening," the woman said, pulling on the lapel of her white lab coat. "I'm Patsy Mckail, your social worker. Glad to see you're doing well. Our software notified me of your admittance to the hospital, and I was hoping you had a quick second to chat."

"Yes, I know what you need to talk about, and yes, my Expiration Date is only five days away." Sandra tried adjusting the droop of her eyes, the fog in her brain.

"Right." The woman referenced pages attached to a clipboard. "Only because you'd have to be discharged twelve hours after your baby's born since you'll expire within six months. Depending on your baby's date, he may be able to stay a couple of days, but that'll be determined once his paperwork goes through."

"My baby will go home with me." Sandra let her eyes close.

"Well, depending on his health, which we assume will be *great*, he can stay a day or two to make sure. The father can stay with him here and you can rest at home, if that makes you feel any better." Ms. Mckail spoke through a smile and held it until Sandra's eyes opened with the rage of an awakened dragon.

"I shouldn't have to repeat myself. My baby—is leaving—with me." She spoke slowly and pronounced every letter. "I have no one to care for him while he's here. His father abandoned us and hasn't been heard from since. So, my suspicion is he won't be joining us this time around." Sandra resealed her eyelids and wiggled her head into the pillow. She wanted to cry.

Ms. Mckail waited, tucked the clipboard under her arm, and tapped the heel of her shoe on the ground. Sandra did not flinch.

"Okay. Well, good luck with your delivery. Be well." The woman turned and walked toward the door, her peripheral vision still on Sandra until she crossed the partition.

Sandra opened her eyes, struggling with internal embarrassment. As much as she did not want to admit it to herself, Ms. Mckail had disappointed her. She had not expected the social worker to stay, but a small part of her wished the woman would have at least pried a little, recognized Sandra's fear, and attempted to implode the walls she has vigorously built over the last few years. Perhaps today could have been a day for emotional healing.

The next couple of hours were unbearably lonely. She fought off tears as her side of the room echoed of her roommate's visitors. Cackles. Guffaws. Silly baby talk. The cries of an infant. But visiting hours were over. Just as Sandra pushed the button to alert the nurse of her intolerance, she felt intense pressure followed by the desire to push.

26

"LOCAL GIRL GOES missing while on a dream vacation with her family in The Bahamas."

Shirley's head swiveled away from the crossword puzzle she had almost completed and strained to see the television from the chaise. Her neck cracked and popped in three different places. Janice's face was in a square beside the female news anchor.

"Janice Hellington was vacationing with her family when she disappeared yesterday morning. Her mother said she was last seen on the hotel's surveillance footage leaving her room as she walked toward the elevator. She was on the way to meet her family for breakfast. Authorities reviewed hours of spotty surveillance video, but the recent college graduate was not seen anywhere else. The hotel manager blames faulty wiring for the lapses in recording. She is twenty-two years old and is said to have an Expiration Date of around this time next year." The newscaster paused.

"So sad," said the woman to her male co-anchor.

"Let's hope she returns to her family safely." He pressed

his lips together and waited the appropriate time before changing his expression to coincide with a story about a lotto jackpot winner.

The news blared in front of Shirley, an over-modulated mess adding chaos to her confusion and disbelief. She nibbled on the pen cap. Her eyes floated through the darkness in the kitchen. It was just after ten o'clock.

Thinking, her mind emptied, refilled, and finally clicked into place. Her thumbs scurried across the screen of her phone in search of more; three separate headlines on Janice.

CONNECTICUT WOMAN DISAPPEARS
IN THE BAHAMAS

WHERE IS SHE? RECENT COLLEGE GRAD
MISSING IN THE BAHAMAS

BAHAMIAN POLICE SEARCH FOR LOCAL GIRL

"Oh my. Janice is missing?" Shirley peeped.

She read them over and again as if she had not fully absorbed the information. The backlit letters vibrated and danced in her vision.

Then, another swipe and a click on her phone.

"Hello? This is Norma! Janice's mother!" Her words doubled in an echoed connection.

"Norma? It's Shirley. Are you okay?"

"No, we're not okay." Her mangled speech lacerated words and swallowed letters.

"How is she missing? It was on the ten o'clock news here."

Through gargles, Norma filled her in on what they saw on the video and everything the police had said.

"I don't know how this could've happened," Norma

cried. "She's on medication and needs to take it or she could have a seizure. The cops have been searching everywhere for her in case she's passed out or disoriented."

Something thrashed inside Shirley, the pain of losing a daughter.

"Hello?"

"Still here," Shirley said, clearing her throat. "Sorry. I don't know what to say. I can't believe this's happened." Shirley released the pen and paced through the living room in her nightgown.

"Maybe you can let everyone there know, in case she makes her way back home somehow or is seen somewhere? I mean, she could have amnesia by now." The tail end of Norma's statement had warped into a blubber.

"I'll talk to the boys as soon as we hang up. Don't worry, you'll get her back. In the meantime, we'll keep an eye out for her here."

The call dropped before they could say goodbye.

Shirley called Ernesto.

"Shirley? Everything okay?" he whispered.

"Yes, have you seen the news? Janice went missing in the Bahamas," Shirley told Ernesto while on her third lap through the living room; one foot in front of the other to the door, the staircase, and around the coffee table.

"You know, I thought I heard that as I was getting into the shower."

"I spoke to Norma; she asked me to let everyone know in case Janice shows up at her house. They're worried she has amnesia."

She briefed him on the details Norma had shared.

"In any case," Shirley said, "I have to head to bed. I have an early appointment at the hospital. Tara's undergoing more testing, and I'll finally have some answers."

After brushing her teeth in the kitchen sink, Shirley

flipped off the light switch, spread herself across the couch, and twisted into a blanket. The living room now lit only by the pixels of the TV screen.

A whirlpool of thoughts created havoc in her tired mind: Janice alone on a beach, Tara alone in a hospital room, Sandra alone after putting her kids to bed. She imagined herself in five years. Preparing one breakfast, a sandwich for lunch, a single dinner. Not much would change. She had learned to be alone.

Curled into the sofa, she invited the television sounds to help nudge her thoughts away. Vacuum them from her mind. Tranquilize her by offering the amusement of children answering political questions, the last segment of the ten o'clock news. Yet, she remained alert for another four hours. By the time her mind settled and drifted, there were only three hours left before having to wake to board an express bus to the hospital.

At five thirty the next morning, the streetlamps still glowed through a layer of curtains. When Shirley's phone buzzed and vibrated, she had no recollection of where she was, why she had slept on the couch, or why the alarm fussed so early. Daylight was still a half hour away.

She peeked through the window for a reminder. The sky shined in silver, Gardenia Way behind a layer of mist, but the patter of the slow rain against the window reinforced her memory. Today, she would learn more about Tara's condition.

Numbed with exhaustion, Shirley walked to the bus stop, five blocks in torrential rains and rubber shoes. Stormy winds unified under Shirley's umbrella and dragged her halfway into the road. Engorged raindrops pelted her face every time she positioned it like a shield to keep its metal frame from flipping inside out. With two blocks to go, the umbrella exerted enough force to rip from her frail hands and fly away, contorted and unusable.

Cold and battered, Shirley walked without cover. The rain dribbled from her hairline onto her lashes and into her eyes until she reached the bus shelter. There, she tucked herself behind a crowd of commuters until the bus arrived.

"Mrs. Wilcox, so glad you could make it at this time. Let me get you a towel."

Shirley resurfaced, wind-blown and drenched, nearly two hours later at the hospital. A nurse near Tara's room unfolded a small, tattered towel, off-white with a gray tinge and frayed around the edges; a look of having survived ten thousand washes.

Pressing the rag into her eye sockets, Shirley's ravenous belly called out—hollow growls louder than the TV that mumbled in the corner of the room where she had sunk into a lumpy couch, waiting for Tara's doctor. The slow start to her day had forced her to commute on an empty stomach. The mirror she pulled from her purse and flipped open produced an old woman. Older than the last time she checked. Sharp cheekbones, purpled skin under her eyes. No bright colors. No rouge powdered across her face. Just pruned skin, damp and pale.

Shirley swayed her heavy head across her shoulders, the pain at the side of her neck nearing unbearable. The uncomfortable pillows of the couch where she had spent the past few nights had begun to punish her.

Then, the thoughts again seesawed in her mind: Would Tara take her life seriously after the coma? Would her doctor help in trying to get her into rehab? Tell her she has no choice? Would he legally be allowed to do that?

Before she could fold the flimsy cloth into a perfect square, an Asian man in dark-rimmed glasses appeared in front of her. He wore a matching shirt and tie, and his skin was smooth and free of stubble.

"Mrs. Wilcox, I'm—"

"What's going on?" Shirley stood, eyes bouncing from doctor to doctor as they moved through the doorway, single file.

"It's bad, right? Otherwise, there would only be one of you here."

The doctors talked. Shirley's attention went dormant, neither accepting nor denying the information. One physician finished the other's sentences. The third coughed and cleared his throat, the fourth nodded his head. They showed Shirley grayed images of the human brain, using their pens to point out and circle specific areas. Drawing arrows, arches and connecting lines, as if mapping out directions to the closest coffee shop.

Shirley's skeletal strength gave in. She fell back into a chair. A doctor lurched to grab her elbows.

"Are you okay? Do you feel any pain?" he asked before calling out for a nurse.

"I'm fine!" she yelled, pulling her arms from his grip. "I always told her, stop—doing—drugs! You didn't kill your sister, but she wouldn't listen. I tried so many times and it made her pull further and further away from me. I really tried!" Shirley gave her speech to a swirl of energy in the center of the room. For a moment, she imagined her husband disappointed in her and asking how she could have let this happen.

A nurse rushed in and thumbed Shirley's wrist for a pulse, counting, listening to its rhythm. Shirley continued her rant in the nurse's face.

"This is why you don't try to change your destiny! Do *you* try to change yours? Because you shouldn't! She tried over and over again to kill herself and now look where it got her . . . and *me*!

"And all those kids on TV, the daredevils, throwing themselves out of airplanes, hour after hour. Or the ones on the internet. You know the ones I'm talking about." She motioned to the nurse.

"Yes. Of course," the nurse said with a hurried nod.

"The ones doing all those stunts because their Expiration Date tells them they won't die that day. But this is what can happen, and they don't realize it. You can't play games with the life you've been given and leave your family bearing the burden of your mistakes." Shirley refocused on the nurse's eyes. "Right?"

"Yes."

"Just because you won't die today doing something stupid," Shirley said, "doesn't mean you'll be able to do it forever. They can end up like Tara." She leaned her head back and sobbed. Her gray hair fanned out against the wall behind her.

In the time it took the doctors to draw on pictures of Tara's brain, life had changed. An involuntary surrender of a quarter of the life Shirley had left, now that Tara had managed to lodge herself in a crevice between life and death.

The room made a slow rotation around Shirley. The floor on the ceiling, the lights on the floor. The door sideways. Upside down. The nurse appeared to do a cartwheel just before everything went black.

"Mrs. Wilcox, are you feeling better?"

Shirley found herself dazed, half her face buried in the thick cushions of a musty waiting-room sofa. Ninety minutes had gone by since she had learned Tara's fate.

"Do you want to see your daughter? She's awake," asked the nurse, holding a bottle of water. She dug into the pocket of her scrub top and pulled out a white bottle.

"Take this for your nerves and drink all the water."

Shirley accommodated the nurse's request, throwing her head back with the bottle to her lips.

The women walked down the hall, side by side, Shirley's

forearm pressing down on the hands that held it. A sluggish journey to the furthest room of the hospital wing where they secluded their most troubled patients. They stopped at the entrance and there she was, an immobile Tara in a pseudo coma. Her eyes barely able to glide and see her mother cross the room. Shirley rummaged through her memory and summoned the conversation she'd had with the doctors, recalling one of them saying this type of coma happens when a part of the brain stem is damaged. That's where the scribbles had come in, blue and red ink all over a printout of Tara's brain.

"Her whole body is completely paralyzed. She'll have little function and won't be able to move her muscles, aside from her eyes and eyelids. But her mind will still be aware." The doctor with the glasses had said, finger combing the little hair he had left on his head.

"It's the only way she'll be able to communicate . . . through blinks," they told her. "A rare condition. She'll be fed through a tube and needs a respirator."

Beeping. Clicking. Puffs and wheezes. The sounds of Tara's monitor and ventilator scrambled Shirley's senses. She imagined them in her home, while cooking, while getting ready for bed . . . and she had just adapted herself to sleeping with the television on. Volume at one.

Mother and daughter locked eyes, and Tara managed a few blinks. Slow, with one eyelid lagging as if something hindered their movement. A lack of oil, grease. At any moment, Shirley expected them to squeak.

"Tara, your mother's here."

A pause.

"She cares about you."

A second pause.

"Okay?"

A third.

"She'll help you with everything when you get out of the hospital."

The nurse spoke in spurts, giving Tara's mind the time it needed to catch up, register the information. At first thought, Shirley had decided she would not speak like that. It would be Tara's problem if she couldn't keep up.

"She'll be discharged tomorrow afternoon. One of the physicians' assistants will be in to show you how to run the all the monitors," the nurse informed Shirley.

"Does she even need monitors? I mean, her Death Date isn't for another five years; what's the worst that can happen now?"

"The respirator will make it easier for *you*; otherwise, she will choke a lot and it makes it worse for you to deal with. She *can* live with the little lung function she has, but it will be hard for *you* to see her struggle." And like a ballerina, the nurse spun on her toes and left the room.

Shirley inched around the side of the bed, pulled out a comb from her purse, and with loose strokes, began to untangle Tara's hair.

27

THE HOSPITAL SURRENDERED to the evening. Few doorways glowed. Visitors were gone. A single attendant made rounds through the nursery.

Ninety minutes earlier, in the midst of controlled breathing and grunts, Brian had been born. Wrapped in a striped blanket, the seven-pound baby slept in his mother's arm rounded into a ball as if nothing had changed. The illusion of still being nestled inside the safety of a womb. Sandra's head nodded and slipped, but she kept herself awake. Her arm flexed around her son's shape. She did not want to let go.

"Hello, Mommy, I can take the baby now so you can rest, okay, sweetie?" The voice was unnecessarily loud this early into the day. One a.m.

Before she knew it, the woman in scrubs invaded her cramped space and in one scoop, Brian had vanished. Drunk with exhaustion, Sandra gave in and allowed distance between her and her newborn.

The room had quieted. The new, young woman sharing

it had left to prepare for delivery, all her visitors long gone. Without the distraction of Brian, the distressing thoughts Sandra had warded off regained their vigor, but once she dropped her head into the pillow, she gave in to the sleep that had tugged at her for the last twenty-four hours.

But just as quickly as her eyes closed they were open again, awoken by a pair of nurses holding Brian.

"Good morning, it's time to feed your son," the same woman with the loud voice roared from the foot of her bed.

Sandra, hazed and disoriented, restored her awareness. Back to the existence of a newborn, back to the horror of her reality. She felt the baby's weight in her arms and slipped him under a feeding cover.

"What time will his paperwork be ready?" she asked. Her jaw jerked with a slight tremor.

Since the final push of her delivery, Sandra had brooded over Brian's Expiration Date. The faster she found out, the quicker she could complete the adoption agency forms. Work to be done from her hospital bed. After weeks of what felt like begging to get the attention of her case worker, she still had not received a call back. She drove to his office two days before going into labor, only to be sent away by his secretary. Sandra assumed his efforts had waned because of her unique position: three kids, a newborn, no father, and no relatives to care for them, and the only adult in their lives was headed for death in four days. Too much for one case worker and his assistant to handle, Sandra guessed.

The only task she had completed during her hospital stay was her burial, next to her father. No wake, no funeral, no service.

"It should be ready by ten o'clock, and your discharge is at noon."

The next part of the morning felt forced. Every hour passed with a screech only she could hear. One hundred eighty minutes of detainment for a freshly printed piece of paper. She imagined herself taking the elevator down in her hospital gown and demanding they make an exception and release Brian's Birth-Death Certificate right away, raising her voice at the person who manned the little window. But the thought ended with her being escorted back to the divided room by female security guards who would linger until her discharge time. Sandra decided it would be safer to wait and allow her valuable time to be sucked away by hospital procedure.

All around her heels clicked, rubber wheels squeaked, voices spoke, and monitors bleeped. Drowsiness had surged once again, and sleep fought to overtake her for a second time today. With every elongated blink, her subconscious flashed a worry in the form of a dream: Brianna looking for her, standing alone in the middle of the street with her doll's hair in her fist. Christopher and Christina crouched in the corner of a room at an orphanage, slapping the hands that came near them. Brian squirming in a crib at someone else's house, someone he would eventually call *Mommy*.

Sandra straightened up in her bed, immersed a cupped hand into a pitcher of ice chips and water, and sprinkled it across her face. Determined to not lose a single minute with her kids, she would fend off sleep for the next four days. At this point, Sandra felt it was the least she could do for them.

A wave of guilt had furrowed in her gut. Overlooking the obvious and tolerating Logan's unresponsiveness to their circumstance had propelled her kids into a situation much worse than she had imagined. Selfishly, she had put off contacting the adoption agency to focus on winning him back. Now, her efforts would be crammed into ninety-six hours. The adoption agency had a two-year waiting list.

Just after eleven a.m., a set of large knuckles slipped past the partition and knocked on her side of the wall. A deep voice asked if she was decent.

"Yes, come in."

A young man entered her side of the room with a thick envelope in his hand. His dirty blond hair had the same cut and style as Logan's—messy and slick.

"Good morning, ma'am. I have your son's certificate and your discharge papers."

"Thank you. Please leave it on the table. I'll take a look at it in a minute." She pointed to the table with an untouched food tray. She watched as his long fingers released the sealed envelope.

"Ma'am," he took a short breath, "is there someone we can call for you? You'll be discharged in about an hour, and usually we have a name or two on your paperwork of who is expected to pick you up."

She had lost herself in his looks. His cool eyes, his tall stature. Microscopic stubble.

"Because if not, we can arrange a car for your ride home, and Brian can be looked after for the next two days."

His words had upset her, but she could not look away.

"I'm taking a cab, and my baby's coming with me. As you probably already know, my Expiration Date is on Sunday and I don't want to waste a second not having my son around. You'd think the hospital was lacking babies with the number of times you've all tried to get me to leave him here." Sandra filled her lungs. "In addition to that, it doesn't interest me for him to be cared for by a hospital that doesn't show the least bit of concern for a mother with severe obstacles, clearly having no one to help me *and* having an upcoming Expiration Date. But thank you for the offer. Please see yourself out. I have to get dressed."

"I understand, but compassion doesn't have anything to do with it. There are policies in place for—"

"Please see yourself out. I have to get dressed." Her voice, like stone.

Again, he tried pleading with her, but Sandra continued before he could get another word out.

"I've heard of hospitals bending the rules for some people. No, I'm not a celebrity, and no, I'm not rich. I'm just a woman without a husband and family. I delivered a baby by myself for God's sake, without a single person to help me through it or an ounce of support by my side." Sandra eased herself off the side of the bed. Overbearing pain in the lower half of her body disabled her for a moment, but she managed to get her arms behind her to undo the knot of her hospital gown.

The young man's authoritative presence had reconstituted itself into that of a scolded boy, and with a sigh, he turned and walked out just before the gown slid off her shoulders. He moved quicker than Sandra expected, and she tried to get one last glimpse of the man who had caught her eye as he passed the curtain and turned out of the doorway. She wondered if that's what Christopher and Brian would look like as adults.

At the end of it all, Sandra was unsure of what she expected the hospital to do for her or which rules should have been bent in her favor. Her mind ran a list of suggestions of how the staff could have made her short stay, at the very least, mediocre. Without the emotional energy, she conceded. Nothing would have helped.

As she struggled to change back into the now oversized dress she wore to the hospital, another set of manly knuckles thumped against the wall.

"Come in," she huffed.

A bouquet of flowers erupted from behind the curtain. Lavender and pink lilies in full bloom; a crowd of dark green stems visible from inside a glass vase. Above it at the ceiling danced a teddy bear–shaped balloon. A light blue bowtie clung to its neck.

The hands that held it belonged to Jeremy.

"What are you doing here?" asked Sandra. A sting of electricity zipped through her.

"I'm your ride home." He held the flowers out in front of her. "These are for you, the bravest mother to date."

Sandra, wedged between bewilderment and regret, thought of the last time they had been together. The harsh words she had flung at him. How his head had dipped when he walked from her house after she had dismissed him.

"And this is for your little one. I'm sure he'll have a good time looking at it since it's likely to have lost helium before he's big enough to play with it." Jeremy smiled.

More sparks of electricity tingled under her skin. But before she could determine whether to react with fury or relief, her thoughts strayed to wishing her roommate was there to see she finally had a visitor and questioning, to herself, whether it was possible to get all the nurses she had come across since yesterday into one room to witness Jeremy and the bloated bear he was carrying.

A fraction of a smile eventually penetrated Sandra's strained lips. It had occurred to her that she had not spoken a word since Jeremy slid past her curtain.

"Thank you."

In the forty-five minutes it took to prepare Brian for his first ride, the nurses moved slower and seemed more at ease now that Jeremy sat in a seat beside Sandra. By that time, her roommate had reclaimed her spot in the next bed, catching eyes with Jeremy who walked in and out of the hallway to answer his phone. Half of the nurses Sandra had met peeked at Jeremy as he walked by, jabbing elbows into the rib cages of their co-workers to take notice of the tall, golden man hovering in the doorway. In Sandra's wishful mind, they would repeat the story to the other half at the turn of their shift.

Heads and eyes followed their slow walk down the hall. The expressions had changed. Men looked at Jeremy; women looked at Jeremy. She felt as though this were her revenge, sensing the shock and suspicions of those who had tended to her. Even the head nurse of the maternity ward had not dissimulated her whispers on the previous day:

That woman is the unluckiest person on earth. Maybe she did something so horrible that not a single person wants to help her now.

As Sandra walked by the nurse's station, her arm looped inside Jeremy's, the head nurse asked to speak privately.

"Good luck with everything," her voice rattled. "I know this is a difficult time for you, but we're glad to see you have help now," the nurse said with a coquettish vibe and a wink. "Whoever he is."

28

THE CRYSTAL BLUE waters, the warm salty breeze, and live Calypso music on a tropical island create an astounding break from ordinary life . . . except when your daughter goes missing and a grave medical condition looms over her safety.

Everywhere Norma turned, Janice's face appeared—in color—on an eight-by-twelve-inch poster. Everywhere, only because she had fought for it. Held back by Barry, his hands in the crook of her elbows, she lobbed herself toward the resort manager who had not wanted to scare the other guests into leaving.

"Ma'am, a missing poster brings forth the assumption there is foul play. Your daughter is ill. The other guests will not understand."

But soon after their near altercation, she got her way. Under the image, they had agreed on the words:

May Be Disoriented or Have Amnesia

Still, with the number of signs taped up around the café,

on the revolving doors, inside the windows of the lobby, and on a bin to discard pool towels, there was no sign of Janice's immediate return.

Norma paced the walkway that led to the beach, knocking into other vacationers who hardly noticed her displeasure. The view from where she stood infuriated her: roasted-looking bodies on every lounger on the pool deck, thonged woman, young and old, children splashing and chasing each other. If it were up to her, the resort would shut down and every person, guest and staff, would mandatorily join the search for her daughter. She would then tread through the sand toward the man playing the steel drums, swipe the sticks from his hands, pluck the instrument from its stand, and with a running start, hurl it into a crashing wave.

Before worry, she felt anger. Out of all the vacationers on the island, how had *her* daughter gone missing? Why was it *her* duty to go through this pain? Additional pain to what they had already experienced and would endure within a year? Her gaze landed on an extended family, bodies of all sizes, swarming around a single table. Shirts, dresses, and hair all flapping in the breeze. Pandemonium contained to one group. Their noise louder than the waves that slammed into the shore. Did they have to be this loud? They cackled while slamming fists into the table, spoke in high-pitched voices, and then huddled in one big group to take a photo. It was all very irritating to watch. Norma's fatigued eyes bounced from group to group as the cluster separated, mulling over the circumstances that led to *her* daughter going missing and not one of the loud-mouthed brats smacking each other with giant foam noodles. The blood in her veins ran cold, and for a second, wished her misfortunes on someone else's family—the girl with the white bikini and charred skin; the guy snapping open cans of beer; the child in the neon goggles splashing the area where she stood. To her, the corrosive thoughts banging inside her head were justified because quite frankly, hadn't she been through enough?

"Mrs. Hellington, they're here." A female hotel worker held the heavy glass door of the lobby, waving Norma inside.

The lead investigator in Janice's case had scheduled an update with the family just after three in the afternoon. She had disappeared four days earlier and in two, the Hellingtons were scheduled to fly home.

Norma, arms folded, slid in sideways through the doorway, making it through just before it closed all the way. She power walked through the corridor and entered the empty room where she had spent most of her vacation.

"Anything?" she asked, her winded lungs barely able to dribble out the question; her scurried steps still echoing in the hall.

The investigator's dispirited slump said it all. He flipped through a notepad. His lips moved as if reading through a lengthy article, though only a few words were written on the page.

His distracted eyes met Norma's.

"We completed the interviews of all resort employees that were here the day Janice disappeared. Some do remember her from the previous dinner and dance event on the deck. Two were from the bar she went to later that night. However, none of them recalls seeing her after that." His lips tightened around his teeth, his eyes like flames trying to ignite the pages of his notepad, searing the lack of information he had for the distressed family.

"So, your thoughts on her disappearance have more to do with the brain tumor? Is that correct? You believe she has amnesia and could have wandered off?"

"No! No!No!" Norma spun on a heel. "I can't keep

answering the same question. I'm worried she has amnesia *now*, after not taking her medication."

"How often did she experience it?"

"She *never* did. You're NOT PAYING ATTENTION. Amnesia is a possibility only because she's not due to die for another year *and* because an entire police department can't locate her. The tumor will only get worse, and the medication was helping with her symptoms of dizziness and seizures.

"Obviously, she's somewhere. And now I'm just scared that—" She paused. Her mind bubbled with images of what life could be like after they found Janice. "That she won't remember who we are or who she is when we finally get her b—"

But the clomping of footsteps disrupted her foresight.

A police officer ran into the room, elbows bent, arms pumping; a petite woman at his heels. She wore a white towel over her bikini. Her wet head dripped down her shoulders and onto the floor behind her. The investigator's eyes begged the officer for new information.

"I'm Officer Barry and this is Julissa. She's here on vacation from New York, but at the adjacent resort. Do you want to tell her what you saw?"

The woman shivered in the air-conditioned room. "Well, I've seen the missing flyers posted everywhere for days and the girl on it looked familiar, but I thought I was confusing her with someone I knew from high school. Just now, as I dove into the pool, I remembered exactly where I saw her and jumped out to tell the manager to call the police." She wrapped the towel tighter around her chest. "On Tuesday morning, I woke up early to do some yoga stretches on the beach and saw a guy and a girl holding hands, but to me it looked like he was more dragging her than anything. I thought maybe they'd had a fight or something and she was mad, but he kept whisperin' in her ear. She looked annoyed . . . or so

I thought. They walked into the water and stood there for a little while—they were the only ones around, which is why I remember—and a boat came with three men in it. Two got off and huddled around her. I continued doing my yoga and next thing I know, she's screaming and her and the guy are strapped to a parasail and it lifted them out over the water." Julissa's teeth chattered. "Her screams faded away and they disappeared, but I thought she was screaming because she was scared to parasail. I thought maybe her boyfriend surprised her or something. I didn't realize what happened until today," she said apologetically.

"An hour later, at about ten thirty, I finished my yoga and cooled off in water. Today, I remembered they never came back . . . because they're supposed to come back to the same place, right? If you parasail?" the frigid young woman asked the officer.

"Yes, they always drop off at the pick-up location," he admitted. "But we'd have to verify with your hotel if they contracted a parasailing company for that day."

"Right. I'm so sorry, but I didn't remember any of this until I dove into the pool today. As soon as my face hit the water, everything came back to me."

Norma went pale, paler than she had looked in days despite having walked miles in the sun searching for Janice. Her face contorted itself into a knot as if from the torment of her brain grinding and computing all of what Julissa had just said.

When Norma finally lifted her head, her eyes looked like pools of stagnant water: wide, lifeless circles.

"Someone took her then."

29

IN THEIR HEADS, each counted the seconds it took for red lights to turn green, looked over the make of the cars during their slow roll on the highway, and took notice of all the license plates that were not from Connecticut. After several miles and no more than a few words spoken between them, Jeremy and Sandra arrived at her mother's house.

The caretaker who had watched over her kids answered the door looking weathered: sloppy ponytail, bloodshot eyes, wrinkled clothing. All indications Brianna, Christopher, and Christina had worn out their welcome.

Letting Sandra know she could take all the time she needed, Jeremy parked in front of the adjacent home and texted Priscilla:

> *Working late.*
> *going out 4 drinks after.*
> *dropping the car off at home.*
> *jerry will drive me back*

He ended his communication with a heart emoji.

In less than an hour, the front door swung open and a steady stream of children spilled out, hopping and jumping down six steps. Their heads twisted and turned until they spotted Jeremy's glazed smile through the windshield. Brianna, Christopher, and Christina raced to the car and in a few handle pulls, were bumping heads over their baby brother.

"His hands are really small!" Christopher shouted.

"When will he wake up? It's day time," asked Brianna.

"Let's pull up his eyelids so he can see us!" suggested Christina.

Jeremy extinguished the chatter by placing his finger on their lips. One by one, they quieted. "Remember, he's a newborn. They need plenty of sleep or else when he grows up, he can't play with you. He'll be too tired."

Their little mouths formed O's. Their eyes widened in horror. The consequences of speaking loudly around Brian spun circles in their minds, and in two collective head nods, each rear had found a seat in Jeremy's car. Millimeter by millimeter they drew their seatbelts and buckled themselves with subdued clicks. Nearly soundless.

Amazement had exploded inside Jeremy and settled like shards of glass. A few simple words mellowed out three ordinarily unmanageable kids. Muted them.

The ride home would be bearable.

The sun had slid into Jeremy's eyeline by the time Sandra reopened the door. Two overnight bags swung out of rhythm from her shoulders. Her back had hunched, and a sense of pain rose from her skin. The time spent inside had weakened her, left her stiff. The blood vessels in her eyes were damaged. Would this be the last time she would see her mother?

Jeremy rushed to her side and accompanied her shortened steps to the car.

"Is classical music okay?" Jeremy asked.

"It's fine."

This ride was as quiet as the last, despite the extra passengers.

Before turning on the main roadway into their neighborhood, Jeremy's mind ran numbers: The current time. Minutes. Hours. Adding and subtracting distances to determine how long it would take Priscilla to escape rush-hour traffic.

He was safe.

Jeremy pulled into Sandra's driveway, untroubled.

"I'll help you get settled if you'll have me," but Jeremy did not wait for a *yes* . . . or a *no*. With his fingers tight on her waist, he helped Sandra inside, guiding her to the tallest seat in the living room.

Jeremy came and went; Brian's carrier hanging from his forearm, overnight bags deep in his grip. The third trip amassed sticky snacks in his open palm. Sandra's fingers curled around the armrests as she watched Jeremy. At the turn of his back, she tested her capabilities. Bending her knees. Lifting her arms over her shoulders. Checking the speed of her movements. The activity winded her. She would not manage on her own.

Her frailty added to the disorder she had left behind before heading to the hospital the previous afternoon. Crusted dishes on the coffee table had bonded to the wood. Unsoaked pots in the kitchen sink were lined with a layer of slime. A pile of whites on the floor by the basement door had circulated the scent of sweaty socks throughout the entire first floor.

Then, she watched it play out. Christina tugged a jump rope out of Brianna's hand and skipped around the coffee table, the rope skimming the ceiling fan with every swing. In her mind, Sandra finally responded to Jeremy's request:

I'd like that. Thank you, Jeremy. You've been a big help.

Jeremy pumped the break on his roll down Sandra's driveway and in two revolutions of the steering wheel, had parked his car in his own driveway and hurried back to Sandra's house.

"If you'd like, I can watch after Brian and keep the kids entertained while you nap. You need to refresh yourself if you want to spend as much time with them as possible. Just let me know what time Brian needs to be fed." But the words that slipped from Jeremy's mouth did not align with his attitude, as if asking for permission only out of courtesy. He had cleared a pile from Christina's skipping path, shuffled the overnight bags to the foot of the staircase, and smacked the start button on the dishwasher—responsibilities for which Sandra lacked strength. Her vocal cords were too weak to tell Christina to jump rope in the backyard; she was too tired to show Jeremy out for doing nothing wrong.

Without further thought, she took Jeremy up on his offer and fell asleep as soon as she stretched herself out on the bed.

One level below, with just a few firm words from Jeremy, Christina understood. Her large, rounded eyes absorbed his mannerisms and quietly wound the jump rope around her arm and slipped it into a drawer. She winced at the squeal that came from the unoiled metal track beneath it. After all, her mother and baby brother were sleeping. By the time she made it back to the living room, Christopher and Brianna had settled on the couch, leaving a space between them for her to sit.

Everything was different. The kids felt it; Jeremy knew it. No screaming, no fighting, no crying. Two DVDs chosen by each of Sandra's kids rested side by side on the coffee table. All movies they had seen dozens of times before, but the atmosphere had changed.

Once the dishes had been confined to their cabinets,

Jeremy gave in. Hypnotized by the animated colors that filled the TV screen, he filled an empty spot next to Christopher. The movie was one he had seen before on a day he surprised Austin with a trip to the local theater after his diagnosis. Every scene that flashed unspooled another thread of memory. Christopher's warm arm bumping up against his felt like Austin's fevered limb. Their collective breaths thrumped in his ears, like the rattle of his son's pneumonia. Before he knew it, Jeremy was inhaling the warm butter aroma that Austin had poured onto an overflowing bucket of popcorn, bear-hugging the tub under the spout to catch every drop. The other patrons waiting their turn did so patiently, pointing and smiling, captivated by his determination to do it himself and the cuteness of his positioning as he bent back to fit the tub perfectly beneath the dispenser. One admirer even said Austin would break hearts when he got older.

Jeremy was there again. Watching Austin; re-experiencing every lip curl, every twitch, every grunt. But giggles between Brianna and Christina hit him like a blow to the jaw, ejecting him from the memory and depositing him back into Sandra's living room. The movie had ended, and the television had gone black.

"Which movie's next?" Christopher asked.

Jeremy's duties came in waves. He changed the DVD while rocking Brian, who had just woken in a fuss, working the remote with one hand while the other held a bottle to the baby's lips. Two ounces into his formula, Brian fell asleep again in Jeremy's arms. By this time, it had been three hours since Sandra disappeared up the stairs.

Tired and mentally calculating the amount of work he had at the office the next day, he still felt himself lucky to play daddy again to small children. He embraced every laboring minute that led him to the next task.

An hour later, he had served dinner with lopsided smiley

faces. Using pasta as the mouth and vegetarian meatballs as the eyes and nose, he had scrounged up whatever ingredients the cabinets and freezer held. He had produced the meal while the kids watched the second movie of Jeremy's double feature, quietly discussing the plot and their favorite characters. At one point, Christopher rose from his seat to compliment the chef, commending his ability to get the house to smell like a restaurant. Maybe, Jeremy thought, what the kids had lacked the entire time was another adult to help guide them when Sandra could not.

"This spaghetti is great! It's so great!" Christopher expressed his elation in an emphatic whisper. Brianna, the subdued of the three, made polite dinner conversation, explaining to Jeremy their time at their grandmother's house and how she struggled getting around in a wheelchair. A thought flourished in Jeremy's mind. If he could stay in this dining room forever, he would.

Just as the kids crunched on their last piece of garlic bread, Sandra's groggy stomps reached the entryway.

"What's going on? Where'd this food come from?" Her eyes had swelled and reddened. Pillow creases had formed a crisscross pattern at the side of her face. Her hair was flattened and lifted on one side like the tail of a peacock.

"I made dinner for the kids with whatever I found in the pantry. Hope that's okay." Again, more of a formality from Jeremy. He had wiped Christina's mouth and swept the crumbs from her place setting before Sandra had a chance to respond.

"Sure. Thank you . . . and sorry, I slept longer than I wanted to. You should have woken me. How's the baby?" She leaned into the recycled double stroller where Brian lay.

"He fell asleep before I started boiling the pasta. He should hang tight for another hour." Jeremy slapped his hands clean over the sink.

Rolled-up shirt sleeves, missing tie, a small sauce splatter on his dress shirt. Sandra wondered why he had given up his whole night for her children.

"Are you hungry? Do you want some pasta?" Jeremy asked while pouring sauce onto a clean dish. Although the rumbles of her stomach had acted as an alarm clock, Sandra wanted to say no. But Jeremy put down a fresh plate at an empty place setting and steered her to the seat.

At first she hesitated. The serving looked double the size she normally ate in one sitting. Discomfort, pain, dizziness, and nausea all hit her at once when she took her seat at the head of the table. But her hand automatically gripped the fork and spun a spool of spaghetti at the end of it. A few mouthfuls and her stomach had settled, her lightheadedness diminished, and her discomfort was minimal.

She looked up at Jeremy with pasta sauce squeezing out of the edges of her mouth: "Thank you."

Jeremy pounced with a napkin. She wiped it across her lips.

There had been more bad moments than good, according to her memory. The short-lived friendship with Priscilla had collapsed after Sandra had decided she did not need a best friend. She did not offer support during Austin's final weeks, and she had thrown Jeremy out of her home amid his persistence to help her in a true time of need. A time when abandonment had situated itself upon her and her three kids. A time when her Expiration Date showed itself in a red circle on the next calendar page. Yet, Jeremy stood in front of her and had waited with a napkin weaved between his fingers until she needed it.

The kids were fed, the baby slept peacefully in a stroller next to her, and she had gained sufficient sleep to equip her with the mental capacity necessary for her final hours with her children. Jeremy's intrusion was a debt she could never repay.

"You didn't have to do this," she mumbled with a pasta string swinging from her chin. Her appetite had uncoiled itself and sent her into a state of famishment, scooping in gobs of sauce faster than she could gulp. For a moment, she ceased chewing to count her blessings. With inflated cheeks, she thought of how fortunate she was for Jeremy's persistence.

"I did have to. You need help, and that's what I'm here for." His smile twisted up the side of his face.

It had crossed her mind to ask if Priscilla approved of his absence at their home, but instead she sealed off her curiosity.

"Thank you again for everything."

"If you don't need anything else, I'll get out of your hair and leave you to your kids." Jeremy kissed her forehead and hurled a couple of high fives at the twins. Brianna opted for a hug. With his belt loop on her cheek, she thanked him for the best spaghetti dinner she had ever tasted.

The night was quiet between the homes. The moon on him was like surveillance, watching his deceitful steps through Sandra's driveway and up his front lawn to where Priscilla waited, checking the time on her phone and skimming her nose on the front window whenever a stream of light seamed to pass through her.

"Hey, Pri." Jeremy came in through the side door. "Sorry, I'm late. That Jerry can surely tell a thousand stories."

"How *is* Jerry?"

"He's good. You know, he hates his job, hates his wife, his dad's a drunk. Same stuff with that guy."

"He drove you home? I didn't hear a car or a car door or anything."

"He let me off a few houses down. I didn't want to wake

you in case you were sleeping. So, what are you watching? Put this up. Is that Ellen?" His words had overlapped. He kicked off his shoes and curved himself next to Priscilla.

The rest of the night was soundless. Priscilla fell asleep on the couch, and Jeremy spread a plush blanket over her before heading up to bed.

30

NORMA FELT WEIGHTLESS, rocking back on her heels, head swaying. She reached for the edge of the room and stood firm against the wall, slipping in and out of consciousness; fighting for respiration as if with constricted nostrils. Her pupils offered her an array of colors. They blended, sorted, and left tracks as they faded. A war had ensued with her eyelids, battling to keep them up when they wanted to slide shut. For Janice's sake, she would not misuse another valuable minute. Waste no time on fainting.

"Are you okay, ma'am?"

"Should we call an ambulance?"

"She's in shock; she needs air; give her some space."

Small puffs of air landed on Norma's face. She was fighting to stay alert. A dozen more gusts and her nostrils widened, her lungs swelled, and her breathing regulated. The silhouettes she fixated on had ripened into people. A moustache. Hair. Brow bones. Eyes like marbles mired in her struggle.

"I think she's feeling better. Let's keep fanning her."

A set of lips surged from the haze and dangled in her view.

"Mrs. Hellington, do you need a doctor?"

But they did not synch up with the words yet. Her waist folded under the weight of her torso. She took a step, lost her balance, and windmilled her arms backwards, bumping into a wall on the opposite side of the room. Her back flat against it, she slid down with poise and gracefully slumped toward the ground. Her cheek rested against the cool floor.

Through a pant, she said, "I need a minute . . . to gather my wits." Norma's voice could have been mistaken for that of a seductress.

Semi-circling around Norma's collapsed frame, the onlookers hung their heads over her.

"Let's give her a moment."

Norma could not distinguish the voices yet. From her spot on the floor, her vision worked to unscramble a set of flip-flops, shoes, and laces. Her mind actively recalled where she was, what she had just learned. With knees drawn to her chest and elbows tangled by her head, she imagined Janice screaming, crying, and then dancing at the sunset dinner. The surveillance video—graduation—gliding through clear skies on a parasail—escaping from her abductors only to be caught and dragged back by her wrists on her knees—a punch across the face.

She had to separate reality from imagination. Squelch the distorted theories.

Like freshly oiled gears, her thoughts kicked into motion, flowing from one fact to another:

Janice had almost a full year left to live.

She could be saved.

It was a matter of finding her.

They had a witness. She saw everything.

Adrenaline raced through her veins, bursting through her joints and limbs.

Invigorated, she sat up. Her legs twisted at her side.

"Let's get a good description of these guys and get another flyer going. We can find her now that we know what happened. Obviously, she's not dead . . . and they won't kill her since she'll be alive for another year."

Different sets of fingers closed around her arms, propping her back up to her feet.

"Ma'am, we have asked for help from the Federal Bureau of Investigation."

"Great!"

"But we don't know who these men are. She can't remember what they look like." The investigator pointed to the soaked witness who frowned when Norma's eyes found her.

"And we worry if this is a human trafficking case, she could have been turned over to someone else out at sea and then the chances of finding her are slim," said the officer.

In Norma's opinion, this tiny piece of paradise had not experienced its share of atrocities. How could they know how to efficiently manage abductions? Her guess: they were underqualified.

"We'll rent a boat? Look for her out at sea. Contact the coast guard."

"They've already been dispatched," the officer assured her. "But I'm sorry to say, sometimes these cases never get solved."

"We have a whole year," Norma said. "But we need to start now. What about surveillance footage at the other resort? We need to pull them and see if those men can be identified. They have to be seen somewhere." In Norma's mind, she had appointed herself lead investigator. The chirps coming from the two men in the room sounded like nothing

275

more than surrender, inexperience, a lack of understanding. Norma leaned on the young woman with one arm around her shoulder and thanked her for coming forward.

"I'm sorry I didn't realize earlier," Julissa said. "I didn't think she was being kidnapped. I thought she was scared to parasail."

Norma examined the young woman. How had Julissa been so lucky? To be in the line of vision of the two men who took her firstborn, only to be passed over. Long brown hair, like Janice's. Some five inches taller, but still petite like Janice.

She turned to the two men in the room and asked, "Why do you think they chose Janice? Could it be possible they targeted her prior to that morning? Maybe, at the deck party the night before?" Norma's brows shifted back and forth between them. "If they did, then they may do it again."

"Can you help us tonight?" Norma asked Julissa. "Will you still be here?" She threw an arm around the bikinied witness and hung off her like a drunken companion. "My husband and I will pay for you and whomever you're traveling with to come to the sunset dinner with us. We'll dance and see if maybe you spot these guys? I know you said you can't remember, but if you see them, maybe it'll jog your memory."

Julissa flung the towel across her shoulders and pinched two corners at her neck like a cape. "Would that be okay?" she asked the men. "My boyfriend and I leave tomorrow morning. I don't see the harm in helping. He'll be by my side the whole night and until we get on the plane."

Norma recognized the looks on the men's faces: skepticism.

"If she agrees, we're doing this. It's our only chance." Norma retracted her arm from the damp woman and stood in front of the investigator, her head a whole foot shorter than his.

"This has to be done for Janice . . . and for all young women who have gone missing under these exact circumstances."

"Ma'am, hardly ever do criminals like this strike twice in the same spot . . . in the same week. We haven't had a disappearance like this in quite a—" He stopped himself before disclosing the time frame.

Norma adjusted her dress at the shoulders and slid her palms across her lap. She set her hair free from the sunglasses that sat askew on her head and approached Julissa.

"If you can meet us at our room before the dinner, we can go over the details. If the men are there, my husband and I will take care of it. You won't need to get involved."

Norma did not solicit permission for her plans. Before the group disbanded, the two women exchanged phone numbers, details, and agreed on a time to meet later in the evening—positive interaction inside the uninspiring blank walls of the room where they stood. Norma's resolve had earned the admiration of the investigator, who opted to send plain-clothed officers to the waterfront restaurant and supervise the ladies' strategy.

Norma had felt herself explode into a million pieces when Julissa recounted her story, but inch by inch, the fragments restored themselves. If the men originated from a different island, then she imagined a second and third victim would make a long trip worth it. Their biggest lead would come tonight; she was sure of it.

Norma exited the lobby onto the pool deck and took a break under the sun, suspending her worry. Her eyes perceived the angles of the palm trees differently than they had forty-five minutes earlier. Taller, straighter, less slanted, allowing for more of the blue skies to be seen beyond the leaves that contained it. Her renewed breaths fell deeper into her lungs, as though the palms pulled from the atmosphere to pump fresh oxygen just for her. The pool water had adjusted its color from dingy blue to lustrous aqua. Women's bikinis had brightened to yellows and hot pinks. Less than an hour before, the roadmap to finding Janice had looked like a pile of spaghetti strands. No real beginning, no real end. Twisted and tangled paths that led them nowhere. But now, they had the exact information needed to begin a trail.

Two more draws of fresh air and she was ready to tell Barry. Norma entered the cold lobby of the resort where he and Lacey waited for Norma after their flyer distribution.

"What? So, she's been kidnapped?" asked Barry, shifting his foot and stepping on the heel of his other sneaker, stumbling backwards. Another inch and he would have toppled over. Lacey grabbed him by the wrists to keep him upright.

"I'm fine; I lost my balance," he assured them, but he was not fine. The minimal precautions he took before standing out in the sun all afternoon, day after day, had landed him in the emergency room. A needle deep in his arm the previous evening as an IV replenished his fluids. He had not told his wife or daughter about his ordeal. Norma grabbed Barry's hand and tweaked his chin to face her.

"We'll get her back. We're going to find those men and take our daughter home."

Sandra: Three days until death

31

THE ONLY OTHER car that had inhabited Sandra's driveway over the last month had been the ten-year-old sedan borrowed from her mother's live-in nurse. So to Jeremy's surprise, the new, infuriatingly shiny Mercedes parked there could be none other than Logan's. No doubt, thought Jeremy, already spending money the deadbeat no longer needed to utilize on his kids.

Jeremy sat in his four-year-old BMW after arriving home, turned off the engine and, in his head, interrogated the extravagant vehicle.

Why had it transported Logan back to his family?

How much had it cost? The price would likely be enough for the kids to live comfortably for a few years.

What was it doing in Sandra's driveway?

For half a second, he wondered how long he could ponder these questions while sitting in the car before Priscilla took notice of his inactivity. She would press him on the tenacity of his interest, an encounter he'd rather avoid. But the thought of such conflict flushed away just as quickly as it had arisen once his eyes started playing tricks on him; his stillness, his glare inciting the imaginary flitter of other objects. The curtains at Sandra's house seemed to wiggle and the doorknob to twist back and forth; the wheels on the Mercedes looked as if they had made half a revolution. Even the shutters appeared to have listed a bit. But resetting his vision with a shake of his head concluded no one had peered through the curtains, opened the door, or disconnected the shutters from the windowpanes. Most importantly, the driver-less Mercedes had not moved up the driveway.

Jeremy forced a change in his attitude. It was all the same to him. Besides, what difference would it make if Logan *was* there? Perhaps he had come to his senses and decided against the karma that had assigned itself to him.

Ignoring the desire to seethe in the car until someone came out of Sandra's house, Jeremy gathered his things, exited the car, and pushed the door closed, using more force than required. The slam made far less of a sound than necessary to prompt interest by anyone at the neighboring home.

He had decided it was none of his business. But in the few steps it took to get around the front of his car, he cared again. This time more than before, angered over the tranquility of the house that stood next to his. Logan was impulsive and irrational; it wouldn't surprise Jeremy one bit if by the time he made it to his front door, the deadbeat would have already jumped into his car, tires peeling, yelling obscenities as he drove away. But standing around to wait for it would risk more suspicion from Priscilla.

It doesn't matter, he thought. *It's Sandra's problem*, and from that moment forward, he promised to leave it alone.

"Hey, honey," Pricilla greeted him from the recliner while putting on her shoes. "Do you want to go out for dinner tonight? The day kinda got away from me, and I don't have the least bit of interest in standing in front of a hot stove all night. Jenn's upstairs; she wants Italian. Ya'good with that?"

"Pri, I'm exhausted. I feel like staying in tonight. Maybe you guys can go without me. I won't mind. I'm not even hungry." He had already made it halfway up the stairs, loosening his tie and unbuttoning his shirt.

"I'm going to jump in the shower," he said as he reached the top step.

Jeremy closed the bathroom door and the annoyance of Priscilla's dinner questions slipped off him with a twist of the lock. Convincing himself it was mere curiosity and nothing more, he ran the shower, stepped out of his shoes, and slid the miniature frosted window up several inches, trying to get his face through the opening. From outside, Jeremy looked like a man held captive, attempting an escape; his head tilted, nose pushed halfway through, the side of his face smashed against the windowsill. Across the way, from the sliver he could see, it was quiet. No yelling. No bickering. Not a single curtain fiber had wavered. Not a thump or a crackle from inside, as if the occupiers had abandoned it, leaving the Mercedes to fend for itself.

Curiosity kept him in the gnarled position for the next thirty minutes, waiting for a single molecule to rise from Sandra's house—something. Anything. Behind Jeremy, the steam from the shower had begun to creep toward him in a whirl of mystery, ready to smother him once and for all.

Enough was enough.

The dormancy of Sandra's house had tested Jeremy's patience, and he failed. With the shower still running, he moved sideways down the stairs, his back up against the wall, slipping out of the house. Priscilla stood at the kitchen counter engulfed by her own agitation and the unwanted dinner she was preparing. Her heavy hands made vegetable chopping sound like a brigade of gunfire.

Jeremy walked across the lawn in his dress socks, the thick grass flattening under his feet. He rang the doorbell once and waited with his heart hammering under the disheveled look of his shirt and tie.

The door swung open quicker than he expected.

A cough and a throat clearing preceded his words. "Is everything okay?" he asked, looking past Sandra's frizzed head, which blocked most of his view into the living room.

"Yes, Jeremy. Everything's okay. What's up?"

"I wanted to see how everything was. Everything okay?" he asked again.

"Yes, everything's fine. Why? What's the matter?" Sandra's eyes immediately dropped to his feet, or rather, his socks. His attire indicated he had just gotten off work, but lack of footwear implied something more.

"Are you okay? Do you want to come in?" To Sandra, Jeremy looked crazed.

As he walked into the house, he scanned every corner of the room, hitting all the immediate targets for any sign of Logan. The couch. The coffee table. Down and across the carpeting. No briefcase. No men's shoes. No blazer thrown over the back of a chair . . . And where were the kids? But before Jeremy could demand Logan show himself and settle things man to man, lawyer to lawyer, Brian let out a tremulous roar from the room upstairs.

"Give me a minute," she said.

The room was Jeremy's now. He was free to look around without the hindrance Sandra imposed.

Voices.

He could hear the kids muttering upstairs as they watched a movie in the bedroom directly above him. Is that where Logan was? Trying to win father of the year? A title Jeremy would never allow him to earn.

But in a sudden shift of interest, Jeremy opened the

drawer to Sandra's desk and grabbed as many pages as he could from the pile inside it. His nervous fingers stuck like glue to the corner of each page.

A quarter of the way through, he came across the first critical document, Brian's Birth-Death certificate. He would live into his sixty-seventh year. Jeremy searched through the other pages looking for a response from the adoption agency, but the ransacking came to an end when Sandra's footsteps loudened. He neatened the pile that had become unruly in his hands and dumped it back in the drawer. Sandra trotted down the stairs while humming to Brian.

"Sorry, Jeremy. He's been fussy today. What's going on?" she asked with two empty baby bottles clamped in her underarms.

"I wanted to make sure you and the kids are good. Do you need help with anything, and is Logan here?"

"I'm managing. The kids and I are watching a movie."

"But is Logan here?"

"No, Logan's *car* is here," she said. "He should be by to pick it up tonight. He came to take a dresser that was handed down to him by his grandfather. It was in the basement. He used his friend's pick-up truck to haul it away." She transferred Brian from one fatigued arm to the other.

"He also said he wanted to talk." Sandra displayed skepticism, shrugging her shoulders. "Maybe the kids have a chance? I don't know. Hopefully, he's reconsidering and will do the right thing for once."

"Right thing? You mean take custody?" To Jeremy, everything she was saying was out of the question. Even the part about letting him park his fancy car in the driveway seemed unreasonable.

"Hopefully, they need him."

"Great . . . that sounds great. Well," He let out a sigh that wheezed through his chest like a distressed whistle. "I wanted to stop by and make sure things were running smoothly. Give the kids a kiss for me." His lips smiled, but his eyes flamed a vicious fire.

He left the house in his socks and made it back up to the vacant shower undetected by his wife and daughter. There, he sat at the edge of the tub and stewed over Sandra's foolish idea. Even if Logan agreed to take the kids, there was still a good chance he wouldn't follow through with it. How could she make sure he would take care of them after she's gone? Perhaps, it was her way of exiting this world with peace of mind. *Selfish*, thought Jeremy.

32

BARRY AND LACEY had already braced themselves for the news about Janice, though the confirmation still came like a punch in the gut. The day before, while waiting for a fresh batch of printed flyers, they had confided in each other, discussing the possibility of an abduction—a bag thrown over her head, a rush of thugs swiping her from their hotel, a shove into a van. Whatever scenarios they concocted while lingering in front of the printer, Barry had not shared with Norma for fear uttering the words alone might make it a truth. But now, with a solid version of what might have happened to Janice, he felt an obligation to keep his opinion on the matter buried within him.

Norma sat on a chair in their hotel room, feet up and resting on a low windowsill, looking out into the ocean. A doubly effective activity; this high up she acted as a lookout for suspicious boats bobbing along the coast, while taking in the view she had missed out on since the start of their vacation. Her memory told her this was the first time she had stopped to admire the seascape. The sun had begun its descent toward the ocean.

"Honey, we're going to find her," she said to Barry's window reflection. "We have a witness willing to help. We're getting Janice back."

His barren eyes caught Norma's through the glass despite the glare as he threaded his belt through the loops of his pants. She smiled and he shook his head, but Norma didn't notice. Her eyes had already made it back down to the late afternoon glow of the ocean. Having a probable account of what happened to her daughter had boosted her spirits, eliminating the burden of guessing.

Since the news, activity throughout the resort had normalized. Fewer police, less vigilance. Norma had agreed on letting the manager take down most of Janice's missing posters. It wouldn't have made much of a difference. During her daily inspection of the lobby and pool deck, she noticed most people walked by without giving them so much as a glance. They had become fixtures like anything else, and the longer they remained posted, the less noticeable they became. In the café, Janice's dimpled smile blended with other posters on the wall—excursion advertisements, images of snorkelers, boat tour pricing. Even a picture of a hot, oozing sandwich seemed to have gotten more head turns from vacationers than the girl who had gone missing from the exact resort in which they stood. The posters Norma requested stay intact were the ones taped to the revolving door and the single one taped inside the glass window by the pool exit.

At 6:45 that evening, Norma's plan kicked into motion. Lacey had arrived in Janice's black dress. The same dress she wore on the night of their first sunset dinner. Her thought: *If I can make myself look like Janice, maybe that will lure a kidnapper.* Barry hated the idea. He sat at the edge of the bed, his teeth clenched, his knee in a kinetic bounce. No objection, no discussion, no attempt at rationalizing. In his mind, he would allow it to play out alongside silent, pleading prayers that his suspicions proved untrue.

Then, pounding on the hotel room door shocked them stiff.

"Sorry we knocked so many times," Julissa said once the door opened. She stood beside a broad man about her height, her fingers crawling like spiders around his arm. "We wanted to get inside quickly so no one sees us. I don't want anyone putting two and two together. This is my boyfriend, Xavier." She gripped his ample bicep with tremulous fingers. "We're a little nervous, but don't worry, we're definitely doing this."

After an exchange of clammy handshakes, the group considered other ways of attracting attention: a scene in which Julissa faked inebriation to entice an effortless kidnapping, but in the end they settled on keeping it simple, the way they had originally planned.

Scooping her beach waved curls from her eyes, Julissa explained her insistence on helping them instead of reveling their last night of vacation:

"I'm Janice's age, and my date isn't for another forty-nine years. I have plenty of time. She only has a year and needs her family as much as you need her. That doesn't go lost on me," she said. "We'll get going so we can be seated."

Separately, they arrived on the deck, a safe distance and unknown vacationing bodies between them.

"Mom, do you think it's weird we're acting like nothing's happened? People have seen us searching for Janice. Won't it look strange that we're going to have dinner and dance afterward, like we've accepted what's happened and moved on?" Lacey asked her mother.

"I didn't think about that, but we can't leave it up to anyone else. We don't have to dance, but we have to be present in case anything happens. What they think of us is not my concern right now." Norma defended her plan, but immediately thought it through. "Well . . . maybe we should eat as normal but sit out the dancing and singing."

Though they knew where Julissa and Xavier were at every moment, the Hellingtons avoided eye contact with the couple. They stared straight ahead, down at their plates, or into their water glasses and made polite dinner conversation with the family at an adjacent table. Behind them, the burnt orange sky now only showed a quarter of the sun, and by the time dessert arrived, dusk had faded into the night.

Dinner ended, and the music began. Most rose from their seats to join the dance train making a figure eight through the dining deck. Barry, Norma, and Lacey remained in their chairs, sipping water and clutching the cloth napkins that lay across their laps. Julissa and Xavier hesitated with heightened senses, then attached themselves to the end of the dance train to fit in. Their moods regulated, their hands on the hips in front of them, feet cadenced with the gongs of steel drums, heads thrown back in laughter. But Norma spotted Julissa's eyes in a steady scan across the deck. The young woman studied the height, saunter, and facial features of every man at the dinner, those standing off to the side on the sand watching the show and even closely examining the male members of the band. Two and a half hours passed and still, she analyzed every male figure in her sight though none resembled the two men she saw the day Janice was kidnapped. By the end of the dinner show, Julissa and her boyfriend walked hand in hand toward the main building of the resort, her head bowed to her phone thumbing a text message to Norma.

> *Nothin! X & I will walk around*
> *to c if they r here at ur resort.*
> *If not, we'll go to my resort n check there*

Waiting to hear back from Julissa seemed to take longer than expected, but at last, two hours later, Norma's text notification dinged and her screen shone in hope.

Still nuthin. sorry

A text Norma feared receiving. Her phone dinged again.

Going to bed.
Tomorrow X says we can look around
the beach early in the mornin
before we leave, just in case
Norma texted back.
U don't have to do that,
but thank u so much. Sleep well.

She slid into the comforter next to Barry, who had been snoring for over an hour. Lacey slept on the pull-out couch.

Just as Norma clicked off the lamp affixed on the wall, Lacey's low voice filled the dark room.

"Mom, what if we don't find her by the time we're supposed to leave? What do we do? Do we leave or stay?" she asked her mother with a crackling whisper.

"We can't think like that. We have to stay positive and keep battling. Let's only worry about that once that day's here. Until then, we stay focused on getting our girl back," Norma said, her tone in competition with Barry's throaty snore.

Lacey turned to her side. The cool air from the vent above her landed across her cheeks like a thin layer of ice. Sleep took her within seconds.

33

AFTER SWALLOWING UNMASTICATED chunks of a rubbery sandwich from a hospital vending machine and an hour-long ride on two buses, Shirley arrived at her stop feeling nauseated. The journey had tossed her limp body around on a corner seat as she slept; her head hanging in front of her, arms dangling and jerking at her sides like an inexperienced marionette. Saliva flooded her mouth. She kept tight lips convinced that parting them would result in regurgitation. Whether it arose from the lack of eating or the gray ham folded inside a soggy bun, it exacerbated the twelve hours she had spent at the hospital. Torturous and boring. Nothing more than talk shows, studying manuals, and the hissing and punching of a ventilator; the search for stale snacks and putrid food when she required it; and Tara's eyes gliding in lazy motion across the ceiling, sometimes with purpose, but the only communication between them happened through blinks. Two for yes, one for no.

In all of her seventy-three years, Shirley had not known old until she pushed off the bus seat and stammered her way onto the concrete. Each step came with soreness and discomfort as if feeling the faulty activity in her body: erosion in her bones, the clumping of free radicals, her heart splashing blood through veins in disordered distribution. The pangs whipping at her head felt as if the instructions she had absorbed about Tara's life support were trying to break free through the top of her skull. Why did she need to learn all this? Hearing Tara struggling for oxygen would be no different than coming home to her daughter lying lifelessly on her good rug.

During the bus ride, Shirley had wished death on her daughter. An unintentional thought that now pulsed through the haggard mother in the form of guilt. Guilt for thinking it, guilt for still considering it as a better option than barely existing until death, and now as she walked home in her thick-soled shoes the doctor recommended for leg pain, more involuntary thoughts flipped over in her mind: smothering Tara with a pillow, cutting through the tubes of her life support. They came and went with the sloshing in her stomach that at times reached high enough to scorch the back of her throat. Perhaps, the sickness in her belly was punishment for the stray thoughts she had about her only living daughter.

Shirley balanced herself on her orthopedic shoes and looked ahead, following the path of the filthy concrete in front of her, counting the doors that passed until she reached her own. Not wondering how Jeremy's day had gone, unconcerned about how Sandra got on with her new baby, not the least bit curious of whether Janice had been found. From behind, Shirley looked ancient, nearly unrecognizable; an old woman with an unstable frame. Her impeccable posture and swift stride had converted into a rounded back and small shuffling steps. Cheekbones poked out from beneath her hollow eyes, which seemed to levitate over purple half-moons.

The skin hung looser around her mouth and gathered in a dozen creases by her chin. And if at all possible, her hair reflected more silver than ever.

As soon as she pushed through the front door, she leaped toward the kitchen and on her knees, vomited into the trash can. Five minutes later she dropped onto the sofa, thick shoes still strapped to her feet and the smell of acid thick across the living room. Shirley covered herself with a musty sheet found crumpled on the corner cushion, sunk into a deep sleep, and dreamt of never waking up.

Sandra: One day until death

34

A T THE BOTTOM of the porch steps at the edge of the front yard, Ernesto dressed himself, shrugging his way into the rest of his suit, straightening his tie, and snapping the clasp of his watch into place. Though summer teetered on twenty days away, the warmth pushed through beads of sweat across his hairline and dampened the inside of his collar, but standing in line with the late afternoon sun in his best suit was the only way to get his girls out of the house in time. It didn't take long. Just as he sized the hem of his pants against his shoes, dresses flickered in the doorway. Ernesto's daughters sparkled in gold and silver at the top of the steps. No sleeves, shoulders exposed. Sequined fabric in the shape of hearts low below their collar bones, the ends of their gowns brushing along their ankles and nothing but straps and heels at their feet.

"You girls look beautiful," he told his daughters as he met them at the bottom of the porch steps and kissed their cheeks. "Now get in the car, we're going to be late." And not a minute later, Mia's legs curved and twisted around one another as she stepped down and turned to lock the door. The red lace that slithered across her torso stopped mid-thigh; its sheen closely matching the four-inch heels that put her eye to eye with Ernesto.

"You look beautiful too." Ernesto kissed her cheek. "Now get in the car, it's almost six thirty."

Ernesto yanked on the steering wheel to reach the center of the road, drove twenty-five yards, and parked in front of Sandra's house; the front tire pinched at the curb and the back end more than a foot away, blocking part of the driveway. His nerves rippled through his teeth as he walked around and examined the severe angle in which the car sat parked. It was fine. They weren't staying long.

The house seemed quiet. Blinds and curtains drawn, no one peeking through the slits, no loud cries leaking out from inside. It surprised them. For some reason they had imagined cries during their approach. Maybe caution tape across the front door. A police barrier by the curb. Broken windows, sirens, or perhaps a medic rushing from the house.

"Should we ring the bell? Knock? I don't know what to do," Mia whispered to the rest of her family, their heads in a semi-circle behind hers.

Something was offbeat, but in a good way.

Dissimilarity from other days and among the skies directly above.

To the Arroyos, serenity rose like a plume of smoke from Sandra's house, as if pushing up through the foundation, clouding and buffing out the sharp edges of the roof. The weakened sunlight streaked across the door like the flicker of a candle . . . a scented one. As if the lavender bush around the bend of the walkway waited until they reached the steps to emit its essence. Such composure on this side of the street, this exact location. An intense calm they had never witnessed in Sandra's space, yet nothing had changed.

Ordinary appeared extra peaceful against the backdrop of what their minds had fabricated. Although they had experienced a handful of Expiration Dates, because it was Sandra's, their imaginations had weaved a state of pandemonium through the duration of their visit.

Mia pressed a finger on the doorbell, and they all waited with their hands clasped in front of them.

The door swung open.

"Hey, guys. You look great. I'm going to say you're off to a party after you leave here. Surely, you're not already dressed for my funeral," Sandra said.

The Arroyos exchanged twitchy glances.

Ernesto coughed up words.

"My—My cousin's getting married. We have a forty-five-minute drive into Hartford. Figured we'd stop by before heading out to make the cut-off time."

Days prior to this moment, Mia sat on the staircase landing hugging her knees, her toes pressed into the wooden floor. With the phone across her lap, she called Sandra on speaker as her family listened. During her skittish explanation, Mia told of how they came to find out her Expiration Date and wished to say goodbye in person. Receptive to the idea, Sandra laid out her rules: entrance to her home would only be accepted the day before her Expiration Date. Anytime between five and seven p.m.

Months before, Sandra had decided to stop answering the door and power off her phone beyond those hours on this night. To maintain awareness. No distractions. An evening of baking with the kids, but with sharpened senses . . . and her sharpest knife accessible under a kitchen towel on the counter.

She had always wondered what a last day on earth would feel like. A count of not days, but hours. The difference was minimal aside from the arsenal of weapons spread throughout the house.

"How are you feeling?" Mia asked as she stepped up through the doorway.

"Fine, I don't have symptoms of anything. I feel healthy and energetic. No different than yesterday, no different than three weeks ago. I'm keeping a positive outlook. You never know, that could be the answer," Sandra said. The curls at the top of her head bounced with enthusiasm.

"I believe it," Sherry said loudly. "Jacklyn and I have interviewed people with stories exactly like what you described. If you don't mind me asking, is your husband still living here?" Sherry's family stood aghast at the personal information she had requested.

"What?" She turned to them. Their expressions worsened with every one of their punchy blinks. "I'm not being nosey; I'm trying to help her."

Sherry turned her back to them and faced Sandra.

"The reason I ask is . . . if you don't have anyone to take care of the kids and you know they aren't set to expire, then you might want to stay home with them all day. Set the security system and have the phone near you in case you have to call the cops. That combined with positivity and your determination to protect them, in my opinion, makes you unstoppable.

"I believe destinies are written loosely. If we have enough fight, then I can't imagine us *not* being able to change them. It's worth a shot," Sherry preached to Sandra as her parents and older sister looked on, a mere audience to the conversation.

"Don't worry guys, everything'll be okay no matter what happens." Sandra's generic response roped around them like a lasso, and within a handful of cheek-to-cheek back pats, they saw their way out . . . four car door slams and they were gone.

Sandra closed the front door and in a rush of anxiety, collapsed behind it on hands and knees. The fevered pressure gathered in her face, strained her eyes, and throbbed at her lips. Her lungs tossed out every molecule of air they had preserved, and in short gasps, recovered them as best they could. Then, her senses malfunctioned. Complete darkness. The patterned patches of carpeting in her view had gone black. A faint tone replaced the clangs in the kitchen. The sharp pain at her kneecaps dulled. Had it happened already? Death? Coming for her a day early? Had the Bureau misprinted her Death Date?

Trying to determine whether she was dead or alive, on her way to another world or still hanging on, she searched for a light. Should there be a tunnel? Should she begin crawling to find it? But like a machine, her lungs powered up into a slow pace and then kicked into gear.

Inhale . . . exhale.

Her nostrils widened; her shoulders rose and fell on their own. The tips of her fingers dug and buried into the weave of the carpeting. She no longer had the task of manipulating her movements to fill her lungs. They were functioning on their own.

Sandra was alive.

A mild glow appeared and the room came into focus; scraping, shuffling, and laughter tickled at her eardrum.

The kids . . . in the kitchen preparing to bake a cake. Right where she had left them.

Sandra moved slowly upward, scaling the door with the heels of her hands. Balancing on her feet, she swayed back to normal. Oxygen flowed in abundance.

As she took her first step back toward the kids, a faint knock shuddered through the pit of her stomach. Loud enough to hear, light enough to have imagined it. Choosing to have imagined it, she moved with careful steps away from the door, but the tap came again.

Sandra's body went into motion. In one swipe, she had armed herself with a chopping knife hidden behind the foot of the curtain and flung open the door.

"Mrs. Wilcox!" yelled Sandra. "Why didn't you ring the bell?"

"I did, dear—three times. Is it broken?" Shirley delivered her sentences in short bursts, wary of the knife still floating between them.

"Sorry," Sandra exhaled her apology. "Your knock startled me. I'll put this away. Come in." She leaned the blade against the wall and swung the curtain around to camouflage it.

"Are you feeling okay?" Sandra asked.

"I'd say today is the best of my recent days."

For a moment, thoughts of her Expiration Date vanished, overridden by Shirley's emaciation. Her lips appeared dried and rough and painful. The dress she wore, a meeting of creases as if it had given in under the weight of a pile of dirty laundry.

Shirley plopped into a corner chair as though letting gravity do its work.

"I wanted to stop by and say goodbye." She reached into her pocket, pulled out a square of old fabric, and blotted her eyes.

"Please don't cry," Sandra pleaded. "My kids are a few steps away. I don't want to scare them."

"I don't know where our lives have gone," Shirley grumbled. "Your life, my life, Janice . . . even Tara, who we knew would make a mockery of her days. I always thought we'd be okay, make good use of the time we had. I just don't know anymore." Distance eclipsed Shirley's eyes, worlds away as if her words were meant to reach beyond the atmosphere, beyond stars for some unknown force to get ahold of them and make things right.

"Wait—Janice? What's going on with Janice?"

"You haven't heard? She went missing six days ago in the Bahamas."

It took Sandra a few loops around her comprehension to accept Shirley's statement. Janice . . . no one knows where she is? And for six days? Although her own grisly reality preyed on her, circling above until it arranged to have her yanked and scooped up from existence, there were still other lives that paralleled hers. People she knew. People she cared for. Someone who lives across the street and babysat her kids on her days off from school. Janice had wanted to live as much life as she could until her last minute of breath, but the decision was no longer hers. It was no one's. Sandra had the urge to do *something*, but she could do nothing.

". . . And with just a year left," Shirley said, pulling on the weave of the soggy fabric to reach across both eyes.

Sandra waited until her vocal cords stopped quivering.

". . . and how is Tara recovering?"

"She won't." Shirley emerged from behind the piece of cloth.

"What does that mean?"

"She'll be in a coma the rest of her life." Shirley's tears paused at speaking of her daughter; collectedness not expected from a grieving mother. "Well, I don't want to keep you from your kids." Shirley eased herself off the seat, bracing a fresh pain in her knee, and leaned into Sandra's forehead, pressing her lips on it.

"Be strong and watch over us."

And just like that, a rush crackled through Sandra's limbs like the strike of a lightning bolt.

No more visitors. A last goodbye.

Seven o'clock and Shirley was leaving her alone to face the unknown. Sandra dropped to her knees and dug her face into Shirley's hip; mouth wide open, face purple, sounds like the shrieks of a heated kettle.

Clatters and bangs came from the kitchen. Brianna, Christopher, and Christina, dropping metal bowls and baking utensils onto the tile floor in pursuit of their mother. bounced off each other as they scrambled to be the first through the doorway.

"What's wrong with Mom?" Brianna asked, turning a heavy shade of pink; tears followed.

"MOM!" Christopher and Christina yelled in unison, throwing themselves at their mother's feet, terror mangling their faces and begging for Shirley's help.

"PLEASE! MAKE HER STOP!" Christina stomped her feet and tugged on her neighbor's wrinkled sleeve, but Shirley could do nothing. No one in the world could cure fate.

In a jolt of consciousness, Sandra lifted her head and sat up on her knees, fighting for breath. This display of fear was not the impression she wanted to leave on her kids.

"Mommy's okay. You see?" Shirley cupped Sandra's jaw, nudging her face toward the children. "She was telling me how much she loved all of you and that made her so incredibly happy she began to cry." Shirley descended back into her seat.

"Look." She pointed. "Those are happy tears, right, Mommy?"

"Yes, kids. It's true. I wanted Shirley to know how much I love you." Sandra's face looked stained of plum, veins bulging at her temples and neck.

"Go back into the kitchen and open the boxes so we can get started." It took Sandra two agonizing steps to lift herself off the floor, hand spread at her belly as if nursing a kick in the stomach.

Not fully convinced, Brianna, Christopher, and Christina stumbled their way back to their measuring tools, shoulders still shuddering, wiping the base of their noses with shirt hems.

"I'm sorry, Shirley," Sandra said through a slurp.

"Don't be sorry." Shirley rose from her seat a final time, gripping the armrests with tightened knuckles.

"Take care of yourself. Stay healthy," Sandra advised.

"I will."

Face to face and hooked at their fingers, the women stared as if each viewed the memories playing out in the other's eyes.

A blink of Shirley's concluded their time together. She released her grip and unlocked the door, reentering the world Sandra would soon leave behind.

The Decision

35

ELEVEN HUNDRED MILES from Gardenia Way, Janice's mother sat at the edge of the bed in a hotel room, flattening the corner of the mattress under the pressure of her persistent knee bounce. It had been the fifth time her phone had battered the wall, as she threw it in a fury of frustration. This last time, the wall retaliated, shattering the screen. Why had Shirley not answered her calls? Message after message and nothing. Would she have news that would put Norma at ease?

Just one minute after presenting Barry with her decision, and already she felt it was a mistake, headed for a mental implosion. How could she leave without having found her daughter? It would only give investigators a reason to exhale and wipe sweat from their brows, going back to their normal lives after being liberated from under her watchful eyes. If she called from her home in Connecticut, they could arrange words and manipulate their tone to allow her to believe they were doing everything they could to find Janice. The FBI, too, had assured Norma they were doing their part, but how could she know for sure?

Her beating heart told her this was all Barry's fault anyway, pressuring her to leave with him and Lacey after the three-day extension they had given themselves to knock on as many doors as they could in search of Janice. His ultimatum: *You can stay here by yourself or you can leave with us.* Then, he put more worries in her head: *Let the experts do their part; we are a distraction. Work is waiting for us. After all, we need to maintain our jobs and funds to take trips back here to continue our search. It's the only way to be effective in finding our daughter.*

She had called the firm four times to quit her job, but Barry wrestled the phone from her hand and replaced it with another glass of whiskey and another and another until she woke up the next morning with her head leaning against the toilet seat, the lid sandwiching it from above.

If Janice did not reappear in the next three days, she would have to step aboard a plane back to the states without her.

The Cakes

36

LIKE ANY OTHER night, the television flashed its series of discrepancies from the living room: animated dogs driving cars, penguins attending school, chickens dancing under the moonlight. On any other night, Sandra's kids could be found embedded in couch cushions, their eyes roving the burst of colors on the TV screen, but tonight they wore aprons and crowded the kitchen. No interest in their regular shows. They wanted to bake.

Knees on stools to reach the counter, each held a box of cake mix, flipping it from one side to the other as if a new picture would appear on the opposite side when unmonitored. Moistening their lips, they inspected the image of chocolate frosting dripped over contrasting swirls of spongy confection. *We're having a party*, they thought. From this moment forward, their minds would know nothing more than streamers, presents, trick candles, and lollipops. Exactly how Sandra had planned.

"Okay, kids. One box of cake per bowl."

Six bowls in total. Individual cakes would take longer, tire them out, and allow them to sleep further into the morning. They would wake, expecting a piece, a party, balloons. If she was not around, they would guess she was off getting the celebration in order.

The kids went to work. Puffs of flour congested the kitchen, and Sandra moved toward the printer and grabbed her instructions.

To whom it may concern,

These are my special marble cakes the kids are hypnotized by. Two cakes will remain fresh, four will be frozen and thawed when needed.

The marble *delicacy*, as the kids saw it, was ordinary. Purchased at the local supermarket, but in Sandra's experience, it had magical powers; she had used it to overturn grumpiness, make them sit still, dry their tears. Perfect angels, they were, when a triangle of cake slid before them . . . and the only way she knew to keep their minds off her sudden disappearance in the immediate days following her death.

The rest of the instructions read:

> *Whenever they start asking for me or crying, please surprise them with a big piece of cake. Tell them it's the special marble cake we all baked together. But stretch it out and make it last. Eventually, they'll grow accustomed to not having me around and forget me as the years go by. It's not ideal, but that would be the easiest form of healing for them.*

> *Sandra*

The End

37

PREDAWN DARKNESS CLUNG to Gardenia Way.
The moon had stuck itself as a crescent at the edge of a navy sky, and the gentle hum of the night crossed into the early morning, soothing the neighborhood's final hours of sleep. But for Jeremy, it buzzed like an angered hive, engulfing him with no escape.

It was late. He had overslept—well into the five o'clock hour on the day of Sandra's predetermined death. Next to him, Priscilla appeared in hibernation, wound up tight in a comforter, the pillow molded around the sides of her head as if it had laid there for months. Her way of withdrawing from the madness of the previous night, a one-sided argument with Jeremy loaded with slamming doors and agitated foot stomps.

"That's so petty, Jeremy!" she had yelled. "Who cares about Logan and what happened that night? His being an idiot shouldn't stop us from being the caring, loving people we were raised to be."

Jeremy had sat with crossed legs on the recliner and a

curled back magazine, disconnected from his wife's grumbling as if her sound could not reach him. He didn't move or flinch or fight back. He had already given his decision some sixty minutes earlier. *We're not getting involved,* he told her when he arrived home from work and powered on the TV.

"How can we *not* visit, Jeremy? At the end of a life, there are no more grudges." Throughout her rant, Priscilla kept her eyes on the clock. Last she remembered, they were down to forty-five minutes.

"What's happened to you?" she asked, staring at him for what seemed like a thousand blinks on his part.

No response.

She waited.

A whole episode streamed through the television and still, Jeremy had not come to his senses. The next time she looked at the clock, it put her twenty-nine minutes past Sandra's cut-off time. Repulsed by Jeremy's attitude and exhausted by her rage, she stomped off to bed earlier than usual and fell asleep within minutes.

Now, at 5:45 a.m., Jeremy needed to make up for lost time. He whipped the sheet back and twisted out of the bed. Heels up, he crossed the floorboards, masking the creaks from beneath his feet. If Priscilla would have awoken, her groggy state would have convinced her of a burglar in the house. The bedroom door closed behind him just as quickly as he wriggled through it. At the bottom of the steps, he stopped at the side window. The area between the houses was hollow. No visitors at this early hour. No Logan.

He stared through a vague reflection of himself. The side of Sandra's house looked composed. Tolerant of the day. A solid enough structure from the outside to withstand an implosion. In the distance, wheels glided over pavement: the momentum of another person's existence, a continuance of life as another ends. The acceleration faded and quiet returned.

He had overslept for a reason. His own subconscious pulling him back, controlling urges to climb through windows, break glass, kick in doors, anything to get into Sandra's house and protect them; guard the little family he built that neighbored his own. Today, it would all go away, and he had no choice but to give up. His feet pivoted on their own away from the window as if his body had relinquished its role as their protector. Pins and needles speckled across his chest, down his arms; regret for not having gone for a last visit.

As he took his first barefoot step away from the window, the bathroom light at Sandra's house brightened. A single light reignited what he had forced to go dormant. His torso spun back, but his feet remained planted in the opposite direction, as though bolted to the wooden planks, maintaining the course on which they had planned to take him.

He cracked his knuckles, tugged at his hair.

Had she already passed?

How did it happen?

Or is she still alive?

Are the kids alone?

Are they scared?

A mesh of concerns and indecision.

With his body in a spiral, he thought it over, chewing down the nail on his index finger enough to expose a fresh piece of flesh.

Should I go?

The pewter framed mirror hanging on the wall responded with an image, reminding Jeremy he was wearing nothing but a striped pair of boxers.

Just go back to bed.

His body realigned and moved unrestricted, as if permitting his limbs to do what they knew was right. Three steps to the coat closet, four fingers under the door handle, drawing it out slowly to lessen the squeal of the hinge Priscilla kept asking him to oil. In a raincoat and a pair of winter slippers, he was ready.

The door opened to a world different than what he had seen through the constraints of the side window. The sky had lightened to royal. The dew glistened from blades of grass. A pair of birds called out, circling one another on their flight up toward a branch. Jeremy set off, his arms lengthened to the width of each stride as he propelled himself in the direction of the frosted window aglow at the side of Sandra's house.

The backs of his slippers dragged on the concrete as though fighting to hold him back and allow him the time to turn around and think it through, but his feet shoved their way to the window. Directly beneath it, he jumped up and knocked twice.

A silhouette approached. Curly hair. A shapely figure.

Sandra was still alive.

"Sandra," he whispered, but the shadow disappeared and the light went out.

Jeremy ripped through the mist for the front door and whispered again.

"Sandra, it's Jeremy."

He could hear a body drifting inside, friction on carpeting.

"Jeremy?" A low voice whispered back from the other side. "What are you doing here?"

"I wanted to see if you needed help. I couldn't sleep and feel bad about not visiting last night." His face pressed against the moist wood of the door, his lips grazing the brass knocker.

Two clicks.

A rattling chain.

Sandra's face appeared in the crack of the door.

"My kids are sleeping. If you wanted to stop by, why didn't you do it last night during my visiting hours?"

Jeremy didn't feel the time limit applied to him.

"Priscilla and I had an argument and it went late. Are you feeling okay?" He bobbed his head for a better view through the three-inch gap that separated them. "Can I please come in? Just for a few minutes."

The door opened wider, and like a magnet, the house drew him inside, his body folding forward, his lips landing on Sandra's forehead, melting like butter on her skin.

She allowed it. For the first time she saw Jeremy through unhindered eyes: Handsome. Even in a raincoat and fleece slippers. She could tell he had spent some time in the sun because the gold had settled evenly across his skin.

"I'm sorry," he told her. "I don't know what makes me keep bothering you. You're a dear friend to us all, and we weren't there for you the way we should have been. I know Logan had a lot to do with it, but that shouldn't have pushed us away. Even though I tried, I feel like it wasn't enough." He carried her hand in his and placed it on his lips . . . like warm puffs of clouds across her knuckles.

His fingers tightened around hers as though transmitting a current of all his affection in one squeeze. Her belly tingled. To her, it felt like his lips stippled all over her body. It was nice to feel cared for, even a little wanted. But it was too late. Sandra retracted her arm and turned away. Beyond the translucent curtains, she saw a world that began to show the signs of daybreak.

"Do you want to see the kids?"

Jeremy nodded.

The second floor pulsed with innocence, lives adrift in unconsciousness. Sandra tapped on a door until it opened wide enough for them to peek inside. Brianna, Christopher, and Christina slept scattered like pieces of a puzzle across a king size bed; different shapes and sizes, but somehow they fit together perfectly.

Jeremy gestured to his ears, but she shushed him with a finger to her lips and closed the door. "That's their white noise machine. They love it. It helps them sleep through the night."

Adorable, thought Jeremy. He had never seen them so at peace.

"I taught Brianna how to call the police if she needs to," she whispered. "She has a cell phone now. I told her if she sees Mommy sleeping during the day, to call them immediately." Her face stiffened. "I also put Logan's number on speed dial for her. Maybe when I'm finally gone, he'll think about caring for his children."

Jeremy's pout reshaped itself into enraged bewilderment. Two hard wrinkles like a set of quotations between his eyebrows.

"Is that the best way to handle this?" he said, in a pitch to match his temper. "He abandoned you. You can't *possibly* still hold out for hope that he'll decide otherwise."

She shushed him again. Sternly, this time.

"He's still their father. The only way they'll stay together. It's all I can hope for."

As she pushed the nursery door open, gurgling echoed through the quiet hallway.

Brian was awake.

"He should be getting hungry soon." Sandra walked to the crib and lifted him up with one arm as Jeremy watched from the doorway. Anxiety jabbed at him.

"Should I hold Brian? Just in case—in case something happens to you while you're holding him?"

"Jeremy, that's absurd. I'm his mother, and I'm alive and well right now. I won't waste what little time I have left."

Annoyed, Sandra turned away from him and rocked Brian back and forth, humming an unfamiliar tune.

Then, the swaying stopped.

"This is hard, you know," she said, her tone pungent. "Knowing you'll be dead by midnight, leaving kids behind that need you. This isn't like Austin, where *you* were the one at *his* side until the end. I can't be there for my kids after today."

His teeth clamped down on the underside of his bottom lip. The salted taste of blood spilled inside his mouth. He leaned in to grab Brian.

"I'd love to hold him. Can I?" he asked with a smile he quickly assembled, already with a hand tucked under Brian's neck.

"Jeremy!" Sandra swung away. "You're being intrusive. I think it's time you go."

He reached again. His fingers elongated like extending antennas, but she kept moving as he swayed behind her.

"Hold on, that's not fair. I've helped you through all this, when your husband wouldn't. I acted as a stand-in father to your kids and a stand-in husband to you. I should be able to hold him."

She looked back at him. To Sandra, Jeremy had suddenly grown a few inches, widened, amassed bulk. The sincerity in his eyes had vanished behind a solid glaze of fury. His even larger shadow followed and doubled his moves as if at any moment, she would have to fight off two attackers.

Their eyes met and stares collided.

"Get the hell out of my house!"

Jeremy's arms wound forward and dropped over her like cranes. In one scoop, Brian was gone.

"Are you crazy? Who the hell—" She lunged. He bobbed and weaved from her swipes, pulled back out of her reach, circled away, and twined his arms around Brian to protect him from his mother's mania. Sandra jumped up, clawing at the collar of Jeremy's raincoat. The following swipe stung the back of his neck. A warm drop rolled down his spine.

"Be careful! You're going to hurt the baby!" He rounded his shoulders around Brian.

Sandra hoisted herself up on the banister to equal Jeremy's height, becoming larger, taller. She arched a foot over the handrail, the other pressed firmly into the wall to create balance. In her mind, she could have had the next seventeen hours with her kids, free of interruptions.

Why had she let Jeremy in and granted him a different set of rules?

All the help he provided, she had not asked for. Now, he was here demanding things for his service, causing a disturbance a quarter of the way into the last day of her life.

She latched on to his forehead from behind, pulling his head back. Her sudden movements confused him. Unprepared for her assaults, he tried to shrug her off. If he could free himself and safely put Brian back in his crib, then he could talk some sense into her, have a level-headed discussion about why he may need to be around for her last day. Protect the kids, even protect her from an intruder. Maybe it would make a difference if he were there to administer CPR. All the stories the Arroyo daughters had relayed bubbled in his head. The different accounts of those who claimed to have lived past their Expiration Dates could be true, at least one or two. He could test it. That could make all the difference. If she would just stop and listen—but his scalp tingled, burned. She had bitten his head.

Then her forearm closed around his neck and he began to cough. He shrugged again, a little harder, more forceful with his arm. His elbow in her ribcage felt like the stabs of a dagger. Losing her balance, she squeezed tighter around his neck and he could feel the pressure building in his face, no longer able to swallow. He was fighting for breath, fighting for his life. He gathered all his strength and pushed back to loosen her off. She lost her balance, and with another forceful shrug, he sent her falling back over the staircase. Her legs swung high above her head as if she had released herself backwards off a diving board. She was headed straight for the bottom of the staircase.

As Jeremy caught a glimpse of Sandra's fall, the sound of one loud wail and a heavy thump knocked in his chest, rattled through the surface of his ear canal. He ran to put Brian back in his crib, calling out to her.

"Sandra!" He fumbled down the stairs in his slippers, losing one along the way.

He dropped to his knees beside her, his heart pounding in his throat.

"Sandra." He tugged at her chin, but her jaw hung loose.

"SANDRA," he grunted.

Putting his ear to her mouth, he listened for breath.

"Sandra!" Jeremy cried through clenched teeth. "Sandra, get up!" Tears spread on his face like the splits of a river, channeling in different directions, lazy in speed as if hesitant to flow. There had to be some way to make this untrue, fix what he had broken, go back to before he left his house, swap out this morning for last night and decide to stop in with Priscilla at his side.

He needed to wake her. He pulled at her chin, but her head moved freely, as if the bones had disconnected in her neck. Nerves burned through his fingertips.

"Sandra!" he yelled out again, jumping to his feet and stomping them next to her head like a frustrated child, but her eyes looked past him, lost as if uninhabited.

"Why? Why did you have to fight me! I was only trying to help." Jeremy wiped his cheeks and dripping nose with the sleeve of his raincoat. "It didn't have to be like this. Look what you made me do." His eyes skipped around, absorbing what he had done. Her hair waved out from her scalp like a headdress; her arms extended.

He froze. The crying stopped, the desperation subsided.

His legs moved on their own again, separate from his mind; up the stairs, into the kids' room, turning up the volume of the white noise. His feet treaded to the nursery; his hands searched in a closet and through drawers and closed around the things he desired.

A bag.

Diapers.

Clothing.

A baby.

With a stuffed bag hanging at his side and an arm curved around Brian, he hopped down the steps and took a giant leap over Sandra's body. In the kitchen, he clawed over counters and through the pantry.

Baby formula.

Bottles.

He pressed them into the bag until it bulged, walked out of Sandra's house and into his.

Sweat dripped from his temples. He removed the raincoat and changed into a pair of shorts and a tee shirt he found on the floor of the laundry room.

Out of breath, he sat at the kitchen table, thinking; Brian squirmed in his arms. He held him snug in the bend of his elbow and swirled a bottle of baby formula. Brian curled his lips around the end of it and slurped himself to sleep.

Ninety minutes later

The New Baby

38

PRISCILLA WADED IN the water on a beach in St. Bart's when she heard the screaming. It pierced through the cloudless sky, tumbled through pockets of sand, skidded over the water, mingled with the waves, and came crashing back to shore. The water settled, then pulled away, but the screaming remained.

She opened her eyes.

The sunlight diminished. The warmth of the sun on her skin, gone. The light blue sky replaced by the spin of a ceiling fan. The crystal waters around her, now rumpled bedsheets.

Screaming. Crying.

She thought, *Is that Jen? Wait. Is that a baby? Am I still dreaming?*

The blubbering, she did not recognize.

Is it a car? It's a cat.

Her mind flitted through a thousand more possibilities for the shrieks she heard around her. She sat up and swung to the side of the bed.

"Jeremy... *Jeremy?*"

She turned the knob of the bedroom door and poked her head through.

"Hello?" Priscilla called out, taking slow, spinning steps down the hall, as if the noise orbited her head, her eyes chasing what she couldn't see.

"Mom? What's going on?" Jen asked from her bedroom doorway. A loose bun flopped at the top of her head appearing just as disoriented.

"I don't know. I just woke up."

The two met halfway down the stairs and continued the rest of the way together with Jen following close behind, using her mother as a shield—hiding from the sound and concealing herself from its source. As they turned off the last step, grasping the banister in their half-rotation, Priscilla stopped short as if she had crashed into an invisible wall. Jeremy held a bottle to the lips of a squirmy baby.

"Who—who's baby is that?" Priscilla asked.

"Ours . . . for now." Jeremy winked as if he had just granted his wife a wish. "Sandra called my phone a couple of hours ago and begged me to take Austin," he said. "She worried about him getting hurt since she constantly has to tend to him." He looked down and spun the bottle in the baby's mouth to stop bubbles from forming.

"Austin? Did you call him *Austin?*" Priscilla was not sure. The fog from her sleep still lingered.

"Sorry—I mean Brian. She asked if we'd adopt him, but I told her I'd have to talk to you first." He lifted his head and searched for her eyes.

"He'll have a long life, Pri," Jeremy whispered as if letting her in on a secret.

"Alright," Jen said. "This is obviously adult talk. I'm going back to bed." She turned and retraced her steps back to her bedroom.

"I don't know about this, Jeremy. I mean, on one hand,

I would love to complete our family with him. He needs a home, but what about the other kids? Wouldn't they want to grow up with their brother?" In her mind, she deliberated an adoption, listing pros and cons to herself like footnotes to their conversation.

She lowered herself into a chair across from Jeremy and watched. Already, this new baby had found comfort in her husband, gripping a tiny hand around Jeremy's pinky and nuzzling into a corner between an arm and a chest. Like a movie, each scene revealed the likelihood of its ending. In her frame of vision, a diaper bag sat at the table next to them filled with everything this baby needed. Jeremy's arm poked around inside it, familiar with the placement of its pockets and zippers, reaching into a corner where he knew to find a bib.

Something in her husband had settled, like the laying of bricks in perfect angles. The torment of having lost a son buried deep beneath its layers. It softened her. The pros were stacking. An opportunity to start over without the worry of waiting for the announcement of another Expiration Date, avoiding the grief of having it happen again the way it did with Austin, going through another pregnancy just to receive devastating news about their newborn's short life. All of it bypassed with a few signatures on a piece of paper. Would it be that easy?

"Well, Pri. Think about it. Until then, we can help take care of him."

"How would the whole process work? *If* we did decide to keep him, can we do it right away? Is she drawing up a document or something? Should I go talk to her?" Priscilla's piling questions led her back to their torn friendship. "I'm honored and a little taken aback that she trusts us enough to raise her newborn."

"You never know what's going on inside someone's

head." He winked again. "We're great people, and I think she knows that. As for the adoption process, I can handle it."

Priscilla walked over to Jeremy. A pleasant road ahead had presented itself, another chance at a fulfilling life, taking in a child in need of their help. A way to honor Austin.

"Can I hold him?" She extended both arms. Jeremy placed Brian over them. She sunk into a seat and lost herself. The world withdrew, falling away as though giving her the space and stillness she needed to connect with Sandra's baby and perhaps, her new son.

But lights disrupted the quiet, encircling the walls of the kitchen in which she sat, beaming in through the window at every half second.

"She's gone," Jeremy said, standing in the middle of the kitchen. "That's the ambulance. I should probably go talk to them." He rushed out of the house in his winter slippers.

"Good morning, officers. Did she pass already? She told me she would have her oldest daughter call 9-1-1." Jeremy held his hand out to shake theirs as they met on Sandra's walkway.

"Yes, we're looking for a baby. The kids say they have a newborn brother?" one of the officers asked.

"Yes, Austin." He drew a long breath. "I'm sorry, Brian. She knocked on my door this morning asking me to take him, worried she was putting him at risk."

"Good thing she did. Looks like she had a bad fall. He could have been seriously hurt."

The two officers turned to head back into the house, and Jeremy followed.

Inside, Brianna, Christopher, and Christina had burrowed themselves in the couch cushions, crying, asking why their mother lay on the ground, why she couldn't get up, why she wouldn't speak back to them. A female officer wiped their tears, explaining. Her own tears spilled as quickly as theirs. Sandra had not had the chance to tell anyone about the marble cakes.

"I can't believe that's how she died." Jeremy looked from four feet away, sobbing into his forearm. The images of his scuffle with Sandra spun slowly into focus, dangling over him like the mobile he had installed on Brian's crib. How could her life have ended like this? *What if I hadn't come to Sandra's this morning?* he thought. *How else would she have died?* There had to be another way. He hadn't planned on coming to Sandra's in the first place.

Then, one of the officers threw a bedsheet over her. Jeremy looked at her form, the contours of how she now rested under it. A mother with four kids, now a lump under a thin layer that separated her from the life she lived, the life from which she was forced to leave.

But had it been their destiny the entire time? Had it already been predetermined that he would be Sandra's killer, her murderer even if unintentionally?

In a sudden rush of weakness, Jeremy dropped to his knees. The officers tried to keep him elevated, shoving their large hands in his armpits, tugging him back up. They succeeded in placing him in a chair by the desk, where he cried for the next thirty minutes. The children were led up the stairs.

"Sir, her body will be taken away soon. I've called my supervisor; the kids will be temporarily placed in homes. Looks like they'll be split up for the time being."

Jeremy gathered his wits, collecting them one by one as though plucking them up off the ground they had scattered across, his mind accepting the missing pieces.

"She wanted my wife and me to adopt her newborn."

Taking a chance, he opened the desk drawer. He gulped down what felt like a giant glob of salted syrup.

"You see? She didn't send these out to the adoption

agency because she was waiting for us to give her a response. But, we didn't fully decide until this morning after she called me." He handed the papers to the officer and resumed his sobs. Worry. Agitation. Sadness. Remorse. Jeremy's emotions had corkscrewed through him so quickly throughout the morning, creating a force that could drop him at any moment the way Sandra had. He put his back to the wall and looked around. Another female officer he hadn't noticed paced in the kitchen while on the phone with her supervisor. To him, her image pulsed like a strobe of light in the doorway. A strong presence, but too soft spoken for him to hear what she was saying. At the same time, the kids came down the steps one after the other, each with a stuff animal tucked under an arm; all they would have to keep them safe.

"My supervisor says it's okay for you and your wife to stay with the baby for now," the female officer said. Her voice came veering at him from the other side of the room. "Newborns can have a tough time being placed temporarily. If you want to adopt him, you can start the pro—"

"I'm a lawyer. I'll get it handled." He spoke before she could finish.

"Still, you'll likely have to wait for the court to decide and see if any of her family members are fit to be guardians. They come first, before you do. I'm sure you know how it works."

"Of course."

Jeremy feared exhibiting a lack of sensitivity. He nodded at the officer and wiped the area under his eyes that had already dried.

After Jeremy hugged the three kids, letting them know Brian would be safe and they'd be safe too, Jeremy left Sandra's property half heartbroken, half grateful. He was going home to a new son.

On his way back to the house, he met eyes with Shirley

as she peeked out her window. He delivered a disheartened wave, lowered his head, and disappeared through the front door of his house.

The Sunset

39

THE QUIET CAB ride home from the airport rumbled louder than a horde of detonations—coughing, sniffling, throat clearing. Even sighs pierced the silence like missiles cutting through desolate skies. Janice's family had traveled home as scheduled after a three-day extension. Lacey, with an empty seat beside her.

Norma said she wouldn't live through it, the disappearance of her daughter. That it would kill her, send her to the grave quicker than any government software could. That she hoped to be that one person to die sooner than her Expiration Date. Prove it achievable, instilling fear in millions. During the flight, she imagined taking sleeping pills and combining them with her anxiety medication. Knock them back with a jug of water sloshing from the sides of her mouth, get them down quickly so there's no time for second guessing.

But if death did not happen, it would undeniably be the best way to keep her comatose for the rest of her life. On napkins spread out on her tray table, she multiplied the number of pills needed by the number of days she had left, dividing the hours in a day to figure out the times she had to swallow them . . . midnight, six a.m., noon, six p.m., and then midnight again. That would also cancel out all the pain: the feeling of acid flowing through her bloodstream, the sense that billions of tiny spiders lived and crawled within her skin, the crunching in her muscles that came with languid movement. Even the sockets felt too small for her swollen eyes. Living the life she had so far would never work again. She needed to sleep. Barry and Lacey would be better off, she was certain.

The lack of news had pushed Norma over the edge. Zero leads in Janice's kidnapping left her in shattered pieces she could no longer reassemble. Or preferred not to reassemble. She was like a walking corpse, dragging along fragments of herself that would not reattach. In six months, if there was still no trace of Janice, the FBI would call off the search, per Expiration Date policy.

Norma stared past the smudges on the cab window, her head bouncing involuntarily with the motion; every turn like flips through long-lost pictures on a projection screen. Memories she wished to keep tucked away but still accessible in case the pain ever subsided.

They rode through the street Janice skipped down while on her way to kindergarten. Turned onto the boulevard of a ballet studio where she performed her first recital. Passed a strip of stores where Janice bought her prom dress. Norma watched the blurred memories pass as streaks through the window, unable to bring them into focus. Worried that if she tried too hard, she could be wasting them.

She blamed herself. This was her fault. She had planned the vacation no one expected to go on. If she hadn't followed through with the last strokes on her keyboard finalizing their trip, Janice would still be at her side. How could she have let this happen?

The cab turned onto Gardenia Way and like flashing light, the broken rays of the sun guided their path from beyond the leafy branches that hung over the street. For a moment, everything seemed to float and scale back into slow motion; the sound, low and distorted as she monitored movement. Jeremy rounded the corner pushing a stroller . . . and there was a baby in it, dressed in blue. His legs kicked out in jubilance. Jeremy folded forward to tickle his stomach.

It meant nothing to her.

Norma's eyes floated away and across the road where Ernesto and Mia were teaching their daughters to swing a golf club. Dressed in matching polo shirts, they laughed and hopped around their front lawn, chasing the tiny balls they knocked over. Norma did not care whether they learned or not.

Her eyes passed over Sandra's stilled home and a visibly thin and frail Shirley glided into her vision, holding her front door open for two men who wheeled in large machines. The van parked out front read "EERP Medical Supplies." Her hair had lost its shine. Now dingy, yellow, and neglected. Like the squiggles a child would draw at the top of a head. Her outstretched arm looked boney, and the skin underneath it sagged past her elbow.

The squeal of the brakes concluded their ride home. The three unloaded themselves and scattered throughout the house as soon as they walked in. Not a single word was spoken between them. Norma put down her luggage in the middle of the living room and walked to the backyard to mingle with the warmth that had grazed their skin on the first afternoon in the Bahamas. It was all she had left to feel close to Janice. The thought that the giant flame in the sky knew exactly where she was, looked down on her, looked after her.

Norma closed her eyes.

An orange glow lit up from behind her lids, just as bright as if she had kept them open; inescapable brilliance. Norma surrendered to it, begging it to drape its warmth over her daughter, wrap her up in its rays, and send her home. The heat circulated through her now, as if the sun had heard her request, letting her know it would do its best.

Then it slipped behind a cloud and Norma's world went dull again. She opened her eyes to a grayed sky and promised to wait. However long it took, she would stay until it found her again; the sun that looked down on her the day her daughter was born. The one set ablaze as they watched its descent during their last night together in the Bahamas. The same sun that would rise on the day of Janice's Expiration Date.

Author's Note

DURING THE FINAL edits of this book, my dog Oliver passed away. Although pets and their Expiration Dates are not a part of this first installment (and may never be included in future installments), the thought of destinies and Death Dates battered my mind for days, much more furiously than when I decided to write the book in the first place. *Would I want to know?Would I not want to know?* Not knowing seems more appealing. It's all I've ever known and all I will ever know. With every keystroke while writing this novel, I counted my blessings for the lives we do have and the way we live them. Some of the characters I created and their circumstances are not far off from real life when it comes to terminal illnesses, but with them there is always hope. Hope that love and determination can outdo science and medicine. But after Oliver's passing, something inside me changed; a fizzing away of everything I had been grateful for. After intense deliberation, I finally decided that I *would* rather know. Not for me, not for what I would want to achieve before then, not to add check marks next to experiences on a bucket list, not for my own preparation, but *because* of those I love.

Knowing how much time my animals, my family, and friends had left would eradicate the fear of death I have for myself. It would create a balance because I don't just live for myself; I live for others as well, to be here for those who need me. To me, that would be as fulfilling as achieving everything on a bucket list.

Acknowledgments

IT MAY BE a little weird, but I've always been told to give yourself credit for all you've done . . . and so, here I go. As many times as I thought writing this book would break me, it never did. I pushed and pushed until there was the slightest light at the end of that dark, soulless tunnel you lead yourself to when you think there's nothing left for you but to give up. "You can't do this," I told myself; "You're wasting your time." Not sure exactly where it came from, but I heard it every single day. I had unwillingly repeated it to myself to justify backspacing over words, X-ing out of a Word doc, and ending, never looking back. Throughout the process, I took several steps back, but I always made sure to take that exact number of steps forward, adding one more every time. At the end of it all, I had won the battle with myself.

Rich Jodice, my editor, my husband, and the epitome of a support system. The twenty-four hours in a day we spend together don't ever feel like enough. Without you, a novel like this written by me would have never happened. As many times as I fell, you were there to prop me back up, guiding my fingers and allowing them to rest over the keys until I was ready to strike them again. I am grateful for every single emotion we expressed together during the two-and-a-half years it took to complete this book.

My parents were the other half of the support system I needed to get through *The Expiration Date*. Seeing their faces squeeze into different expressions whenever I expressed frustration or told them how I'd tossed aside plans to write through the weekend or when I finally told them the premise of this book was fascinating. Through that, I could feel the emotional link my parents have with their children.

Christine Pingleton, my final editor/proofreader, I am grateful for all your thoughts, feedback, and help you provided during the final edit. Your encouraging words about this book were, by far, more inspirational than you will ever know.

My dogs, Eddie and Oliver. Had they not been by my side to cuddle with whenever I wanted to quit, I might still be writing and attempting to get through this book. Many times they sat on either side of me on the couch, basically incarcerating me, so that I had no choice but to keep going. My heart is yours.

To Sue, the only other person who knew this was a go as I kept it secret from other very deserving souls. Somehow, you always provided laughter just as I was tearing up chapters to shove into the garbage. Thank you for that.

To my nephews, Julian, Cristian and Nicolas. They provide endless amounts of hugs and laughter, and bucket loads of all the *critical* support I need in order to make them proud.

My friends and family, without you, I would be nowhere . . . and that doesn't just pertain to writing this book.

CPSIA information can be obtained
at www.ICGtesting.com
Printed in the USA
LVHW112002121119
637141LV00001B/100/P